TOO TOUGH TO DIE AND THE VALIANT BUGLES

Two Full Length Western Novels

GORDON D. SHIRREFFS

WOLFPACK PUBLISHING
— EST 2013 —

Too Tough To Die and The Valiant Bugles
Paperback Edition
Copyright © 2023 (As Revised) Gordon D. Shirreffs

Wolfpack Publishing
9850 S. Maryland Parkway, Suite A-5 #323
Las Vegas, Nevada 89183

wolfpackpublishing.com

Paperback ISBN 978-1-63977-725-9
eBook ISBN 978-1-63977-726-6

TOO TOUGH TO DIE AND THE VALIANT BUGLES

TOO TOUGH TO DIE AND THE VALIANT
BUGLES

TOO TOUGH TO DIE

TOO TOUGH TO DIE

CHAPTER ONE

T he dry wind was a living thing that drove stinging clouds of gray, gritty dust across the cream-colored devil's dance floor of the long dry lakebed. There seemed to be no boundaries, no limits to the naked expanse of the lakebed. It was as though the Creator had prepared this great span of nakedness for some forgotten purpose, then had callously abandoned it, never to return. There was nothing of life upon the flat surface as far as one could see. Not a bush, weed, animal or animal track; not even a bird flying above it. Not an animal track or a wheel track. Nothing but the frightening distances, obscured by the flying veils of gray dust.

In the middle of the afternoon a living thing did appear. A man afoot, walking to the unseen west, planting one boot ahead of the other like an automaton, faded bandanna tied tightly across nose and mouth, faded hat pulled low over borax reddened eyes, worn Winchester carried in a big left hand, and empty canteen bobbing maddeningly at left hip. On and on, as though following an invisible line across that dead and trackless land. The sun was but a faint orange blob in the western sky, and Buck Ruffin was walking west for want of any other way to go. He had no idea if he was walking across the width of the lake, or following the length of it, but he knew that to stop was to die.

Buck Ruffin wasn't the kind of man who waited for death; he was the kind who'd go out to meet it, to try its strength against his, even if he knew he would die in the end.

Somewhere far behind him on the Nevada desert lay his horse, dead with a bullet through its head, a humped shape already drifted with blow-sand as fine as talcum powder. Buck could have turned back when that had happened. He could have walked back twenty miles to Dixie Springs, then made it by easy stages afoot until he could buy or borrow a horse, but that wasn't Buck Ruffin's way. Somewhere ahead of him, through the swirling dust, rode four men pulling leather for the California line, and standing not upon the order of their going. Buck Ruffin didn't know them personally, but he knew their names and descriptions well enough. Those four names were inscribed in a clerkly hand on each of four warrants carried inside Buck's salt-rimed shirt; Hazen Deeth, Quin Scheel, Jack Yering, and a man, a John Doe, known only as "Stinger." It was one of their bullets that had dropped Buck's horse in a dawn ambush. Killing wasn't a novelty to any of the four of them. For that matter it wasn't a novelty either to the man who was following them. There *was* a difference, Deeth, Scheel, Yering and Stinger were *gunmen;* Buck Ruffin was a *gunfighter,* a man who wore the star.

Buck's feet suddenly sank into a soft spot, deeper than his ankles. He kept moving, afraid to go on, afraid to turn back, not knowing whether to turn right or left, and the green sickness welled up into his throat, for there are ways a man really doesn't fear to die, while there are others that sicken a man to the very core, no matter how hard case he is. Deeper and deeper, until he could almost feel the sucking of it, trying to pull him down to the knees, then the hips, then the armpits, until his nose was level with the lake-bed and he would know he had but a few minutes to die alone and unseen, neatly trapped, killed and buried by nature itself.

He was just above his knees when he threw himself forward and bellied across the soft, queasy mass, feeling the heat of it drive up through his thin shirt and undershirt like the top of an oven. Even in his desperation he did not let go of the rifle, driving himself on across the treacherous surface until at last he got to his knees, then managed to stand up, and plodded on to the west, feeling some of the burning salts working down into his boots.

A vicious gust of wind caught him and as he bent his body forward he saw something indistinctly to the right of his way; something that looked like what he hardly had dared to hope for in that waterless expanse. He slit his eyes and saw the pool. It wasn't a mirage. He covered his stinging face with his forearms and turned directly into the whining wind, to walk toward the pool.

He stopped when he saw the riffled surface of the water almost at his boot toes, and sickness again welled through his lean body. The water was chocolate colored, dull and lifeless, like a suppurating sore on the creamy whiteness of the flats. To drink such a fluid was to die slowly and agonizingly, if one could bear to swallow it.

Buck Ruffin turned away and plodded on and the steady rhythmic bobbing of the canteen against his hip was more maddening than ever. The sun was lower now, dropping toward the vague and almost unseen western range. There would be a moon that night. Enough light for Buck to keep picking his way across the lakebed. "To *what?*" he said harshly.

The darkness came suddenly. The light was gone but the wind was still present. The wind needed no light to keep on playing its deadly game with Buck Ruffin. It was rare indeed for man to attempt a crossing of that area, even with water, and well mounted. So, the wind would make the best of what it had that night. A human toy.

Keep it alive as long as possible, like an Apache child torturing a bird to learn its lessons for use against enemies in later life, or a white boy idly pulling the wings from a struggling, buzzing fly. "Ho, ho, hooo..." laughed the wind.

"Ho, ho, hooo, yourself, you howling sonofabitch," snarled Buck Ruffin.

On and on with feet tired and swollen, hot from the chemical reaction of the dead surface of that forgotten lakebed, stinging sweat rolling down hot flesh, dry thirst working from the outer flesh into the bones, slowly and inexorably, positive of success. *Patience*...

Eyes burning as though filled with acid, lips cracking red and swelling, tongue coated and thickening, nostrils filled with burning dust. The dust seemed to be working up into the inner passages of his skull, seemingly working with deadly intent toward his tired brain to coat it, to dull his mind, then to loosen his discipline and sanity so that he would soon begin to mumble and then to rave. He would start to tear off his clothing, then begin screaming at the top of his hoarse, thirst-cracked voice as he plunged on and on to slow death. *Patience*...

The desert kills like a stalking cat. Death out there is never seen as when a man faces a crackling gun, the naked flashing of deadly steel, or the precisely shaped loop of a hangman's noose swinging idly against a yellow sky. Death out there is heat, and loneliness coupled with intense thirst, all of them slow but certain killers. Take your time, Desert! This one is tough. All rawhide and hickory, hard muscle and tough bone. Tough in body, tougher in mind. The game is worth the candle with such a one. *Patience*...

The wind began to rise in velocity and then began to chase its tail, whirling about in gusty delight, with the lone human right in the vortex, seemingly forgotten. Buck Ruffin plodded on, head lowered, bandanna tight about mouth and nose. Time and time again the frightening realization came to him that he wasn't sure of his direction. With the sun gone, and no moon, in that madness of howling, grit-laden air on the move, it could be possible that he was backtracking. There was no way of knowing, for his shallow tracks on the harder surfaces would now be erased by the wind and drifted blow-sand.

Then he hooked a boot toe in something; something unexpected, for the lakebed was as flat and naked as a billiard table. He sprawled awkwardly and found himself lying over a hump on the ground, a hump tufted with sparse greasewood. He closed his eyes. He was at least off the lakebed. Buck began to crawl, feeling ahead of himself with his free hand, sensing, rather than feeling the slow, almost imperceptible sloping of the ground. Now and then he passed drifted sand and clusters of wind-tortured greasewood. He got to his feet, leaned on his rifle, gathered his failing strength and plodded on, and as he did so, he seemed to note a change in the tone and timber of the wind shriek, as though now it wasn't so sure it was going to beat him flat and then bury him alive on the playa.

The wind flailed at him with vicious, staggering blows, like a frenzied woman beating a child, but the inner strength of Buck Ruffin came to the surface and gave firm, rigid defiance to the wind. It was more sheer stubbornness than strength. *Too tough to die*...

He was climbing at a more acute angle now and he saw through the swirling dimness of the furnace wind a huge, vague and indefinite mass. He stopped, steadied himself with his rifle, and stared at the mass, not knowing if it was real, or a vast wall built up by his tortured imagination. Then he knew it for what it was. Naked hills forming the western boundary of the lake valley. He plowed between two of them and whether it was the shelter of them, or the last despairing battering of the night wind, he did not know, but after a final and furious gust, the wind seemed either to retreat to its wild playground on the lakebed, or to die away.

It was then that Buck noticed he could see better. He turned and looked through the rifted veils of dust behind him and saw a faint suggestion of lighter sky far to the east, forecasting the rising of the moon. He walked on, feeling better now, but still, at the back of his tired mind, was the thought that he had no water, that it looked like a country bereft of water, that he faced another day of hell when the sun arose, and this time he was not sure he could last through it. There is a limit. The desert was not through with him yet.

The first silvery light of the moon rose above the humped and shapeless masses of the range far behind him. He saw that he was passing through an area of drift sand, surrounded by the hills, and climbing steadily. His legs began to tire and his throat seemed lined with brass as he slogged on. The moon was lighting the desolate country when he reached the top of the incline and dropped flat on his belly to rest, hardly daring to look beyond the crest for fear of what he might see. Perhaps another naked lakebed, ghostly white beneath the light of the moon, and not a drop of water within many miles of it.

The wind had died away considerably, shifting directions, boxing the compass, moaning softly between the bare hills, rustling the sere brush. Buck lay still, with his face resting against the sand, trying not to think of what lay ahead. He knew he'd never go back across that hell below him, for daylight would catch him somewhere in the middle of the lakebed, and he knew well enough he'd never make it to the other side, much less to distant Dixie Springs.

The faint sound of the bell came to him as he lay there, trying to gather strength. He closed his eyes. He listened, sure it was imagination. Minutes ticked past. The wind shifted. The sound of the bell came again.

Buck raised his head. The wind died away. Buck closed his eyes. His mind was playing tricks on him.

The bell sounded clearly and distinctly.

Buck sat bolt upright. Imagination or not, he could have sworn he had heard the sharp metallic ring of metal upon metal. The moon was higher, etching each shadow sharply upon the silvered ground. Buck got to his feet and walked to the crest, looking down the long slopes below him.

The buildings stood in gaunt array upon both slopes of the valley, with an etched ribbon of road centering the valley floor, from right to left, through the center of the town, to vanish into the distance. The moonlight was just beginning to touch the upper floors of the bigger two-storied buildings. The windows stood out blankly against the light surfaces of the dressed stone buildings. The wooden, false-fronted buildings were dark and somber beneath the moonlight.

Buck slowly drew down the bandanna from nose and mouth. He squinted his reddened eyes. He closed them and then reopened them thinking perhaps that the town would vanish like a chimera, but it was still there, solid and substantial in the cold light. On the higher slopes, hard against the base of the multicolored hills, faulted and banded, fissured and eroded were the gaunt, rusted skeleton structures of mine headings. Many of them. A sagging board flume came down the slopes across the wide valley, like a huge wooden centipede and ended in a chaotic mass of warped and shattered wood.

The moon was beginning to flood the silent valley, showing in stark detail the huge masses of rusted iron equipment and the humped shapes of the ore tailings thoroughly oxidized by time and weather. A church steeple, tilted slightly to one side, thrust its weathered spire up like the warning finger of a prophet. Buck could see the bell, still hanging in the four-sided opening beneath the spire. Even as he watched the wind sang dryly down the valley and moved the bell. It rang softly.

Buck walked down the long slope at a steady pace. Not a friendly light showed in the whole town. It was too early for them to be all asleep, at least in a Nevada mining town, for the liquor always flowed in such places, and the hurdy-gurdy girls worked the same shifts as the miners, three a day, for twenty-four hours. But there were no lights. No steam rising from the mines. No smoke from the chimneys or the smelters. No horses standing patiently hipshot at the rails. Not a wagon, a surrey, a buggy, or an Abbott-Downing to be seen on the main street.

A tumbleweed scurried down the road, gathering speed as it passed down the main street, to vanish. rolling crazily, on the littered flats beyond the town. High on a hill to the right was the graveyard, with fenced-in graves, the fences warped by weather and silvered by the harsh rays of the sun. The rusting wire fence sagged close to the hard ground. A large wooden cross hung drunkenly over a stone monument.

Buck reached the first building and stopped to look down the main street. Not a sign of life. Not a light, a voice, a sound of any kind beyond the soft rustling of the desert wind, and the occasional faint tone of the abandoned bell.

The town was long dead. A rusting, decaying ghost from the past, crumbling into dust bit by bit, in a slow but sure process by time and weather.

Buck took no time to meditate on the transient glories of the dusty past. His throat was sanded raw by thirst and dust. He trotted slowly to a rusted pump that thrust itself up from a warped mass of boarding. It was no use. He could not budge the rust-welded handle. One pump after another he tried. Some of them he could work, but no water came up from the depths. A lurking feeling of panic jibbered and gestured obscenely in the back of his mind. He had come out of the dry hell of the desert and hills to find a dry hell of a town, and this was a worse mockery than the poisonous chocolate-colored pool he had found just before sundown. There had been water in this gaunt relic of the past. Perhaps water too was a ghost, an intangible memory from long ago.

He walked slowly down the center of the moon-lighted street. Stores and saloons, shops and offices, all empty of life, shattered of window, warped of frame and siding, rimed with dust and threaded with cobwebs. Grinning windows like the grinning of whitened skulls.

Buck stopped at the main intersection. A large, two-storied building, imposing even in its abandonment, shone softly white in the moonlight. He saw the sign cut into the stone above the double doorway First Bank of Lodestar. *Lodestar!* Lodestar had been founded during the Civil War, and in its time, millions in rich silver had been taken from the naked looking hills surrounding the town. Lodestar had been known from coast to coast for the richness of the silver deposits, the swift rise of its build-ings and population, the wild profligacy of its bearded, drunken citizens and the five or six hundred girls who inhabited the many bagnios on both sides of Stingaree Gulch. In later years it had achieved great publicity because of the sudden failure of the silver mines, the cataclysmic drop from the heights of wealth and luxury to the depths of empty mines and empty streets. Lodestar had been fully abandoned for more than a decade, as far as Buck Ruffin knew.

Buck slowly drew a dirty sleeve across his raw, cracked lips. His tired eyes flicked from one building to another. A wide, frame building, false fronted, and still showing traces of gaudy paint, stood sagging beyond the bank. The main roof supports had snapped or weakened, and the holed roof was dangerously sway-backed. Buck walked toward it. One of the batwing doors lay on the wooden walk, while the other hung from one rusted hinge. He bent beneath it and walked inside, watching his step, as the floor was slanted to one side and full of holes.

He forgot caution as he hunted about the dusty, echoing building. Thirst was the goad and the lash. He rounded the long and dust covered bar and looked beneath it. His left foot struck a wooden case. It was full of dusty brown bottles. He jerked one from the case and broke off the neck of it against the bar. Fluid bubbled up and cascaded over the jagged lips of the break. He slopped some of it into a dirty palm and sniffed it, then thrust his dry tongue into it. "Sasparilla," he said. He upended the bottle and emptied it. Then he leaned against the bar and grinned. It was the first time in his drinking life that he ever remembered drinking anything but beer or rye in a saloon, abandoned or otherwise.

Buck checked the bottle. Out of twenty-four in the case, nine were still filled with the drink. Enough to keep him alive until he could figure a way out of this forgotten valley. To his recollection, he had wandered too far north, from fairly well traveled country, into a country that was as empty of human life as the moon, at least most of the time. He knew now he was about forty miles from the water at Dixie Springs, and little chance of reaching that on foot, with nothing but sarsaparilla to keep him going. To the north would be nothing but waterless, heat-blasted hills for a good eighty to ninety miles. To the south, beyond the valley, was more desert, stretching on to infinity. He didn't know that country at all, and the odds of finding water in it would be too high against him. That left the west, between Lodestar and the California border, and he knew nothing about that country either.

Buck walked outside with a bottle of sarsaparilla in his hand. He walked to the corner and leaned back against the bank building, surveying his domain.

"Lodestar's only citizen," he said aloud. "The Honorable Buck Ruffin." He laughed. His laugh was echoed by the wind. It was rising again, driving dust and tumble-weeds down the center of the main street.

Buck crossed the street to where a livery stable stood. He forced open the door and slid it shut behind him, cutting off the sharp edge of the gritty wind. The stalls were empty. Dried pieces of harness and leather straps littered the floor. A rickety ladder hung from the wall, held by one rusted spike. A Studebaker wagon lay tilted to one side, two of the wheels having collapsed.

A pile of straw lay against a back wall. Buck walked to it and sat down, leaning his rifle against the wall. He sat there for a long time. It was as though he was a prisoner in Lodestar. No walls and no iron bars, but a prisoner of the surrounding desert, until he could figure out a way to beat it. He lay back and felt the stiffness of the search warrants beneath his shirt. Deeth, Scheel, Yering and Stinger, would be well on their way to the border now. There was nothing Buck could do about it. He closed his eyes, listening to the rising howl of the wind and the scrabbling of its gritty fingers against the warped sides of the stable, until he knew no more.

CHAPTER TWO

I f the wind had been wild during Buck Ruffin's hike across the lakebed, trying to fell him for the final count, it had outdone itself during the night, particularly after moonset. It howled insanely through the valley and battered at the trembling buildings, ripping loose shutters and shingles, doors and sidings. Jagged pieces of rusted tin were torn from the roofs of the mine buildings and hurled with insensate fury down the slopes above the town. Windows splintered in the blast and the roof was ripped from a shed.

Buck had snugged down in the welcome straw, listening now and then to the mad raging of the storm, then dropping off into a dreamless sleep. He thanked his God that he wasn't outside on that mad night.

He had awakened when a bright shaft of sunlight had thrust itself through a hole in the stable wall and touched his face. It was strangely quiet now after the wind had stopped. Buck sat up and yawned. He picked up his rifle and walked outside to survey Lodestar in the bright, revealing light of day. It was going to be a heller that day. Already he could feel the probing heat of the sun's rays, trying to find the well-springs of his sweat, to make them spring forth and then dry them up, as he would dry up in time when the sarsaparilla was nothing but a sweet memory.

Hunger gnawed within his lean belly. He hunted through half a dozen buildings with no success. It was high noon when at last he walked slowly back toward the center of town, eyeing the rusted structures high on the hill slopes, wondering if there might just be food and water up there, but not daring to attempt the climb in that searing heat. He reached the center of town and leaned his rifle against the bank. He felt for the makings. Before this time, he had hardly wanted the drying effect of smoke in his mouth and lungs, but now he wanted to think. The sack of makings was in his left hand when he caught the swift and furtive movement across the street. He swung, crouching a little, drawing, cocking and firing in one fluid motion and the rabbit was flung lifelessly against a post with a .44 caliber slug in its head. The echo of the shot chased itself down the street and died away in the heat-shimmering hills.

Buck picked up the warm and lifeless body. The rabbit was hardly enough of a meal for a man with Buck's appetite, but it was better than nothing. He took it to a nearby building, skinned it, started a fire in a rust-scaled stove, scrounged up an old ramrod for a spit, then placed the meat above the embers. He could hardly wait for the meat to cook. When it was done, he took it, ramrod and all, to the rear of the building and sat down in the dubious shade to munch on the tough and stringy meat, while his eyes studied the mine structures on the slopes high above the town. He'd climb up there when the sun dropped behind the western hills, giving him enough light, without the hell blast of the heat, to poke about a bit. He knew better than to fool around old mine shafts. Many a curious explorer had fallen to his lonely death down those shafts with never another soul to hear the last shriek of the long fall.

Buck rolled a cigarette and lighted it. There was no

use in sitting there like a hermit in his cave. He'd have to fight to live in Lodestar. He walked back to his rifle and picked it up, then began a systematic searching of the town, until by the middle of the afternoon he had accumulated two bottles of ginger beer, a bottle of charged water, a dozen rusted cans of beans, and a sagging spring cot. He set up his temporary quarters on the second floor of the bank building, using an old office for his bedroom, blocking off the path of the wind with a sheet of faded tarpaulin. There was little chance of a building such as this to collapse over him some dark and windy night. Besides, the second floor of the bank gave a fine view of the silent town and brooding hills. He completed his sleeping arrangements by filling some old sacks with straw from the stable.

When he was done, the sun was tipping the western range, although the heat was still heavy and sluggish in the valley. A curious feeling settled over him now that he was no longer busy. Maybe Robinson Crusoe had felt the same way after he had built his crude home and arranged for his food supplies. He descended the wide staircase of the bank and walked out to the back, heading for the mines behind the town.

The bell was silent in the steeple as he neared the faded church. He saw crude lettering on the door. "This church closed," he read aloud. "God has moved on to better diggings." A gray lizard darted from beneath the porch of the church and vanished into the encroaching brush.

He was high on the slopes, close by a tailings dump, when he turned and looked back down on the silent town. Buck suddenly raised his head. A thread of dust was rising from the north. He stared at it. Heat still shimmered up from the valley floor, distorting the hills. The dust was etched against the clear sky like coarse hair drawn across blue cloth.

He watched for ten minutes. His field-glasses were

still in his saddlebags, far back across the desert, and he wished to the devil that he had them now. Some impulse made him work his way down the littered slopes, past the church, until he reached the bank building. He climbed to his quarters and peered again to the north. There was nothing to see but that thread of dust. Then suddenly the sunlight was gone, plunging the town and valley into gray shadow.

Buck walked through the littered corridor to the large office at the front of the building, and took up his vigil there. The valley was fully dark now. There was no sight nor sound of anyone approaching Lodestar. Buck rubbed his bristly jaws. The quartet for whom he was hunting might just have passed north of the dry lake, then turned south again on the long deserted road to Lodestar, searching for water in all likelihood. He checked Colt and Winchester.

There was a faint suggestion of moonlight in the eastern sky when he heard the ringing of a hoof on the hard earth north of the bank. He left the office and padded down the rear stairs, cut through the big main office on the first floor and crouched just below one of the large, paneless windows at the front. Once again he heard the striking of a hoof against the hard packed earth of the street, so close now that he felt he could reach out and touch whoever it was.

Buck stood up and flattened himself against the wall, just within the doorless entrance. He peered around the corner. He could just make out the horse, head sagging, standing just beyond the boardwalk. Its back was strangely humped. Buck bent his head and narrowed his eyes. It was then that he saw the man just beyond the head of the horse, standing there, looking the other way,

Buck moved softly, peering up and down the street. There were no other men or horses to be seen. Buck stepped out of the doorway and his left boot crushed broken glass beneath it.

The man whirled and a gun exploded, driving flame and smoke toward Buck. He felt the slug pluck at his right sleeve and the sharp impact against the stone wall just beside him. The lead screamed eerily off into space. Buck jumped forward, reversing his rifle. As the man raised his pistol to fire again, Buck swung the rifle. The butt struck neatly just above the man's right ear, partly softened by his upthrust arm, then he went down on a knee. Buck jumped forward and kicked out, just striking the man on his chest. He sprawled backward, and Buck had a curious feeling as he turned his rifle and levered a round into the chamber. "Stay where you are, mister," he said quietly.

The man moved a little. Buck walked toward him, still with that curious feeling within him. He bent his head to look down at the man. Then he stared. He placed his rifle on the ground and reached out a questing hand. Instead of striking a hard muscled chest, his hand struck softness, the same softness he had felt when he kicked the man. "Man hell!" he said aloud. *"He's a woman!"*

He took off the woman's hat and saw her tightly-braided hair. "Damn," he said. "I didn't know it was a woman!"

She moved a little and opened her eyes. "Who are you?" she asked weakly. "Where are we?"

"The name is Buck Ruffin," he said dryly. "This thriving *mee*-tropolis is Lodestar, or what's left of it."

"Thank God," she said.

"For what?" he asked, mystified. "Me or Lodestar?" Can't be Lodestar, must be me." He grinned. "Sorry I had to hurt you, ma'am. I ain't used to fighting ladies in the dark of the moon."

She sat up and tenderly touched the side of her head. "My arm deflected most of the blow," she said. "When you kicked out, I moved back, and was hardly touched." She smiled ruefully. "I think a jackrabbit could have easily kicked me over, Mister Ruffin."

He squatted on his heels. "Out of water I take it? Lost too?"

She shook her head. "Yes and no. Out of water. Not lost."

He eyed her. "You mean you aimed to come here?"

She did not answer. She got to her feet and picked up her hat. "Do you have water?"

"Sasparilla, ginger beer and a little charged water. Not the real McCoy, I'm afraid."

She looked up at him and for the first time he realized how pretty she was, despite her dusty, bruised and sunburned face. She had other feminine attributes too, and he was glad he had not caught her with a full booted kick. "Help me with him," she said.

"Him?" Buck stared. "The horse?"

She laughed. "No, silly! The *man* on the horse!"

Then Buck realized that the strange humped shape of the beast was because it had a man lying across the saddle. He helped the woman with the unconscious man, placing him on the boardwalk. He was a big man but rather soft of body thought Buck.

"We've had no water for a day and a half," she said quietly. "Mason became delirious, then passed out. Thank God he was riding at the time, or I'd never been able to get him up onto the horse. I heard what I thought was a shot from this direction earlier today. I started toward that direction. I didn't know what else to do."

Buck nodded. "I killed a rabbit," he said. He looked at the horse. An idea had formed at the back of his mind. He could take the horse, go after his quarry, send back help for the woman and her man. It was no use. The horse was too far gone. Even as Buck watched him he sank down to his knees and his head lolled.

"Will he live?" she asked quietly.

"No."

"There was no water for him," she said. "Mason

needed it. He's so big. It takes a lot of water for a man the size of Mason."

He nodded. "What about you?"

She shrugged. "I'm too tough to die," she said wryly.

The moon was rising. He eyed her face and realized that she was just more than pretty. She was downright lovely, give or take a few too many freckles, a too generous mouth perhaps, but lovely enough for Buck Ruffin.

"I'll get the charged water," said Buck. He picked up his rifle and emptied the chamber. He hurried up to his quarters and brought down a bottle of sarsaparilla and the one bottle of charged water.

"Let him have the water," she said.

He looked quickly at her. "The other is sasparilla," he said.

"That's all right."

Buck held the bottle to the man's lips. The man's eyes opened. He gulped greedily and a big hand tightened on Buck's arm. It was like feeding a huge baby his bottle of milk.

"I'm Edith Young," she said over his shoulder.

"This your husband?" asked Buck.

"Not exactly," she said.

He looked back at her. "Well, he is or he isn't."

"He's Mason Bruce, my fiancé."

"Oh," said Buck dryly. He stood up. The moonlight reflected from the star he wore pinned to his gunbelt to the left of the big buckle.

"You're a lawman?" she asked.

"Deputy-sheriff, Miss Young."

Her eyes widened, almost a little mischievously. "Here, Mister Ruffin?"

He grinned. "Not exactly. Lost my horse beyond the dry lake to the east. Got twisted around in a windstorm. Just made it here last night. Been wondering how I'm going to get out of here."

She nodded. "Matter of water, isn't it?"

"Matter of water," he echoed.

"Water!" cried out Mason Bruce.

Edith handed him the water bottle. He drained it. "More," he said.

"He's had enough," said Buck quietly. "He'll get sicker than a newborn pup if he drinks more."

"Water, damn you!" said Bruce. He reached up and snatched the sarsaparilla bottle from Buck's hand, thrusting the top of the bottle into his wide mouth. He gulped the sweet, and somewhat stale liquid noisily. He did not stop until the bottle was empty. He sat up suddenly, gripped his meaty belly, then spewed out the liquid over Buck's worn boots. "What the hell was that slop?" he demanded weakly.

"It was for the lady," said Buck. He scuffed his boots in the thin dust.

She helped her fiancé to his feet. The man was half a head taller than Buck's even six feet, heavier by thirty pounds at least, but some of that in fat.

Buck led the way upstairs to his quarters. Bruce dropped on the sagging cot. "Any food?" he demanded.

"I'll have the waiter bring up the menu," said Buck. "You want me to ring for room service?"

The man's pale eyes darted at Buck. "Why, damn you! Don't you talk that way to me!"

Buck leaned against the wall and rolled a cigarette. He glanced at the woman. "Feisty, ain't he? You have any ideas as to the disposition of that public nuisance down there? The horse, I mean?"

She looked at him, mystified. "Why do you ask?"

"Might have to eat him, is all," said Buck. He lighted the cigarette. "Hoss steaks and stale sasparilla, plus a few cans of Mexican strawberries." He nodded toward his little store of rusted bean cans.

"Is there no water here at all?" she asked.

"Couldn't find any."

"Did you try the mines?"

"Didn't have a chance. Hardly likely though, from the nature of the country."

"There is water up there, Mister Ruffin."

He eyed her closely. "How do you know?"

"The mines flooded after they petered out."

"Are you sure, ma'am?"

"Positive."

Mason Bruce leaned back on the cot. "Go get some, Edie," he groaned. "Hurry, will you?"

She looked at Buck. Buck shrugged. "Plenty of moonlight," he said. "We can take a looksee anyway. I'll wait downstairs for you, ma'am."

Buck left the room and as he walked toward the rear stairway he heard the quick murmuring of their voices. He had ears like an Apache, but he couldn't distinguish their words. "Go get some, Edie," he jeered softly as he walked downstairs. "Hurry, will you? Jeees...!" He shook his head. "The big soft slob."

The horse had managed to get up on his legs again but it was only a matter of time before he would drop forever. Buck led him slowly to a place where a building had burned long ago. The deep basement was still partly free of the ever present drift sand. Buck led the dying horse down into the hole. After he cut off the best of the meat, he'd be saved the trouble of trying to dispose of the carcass. If they had to stay in Lodestar longer than he anticipated, the stench of the decaying meat would be too much to bear. "Sorry, old boy," he said to the horse. "If there is water up at the mines, I'll bring some back for you." He removed the lariat from the saddle.

Gravel pattered into the basement and he looked up to see Edith Young standing there. He flushed a little. "Well," he said defensively, "if he has to die, at least he won't die thirsty, ma'am."

"Yes," she said quietly. She looked back at the bank building. "I wonder if he would have thought of that?"

"Ma'am?" said Buck.

She walked quickly away. "Nothing. Nothing at all."

Buck caught up with her. "You are sure about water up there?"

"Yes."

He eyed her. "May I ask how you know?"

She glanced at him. "My father was one of the engineers here years ago. I lived here as a child. He always claimed that there was a fortune in silver still in those mines, but no one could figure out a way to pump out the water."

"I had heard the vein just petered out."

She shot another sideways glance at him. "That's what a great many people think."

"Must have been quite a place in the old days," he said.

"Yes. A killing just about every week. Miners, muckers, mistresses and ministers." She eyed the church as they passed it. "Babylon has fallen."

"Then why did you, and Mason, come here?"

"You don't care much for Mason, do you?"

"You didn't answer my question," he said quietly. He had asked her the same question once before and had received no answer then.

She walked steadily on, sturdy and self-reliant, though Buck knew she must be tired and weak from the heat and lack of water. "Mason Bruce is quite a man, Mister Ruffin," she said over a shapely shoulder.

"So?" Buck grinned.

She turned. "He's big. He needs water and food more than people like us."

"Do tell?"

She flushed. "I advise you not to antagonize Mason. He can take care of himself."

Buck laughed. "Yeh, sure can."

They climbed the slope and paused beside a huge, collapsed cyanide vat. Beyond them were gaunt, skeleton-like structures, red with rust. "The shaft head is there," she said, pointing into the thick shadows underneath the rusting structure.

"Yeh," said Buck, with little enthusiasm. He walked toward the structure and saw the shaft entrance, once covered by boarding that had now fallen away from the black hole. Cool air blew about him as he stepped inside and lighted a match. The flooring looked solid enough. He got down on his belly and edged forward, feeling with his hands, until he reached the edge. The old elevator was either down at the bottom of the shaft, or it had been taken away when the mine had been abandoned. The cables were also missing. Buck felt about for a stone. He dropped it. It seemed a long time before the stone struck something far below. There was no welcoming splash of water. Buck dropped a dozen stones, all with the same result. He looked back at the girl and shrugged. "Shaft sides may have collapsed," he said.

They walked out into the bright, silvery moonlight and looked down on the dead town. "I can remember it so well," she said quietly. "Bright with lights. Alive with noise. Steam and smoke drifting over the town, mingled with the reddish dust from the mines and the grayish dust from the desert. Everything was gritty, including your food and water, but it was a lively place. A boom town, Mister Ruffin."

"Buck," he said.

She smiled. "Then please call me Edith! I feel like an old lady or a Sunday School teacher when you call me 'ma'am'."

"Does your father know you came back here?"

"No."

"I didn't think so."

She started toward the next shaft. "My father is dead, Buck."

"Sorry to hear that. Maybe he's buried here? Is that why you came back?"

She shook her head. "He died a month ago. In Utah."

He eyed her as she walked beneath the rusting struc-ture. She was holding something back. Then an odd thought drifted into his mind. Something Sheriff Ward had mentioned to him. "These four men are coldblooded killers, Buck. Yering and Stinger are wanted in half a dozen states on various charges, including murder. Deeth and Scheel committed a foul murder in Utah some weeks ago. Killed an invalid. Mining engineer. Name of Young. I knew Elias Young during the war. He was my battalion commander. No finer man than Major Elias Young, Buck. For his death, if nothing else, I'd like to see Deeth and Scheel strung up higher than Haman!"

Buck walked up beside the girl. "Major Elias Young?" he asked.

She started and then looked up into his face. "You knew him?"

"Not personally, Edith. He was murdered, wasn't he?"

She shot a suspicious glance at him. "Yes." '

He tapped the star at his belt. "So happens I'm looking for four men, names of Deeth, Scheel, Yering, and some character known only as 'Stinger.' They were heading for the California border. Dropped my horse this side of Dixie Springs. I kept on after them." He shrugged. "Damn fool that I am! Beggin' your pardon, ma'am. I'll never catch up with them now."

"No," she said quietly.

"Maybe that's why you came to Lodestar?"

She felt her way to the head of the shaft and dropped a stone. "Listen," she said. Far below them the stone splashed into water. "Thank God," she said.

"Now all we have to do is figure a way to get it," he said dryly. She was beginning to irritate him with her secretive ways. There was no time to speculate now on why she had come to Lodestar. If they didn't get water within the next twenty-four hours, it wouldn't make a bit of difference to either one of them.

Buck saw that the elevator cables were still hanging from the big wheels above them. He picked up a stick and poked at them. They seemed solid enough. "Go back and see if Mister Bruce is able to struggle up here," he said over his shoulder.

"What do you plan to do?"

There was a ladder fastened to the side of the shaft. Buck tested it with a foot. It seemed fairly solid. "Somebody will have to go down the shaft," he said. "The cables aren't long enough to get down to that water. Maybe we can rig up some way to link onto the elevator cables as a safety rig in case the ladder lets go."

She shuddered a little. "It's awfully dark down there, Buck."

"The darkness don't bother me, Edith. It's the depth." She nodded, then left him, striding down the long moonlit slope, and as thirsty for water as Buck was, he took time out to lean against the side of the shaft entrance and watch her. "Thoroughbred," he said at last.

"Thoroughbred...thoroughbred...thoroughbred..." echoed the deep shaft.

CHAPTER THREE

B uck was ready when he heard their voices as they came up the slope, and the big man was grousing. "I don't see why you couldn't have done this without me, Edie."

Buck shook his head as he made his improvised safety belt fast to the thickest elevator cable. He had pulled the cable close to the shaft side, near the ladder. If the ladder broke, he'd have the cable for safety, *If the cable held.* He had no heart and belly to go down that dark, echoing shaft, but he had no other choice. Mason Bruce was too big, and perhaps too yellow to try it, and Buck certainly wasn't going to talk Edith into the job, light as she was.

The two of them came into the shaft entrance. Buck had found several metal containers complete with lids, that would hold about two gallons apiece. He looked at the big man, who was still puffing a little from the climb up the slope. "When I get the water," said Buck, "I'll fasten the containers to the thinnest cable. It'll be up to you. to haul it up. Won't be easy."

"Yeh," growled Bruce. "How deep is the shaft?"

"Maybe a hundred feet, maybe more."

"Helluva lot of cable to pull up."

Buck rubbed his lean jaw. "Maybe you'd like to go down after the water?" he suggested dryly.

"I'm too heavy for that!"

"Then, dammit, you'll have to pull the cable up!"

"Can't you bring the water up by the ladder?"

"Mason!" snapped Edith.

"Oh, all right!" said Bruce.

Buck took off his gunbelt and holstered gun and hung them on a spike driven into a prop. He hung his hat over the gunbelt, then pulled off his boots, hoping Edith wouldn't be too offended at the condition, both of wear and of cleanliness, of his socks. Buck took the search warrants from inside his shirt and handed them to Edith. "If anything happens, get these to Sheriff Dan Ward at Piute," he said.

She gave him several candles and a box of matches. "It's the best I can do," she said.

"Thanks." He stowed the spare candles in a shirt pocket and lighted the one he had kept out. Buck placed his feet on the top rung, checked his safety belt once more, smiled briefly at the girl, then began to work his way down the ladder, feeling for and then testing each rung, with his heart in his throat. The candle flame flickered maddeningly and the containers bumped and jangled at the end of the piece of lariat he had tied them to.

Rung by rung he worked himself down until he could feel the cold air of the first drift blowing about him, and then he could see the dark mouth of the drift. Dirt worked loose from the side of the shaft and pattered and splashed far below him. He was fifty feet down when his questing foot fanned air instead of touching wood. He paused for breath, then lowered the candle as far as he could to see if the ladder had indeed ended. Two rungs were missing. He tested his safety belt, then gripped the sides of the ladder, cursing softly as hot candle wax burned his left hand. The ladder held. He breathed a prayer. Cold sweat trickled down his sides as he worked further down, down and down, expecting each second for a rung to snap, or the sides of the ladder to break away from the shaft side and dump him down through the clinging darkness until he plunged into ice cold water or broke his back on timbering.

The shaft ladder ended after he passed the seventh drift. He crawled into the drift and held out the candle. Faintly, ever so faintly, he thought he saw the light reflect from water. He dropped a stone and heard it splash, not too far down. Buck uncoiled the rest of the lariat and made it fast to one of the containers. Then he lowered it, bumping noisily against the side of the shaft until it struck water.

"Are you all right, Buck?" anxiously called Edith.

"Are you all right, Buck...are you all right, Buck...are you all right. Buck...?" echoed the shaft.

"O. K...." called Buck.

"O. K.... O. K.... O. K...." responded the shaft echo.

He felt the container sink with the weight of the water. He pulled it up, then held it to his mouth to test it. The water was cold and tasty. He swilled it about his dry mouth. He fastened the container firmly to the thinnest cable and gave it a couple of tugs. "Pull away!" he called. He watched the container swinging wildly as the cable was slowly pulled upward. Buck lowered the second container and heard it strike water. He also heard Mason Bruce cussing at the top of the shaft. Buck grinned. "Ought'a made the slob come down here himself for his water," he said. "Oh, well."

Buck rolled and lighted a cigarette as the container filled. He held the candle behind him and looked back into the drift. The shoring had sagged with the vast weight of earth above the drift. Splinters stood out from the stout timbers, clear indication of the intense strain they were under. An empty beer bottle lay near his feet. It would be empty.

He felt the container sink. He let it fill fully, then peered up the shaft. The empty was coming down. He caught it, took it from the cable, made the filled one fast, then jerked the line a couple of times. The filled one began to rise. This was a helluva lot easier than he had expected it would be.

Ten times the filled containers were hauled up the shaft and then one of them broke loose and fell, sinking into the black waters far below.

"You had enough, Ruffin?" yelled Mason Bruce down the shaft.

"Why?" retorted Buck.

"This is one helluva job up here. You got the easy part of it, *mister*."

"Sure, sure," said Buck. He shook his head. "Comin' up," he said. He rolled a cigarette and lighted it, flipping the lighted match into the shaft. It struck the water and hissed out. Buck shivered. He wondered how deep that water was. He fastened his belt to the thicker cable and grinned as he heard Mason Bruce grunting and puffing as he hauled up the last load of water.

There was no taste in Buck for the return trip up the shaft, but he sure as blazes couldn't stay down there. He took the candle and thrust it into the shaft, eyeing the ladder as far as he could see it. It looked all right. He hoped to God he wouldn't have to come down that shaft again under such circumstances, water or no water.

He could hear their voices, and strangely enough, through some freak of acoustics, their voices carried clearly to him, despite the fact they were not calling loudly as they had to him before.

"How do we know who he is?" said Mason Bruce.

"He wears a star," said Edith.

Buck felt the rungs of the ladder. He cocked his head and listened.

"Anyone can wear a star, Edie," said the big man.

"He went down there for the water, didn't he? Maybe he saved our lives, Mason."

Bruce laughed. "I would have gone down, Edie."

There was a moment's pause before she spoke again, "*Would* you have, Mason?" she asked quietly. Buck hardly heard her question.

Buck reached the first drift above the one where he had stayed while he got the water. Their voices faded away. He worked his way up slowly. Dirt pattered on the surface of the water. A rung creaked loudly beneath his weight.

"I don't trust him, Edie," said Bruce.

"He doesn't know why we are here, Mason."

Again the pause. Buck reached the next drift. He was getting tired, not so much from the exertion but from the tense nervous strain. He wanted to plant his socked feet on hard and solid earth.

"You said he was asking a lot of questions, Edie," said Mason Bruce.

Buck reached the next drift. He paused for breath. The thinner cable was being drawn up. He could see the wiry coils moving about at the top of the shaft in the faint light of the moon that was penetrating the shaft entrance. Buck was halfway between drifts when suddenly the thicker cable jerked violently and his improvised safety belt tugged at him. He slipped, gripped the sides of the ladder tightly and raised his head. "Gawd dammit!" he screamed. "What the hell are you doing up there?"

"Sorry, Ruffin," called down Bruce. "I mistook cables."

"I'll just *bet* you did," said Buck under his bream.

He worked his way upward.

"Edie," said Bruce. "Pull the thin cable down the slope so we can straighten it out. When daylight comes we can inspect it. God knows how much more water we'll need before we get out of this mess."

Buck heard the grating, scraping sound of the wire

being pulled against the lip of the shaft entrance high above him. He kept moving upward until he was at the drift just below the shaft entrance.

"Ruffin?" called Bruce.

"Yes?"

"You all right?"

"Just keno, Bruce."

"O.K."

Buck started up the last section of the ladder. He looked up to see the head and broad shoulders of the big man framed at the shaft edge, and he could hear Bruce's stertorous breathing. For a fraction of a second suspicion and a bit of panic crept over Buck. If Bruce didn't trust Buck, then Ruffin sure as hell didn't trust Mason.

Buck heard the girl call out, faintly and almost indistinctly. "Don't pull the cable, Mason! It isn't time yet!"

Time for what, thought Buck.

Bruce's breathing seemed to fill the shaft like the breathing of some gigantic sea mammal that had broken water and was lying on the heaving swells regaining its prodigious breath.

"All right, Edie!" called Bruce.

The big man moved. Buck's eyes widened as he saw Mason Bruce holding a big coil of the heavy wire cable in his hands. An instant later the coil fell directly at Buck's face. It struck him with harsh cruelty across the face, half blinding him. His grip loosened. The heavy coils of wire hung about him, entangling him, weighing him down, wearing down his strength. He sagged. A rusty spike snapped. The rung below his right boot snapped as well. His breath sobbed in his throat as he felt himself being pulled down.

For one awful moment he saw Bruce's face in the pale moonlight above him, then he fell heavily, tangled in the rusty coils of wire. The safety belt caught and then cut into him cruelly. His breath rasped from his wide open mouth. He screamed just once and the echoes slammed back and forth in the shaft, mocking him, then he fell swiftly, with his grasping hands being torn and ripped by the splintered wood of the old ladder. Then he struck his head against something. The last thing he remembered was hearing what he thought was someone laughing, but whether it was the laughter of a man, or a woman, or *both*, he could not tell.

CHAPTER FOUR

He was encased in freezing ice from the waist down, somewhere in a mountain pass, deep with snow, plunged into stygian darkness. His teeth chattered violently and his battered head throbbed like a Piute rain drum. Something incongruously warm trickled down his cold face. He touched the liquid with the tip of his tongue. It was salty and warm. It was blood.

Buck closed his eyes, trying to orient himself. It was a dream, a nightmare, nothing of reality. Maybe he'd drop off into dreamless sleep or awake to reality.

Something was trying to saw him in half, like the lady in the box at the vaudeville show in Piute. His guts were tightly constricted and cold, so cold he wasn't sure they were there at all.

He opened his eyes. It was black as the inside of a boot and cold, cold, cold...

He moved. Water lapped steadily close beside him. He felt the harsh abrasion of something against his face as he looked up. High above him was a faint area of light, so faint he could hardly believe it was there. He moved again. The rusted wire gashed his left cheek.

Buck looked down. He felt about with his left hand and found that he was in icy water up to his waist, held suspended by the safety rope that was still attached to the cable above his head. Heavy coils of rusted wire cable crowned him as Jesus had been crowned with a wreath of thorns. Sharp edged strands of the wire gouged him whenever he moved. He cautiously explored his head. His hair was wet with blood and his questing fingers struck a cruel bump. He winced in pain. There was no use in calling for help. The cold realization flooded his brain that if they knew he was still alive they'd made damned sure he never got out of that dark shaft of hell.

Buck reached out with his free left hand, holding tightly to his safety belt with his right hand. His hand struck the side of the shaft and then the splintery ladder. He worked slowly, pushing and pulling, until he freed himself from some of the entangling coils. If the lariat broke the wire would sink him like an anchor, and God alone knew how deep that shaft water was.

At last he managed to grip the ladder and shrug off the remainder of the wire. It splashed behind him and could not leave him without a parting thrust. The end of it flicked across the side of his head and he felt the quick spurting of more blood. "Have your fun, Gawd damn you," he gritted. "Old Buck has at least a shot glass of blood left in him!"

He managed to pull his freezing legs out of the water. He shook so violently he was sure the ladder would be torn from its precarious fastenings. A hell of a way for a man to die. "Well, I wanted water," he said. He laughed. "Haw! Haw! Haw!"

"Haw! Haw! Haw!" echoed the shaft.

"Shut up you mocking sonofabitch," grated Buck. "You ain't whupped me yet!"

"Whupped me yet... whupped me yet... whupped me yet."

Buck rested his head against the rough wood of the rung. Then he started up the ladder and suddenly it was as though a pair of steely arms, tough and pliant, gripped him about the waist and began to draw him back into the ebony waters. He held onto the ladder with all his weakening strength and knew he was losing the battle. What was it? What was drawing him down to a watery grave? The lifebelt had caught in the sinking wire cable. He held on with one hand, felt for his Barlow knife, opened the big blade with his strong teeth, then slashed quickly and wildly at the wet line, slicing into his own side as he did so, but the cold of the water and the terror of his soul anesthetized him. The line parted. Buck thrust the knife between his teeth and cast caution to the winds. He climbed the creaking, rickety ladder until his hands felt the floor of the drift. He bellied out on the harsh floor of the drift and lay there, streaming water and leaking blood, while his harsh breathing echoed down the drift.

Half an hour passed before Buck could sit up. He felt inside his shirt pocket for candles and the makings. He hadn't gone deep enough into the water to wet them. The matches too were dry enough to make a light. One match did for the cigarette and the candle. He squatted there in the eerie, flickering light, sucking in on the quirly, blowing out smoke in quick spurts, while his mind filled with the killing thought. He looked up at the rough roof of the drift almost as though he could see through those many feet and thousands of tons of earth to the face of Mason Bruce, and the thought of what he'd do to that face was enough to warm his chilled blood for a little while anyway.

There was no sense in sitting there. He felt about for the ladder above him and could not find it. Then the realization came to him that he was in a drift much lower than the one where he had stayed while he lowered the containers for the water, *and that the ladder did not reach from there to where he now stood.*

He tried to reach out for the dangling cable in the middle of the shaft, but it was too high and too far away. Buck rolled another cigarette, lighted it from the butt of the one he had already smoked, then held the candle out into the shaft. He could not see the pale light high above him. The moon had passed beyond the valley.

He looked behind him. There was no choice. He walked back into the drift, eyeing askance the cracked and splintered pit props. No safety engineer would have allowed a cat to walk up that drift.

He stopped after he had walked for five minutes. There was a faint feeling of draft air playing about his battered and bloody face with tiny questing fingers. He walked on, bending now and then beneath sagging props. At one place he had to widen a hole through fallen material. Water trickled from a fault and formed a pool through which he waded, testing each foot of the way with a piece of scrap lumber, until he was beyond it. He splashed out of the water. The draft was much stronger now.

His breathing echoed hollowly about him as he plodded on, seemingly deeper and deeper into the earth, for the drift floor slanted downward. He knew he was trending in a general easterly direction, or at least he thought he was. If so, he might come out on the valley slope above Lodestar.

He had no idea of time, or distance, when at last the current of air increased. He trotted forward and stared into the thick darkness beyond the weak moving pool of yellow candlelight until he thought he saw a vague grayness ahead of him. In a moment he was sliding and slipping through a mass of fallen material, then clambering up a tangled pile of pit props and warped boarding, to reach a hole through which the blessed air of the outside world poured against his battered face.

He forced his shoulders through and bellied out into a deep hole in the harsh earth. High above him winked the stars. He blew out the candle and then lay there resting. No sound came to him other than the rustling of the night wind through the dry brush.

At last he scaled the steep and crumbling slope to find himself far down the slope from the mine entrance. The scattered remains of some sort of mining shack lay about him. The moon was almost gone behind the western heights of the valley. The last of its light showed Lodestar farther below him. There was no sign of life. No light. No sound.

He looked about and found a pick handle, still sound enough for his purpose. He walked up the slope, keeping into shelter as much as possible until he reached a cyanide vat. He peered past it toward the mine entrance. The place was as deserted as it had been for many years.

Buck walked silently up the remaining slope, cursing beneath his breath as his bootless feet struck flinty stones. He paused again and listened. Nothing.

He walked into the shaft. His belt and gun, hat and boots were gone. It was what he had expected. Probably pitched down after him as he hung there unconscious. Destroy all traces of the crime. What better way to get rid of an unwanted person? Who would look for Buck Ruffin at Lodestar?

Strangely enough as he limped painfully down toward the town his hate was more intense toward Edith Young than it was for Mason Bruce. He hefted the handle in his big hand. That would take care of the big slob. But the woman? How could you effect a proper revenge on such a woman? There were ways. He could give her less of a beating than he intended to administer to Bruce. He could take his pleasure from her, and let her scream about it, or suffer in silence. There'd be a certain amount of revenge in that. But Buck Ruffin wouldn't give her the minor pleasure of knowing he craved her body. No, there would have to be another way.

Her lovely face seemed to appear before him, wide of eye, pert of nose, freckled of skin, and lusciously soft of mouth. He remembered too her well-shaped and firm curves, the steady and easy womanly stride of her as she had gone down the long slope to get that fat slob of a Bruce to come up and help get the water. He remembered her soft, melodious laughter before he realized that the humped shape on the dying horse was that of a man. He remembered how she had given up the one bottle of charged water to Bruce, though she herself was suffering from deep thirst as much as Bruce was.

He remembered the feeling of pleasure he had had within him when he had walked up toward the mines with her. Just the two of them although they hardly knew each other. He remembered too her evasiveness when he had tried to find out why she had come to Lodestar. She had sure picked herself a jim-dandy of a partner in Mason Bruce.

Maybe he was weakening in regard to Edith Young. Then one more thought came to him. The last words Buck had heard her utter. *"Don't pull the cable, Mason! It isn't time yet!"*

"Time for what, you witch?" said Buck Ruffin as he increased his speed down the slope, his hand itching about the rough wood of the pick handle.

Buck stopped in front of the church and eyed the bank building. The moonlight was gone, but the white stone of the big building stood out clearly in the darkness. There was no sign of life about it. Maybe they had pulled out, but unless they had gone on foot, there was no other way to go. Maybe they had tried it, with the water to sustain them. The water! He looked back up the slope. Mason Bruce had enough guns to stop a dozen men, his own Colt and Winchester, the girl's Colt, Buck's pistol and rifle. That against a pick handle, and two of them shooting down an unarmed man. There were other weapons for a man to use.

Buck walked quickly back up the slope, forgetting his abraded feet. He reached the mine structure and felt his way about until he found the large container into which Mason Bruce had emptied the water containers from the shaft. The container was almost brim full with water. Evidently they had just taken enough for the time being, sure of the store there at the mine entrance.

Buck whistled softly as he found a number of large cans. He bailed the water from the large container and secreted the cans here and there. His last act was to poke a hole into the thin bottom of the large container. He grinned evilly as he looked down toward the silent and dark town. "Go down and get your own water, Bruce, you slob," he said in a cracked voice.

Buck faded down the slope once again, until he reached the edge of the town. He padded along the street, studying the silent and darkened bank building. Where were they? Maybe asleep up there in the quarters he had arranged. Nice and cozy, with no thought of the trusting man they had dropped to a horrible death after he had risked his life to get water to keep them alive.

Hunger was gnawing again at his lean belly. He swiftly crossed the street and looked down into the basement hole where he had led the dying horse. The horse lay still and silent at the bottom of the hole. Buck slid down into the basement and walked to the horse. The saddle had been removed. The carcass had not been touched. Too squeamish were they? Buck grinned as he took out his knife, ready to cut steaks from the beast. Then he stopped. Let them keep thinking he was dead at the bottom of the shaft.

Buck was bone weary. There was no heart left in him that night. He walked down the old alleyway to his first quarters. The livery stable. He eased inside and looked about. The front door was closed. He braced it shut with a length of timber, then did the same for the back door. He threw himself down on the straw, oblivious of anything else but getting enough sleep to bring back the strength into his battered body. Tomorrow would be time enough to give Mason Bruce a going over. That pleasant thought drifted Buck off into a deep sleep.

It was just before the false dawn when he awoke. He shivered in the cold. As it grew a little lighter he examined his many cuts and bruises. None of them were serious. He honed his knife on a stone, then wrapped his sore feet in strips of canvas he cut from a tarpaulin, binding them with some leather thongs he found. He grinned as he saw the result. Better than skinning his feet further on the flinty ground.

He climbed up into the loft and walked forward until he could peer through the opening at the front of the loft where the hay had been hoisted up in the old days. He could easily see the bank building, already clearly visible in the dawn light. He narrowed his eyes as he saw Mason Bruce come out of the front door of the bank, rifle in hand, looking up and down the empty street. A moment later he was joined by Edith.

Buck's big hands closed into rocky fists. For a moment a paroxysm of rage swept through him, to be replaced by a cold and deadly hatred. Those two were up to something, and before Buck would confront them, he meant to find out just what it was they were so secretive about.

Edith followed the big man up the sloping street toward the mine structures. A paper fluttered in her left hand. Now and then she glanced up toward the mines and then down at her right hand. Buck realized she must be holding a compass in her hand. He waited until they had vanished amidst the clutter of buildings high on the slope, then he left the stable, cut across the street to the bank building and up the stairs into the room where he had set up his quarters. A few empty bean cans lay about. His big canteen was missing. They were leaving no evidence around the place. There were no firearms in the room. He took two cans of the beans and opened them with his knife, wolfing down the cold contents. He carried the empty cans to another room and dropped them behind the plaster in a broken wall.

The sun was peering over the eastern range when he left the bank and worked his way up toward the mines. It was easy enough to stay under cover. The slopes were stippled with a great number of miner's huts, storage sheds, vats and other necessities for large mining operations. For a time, he felt as though he was all alone again in Lodestar until the dry wind carried the faint murmuring of voices to him. He located the sounds as coming from the narrow gulch that drove into the flinty hide of the hills like a deep furrow. Buck padded up the gulch, feeling the molten heat pouring down into it. He stopped suddenly and took cover near the mouth of the gulch when he heard boots grating on the harsh earth. He stepped back into the hot shadows of a sagging hut and hefted his pick handle.

"It's no use, Edie," said Mason Bruce. "We've got to have the map. The overlay is no good without the map."

Buck peered through a crack in the wall. Bruce was standing not twenty feet away looking back at the young woman. Edith shoved back her hat and sat down on a box. A paper fluttered in her hand. "My heart isn't in this thing anymore, Mason."

"You can't bring him back," he said.

She shook her head. "It happened so swiftly."

"There was nothing I could do! I've told you that a dozen times! You know I was going to go down after him. I was willing to go! You know that!"

She nodded. Her face was set and taut. "You did say that," she said quietly.

"You act like I didn't care whether or not Ruffin made it."

She looked steadily at him. "It did seem a little cold-blooded of you to start right out this morning, with never a thought of trying to see if we could find his body, Mason."

"What good would that have done? *I* certainly am not

going down into that death trap! The man is dead! Let's forget him!"

She lowered her head. "He was so much alive, Mason. The way he would grin at you. The way he smiled at me just before he went down that shaft."

"You sound like you liked him," jeered Bruce.

"I did," she said. "He was a real man, Mason. There was much you could have learned from him."

The big man spat. "Real man? Some saddle tramp wearing a star he stole from some real lawman. I didn't like him and his prying ways. He was a wiseacre too! I had just enough of his lip."

"You're talking about the dead, Mason," she said. She stood up. "I've had enough of this for today. I can't stand this heat, the overlay proves nothing, and your attitude is a little sickening." She started past him and began to walk toward the mine where Buck Ruffin, very much alive, was supposed to be very much dead.

"Where you going?" demanded Bruce. "You take it easy on that water! I sure ain't going down that damned shaft, for you or anyone else! You hear me?" He hurried after the girl.

Buck smiled coldly. He left the hut after they had passed from view, then followed them along the slope like a great, lean hunting cat, and the feral look in his eyes would have done credit to any panther.

He saw Edith Young walk into the shaft entrance. His opinion of her had changed again. Her attitude was that of someone who was genuinely upset about the death of a man whom she had hardly known. It renewed Buck's interest in her. It also renewed his interest in Mason Bruce, but in a far different way, for it did not matter to Buck that the girl would see his vengeance on Mason Bruce. Buck could not forego that. She could stay or leave. It mattered not.

Bruce was rummaging around below the mining structure, cursing softly to himself, when Buck stopped ten feet behind him. "Edie! Edie!" yelled, the big man. "The damned water has run out! One of us is going to have to go down after more! We can't live here without it! We can't get away from here without it! Looks like it's up to you! I'm too heavy to go down those ladders! Edie! Edie!"

She came to the entrance of the mine and stopped stock-still as she saw the lean and battered figure standing behind her fiancé, as though risen from the dead, but seemingly very much alive. The odd thought passed through her mind as to whether the spirits of the dead would show signs of the death they had suffered. Buck Ruffin looked as though he had been drawn into hell through the keyhole of the door.

Bruce looked quickly at her. "What's the matter with you?"

She did not answer. She was still staring at Buck.

Bruce turned quickly. His jaw fell. "For the love of God!" he husked.

Buck moved forward like a cat.

"He's alive!" blurted Bruce. He had a feeling what was coming to him. He dropped a hand to his Colt and drew the weapon with more than creditable speed, but Buck had expected a draw. He swung the pick handle, striking the gun. The gun spat flame and smoke and the slug sang thinly through the dry air. The Colt clattered on the ground as Mason Bruce gripped his stinging gun hand in his left hand while his eyes widened in sudden fear.

The girl moved.

"Stay where you are!" snapped Buck.

"I wasn't going to interfere," she said.

"Get the drop on him, Edie!" yelled Bruce.

"No, Mason," she said sweetly. "You're on your own now."

"He's got a club!" Buck leaped in, brought the handle in a full sideways sweep, cracking Bruce alongside the head, staggering the big man. He shrieked in pain and rage but did not go down. Buck stepped back and threw the handle to one side. He pulled up his pants belt and tightened it. "That clout was to whittle you down a little, big man," he said quietly. "You sure as blazes whittled me down."

Bruce stared at him. Then he smiled slowly. "You mean you aim to give me a whipping with your bare hands, *Mister* Ruffin? *You?*"

"You've got the idea, Mister Bruce. Me!"

The big man grinned widely. He threw off his hat and unbuckled his gunbelt, letting it drop to the ground. He spat into both ham-like hands and closed them into huge fists. "Well, I'll be double damned," he said with sheer pleasure.

"Buck!" she said sharply. "Don't underestimate him!"

It was too late, for Mason Bruce was already moving easily across the littered ground toward Buck Ruffin.

CHAPTER FIVE

There was a confidence in Bruce that would have warned any other man, but Buck Ruffin was in no mood for anything but the quick battering satisfaction of hard knuckles against flesh. Bruce tested Buck with a stabbing left and a hard and short right cross that whipped past the tip of Buck's nose. He did not expect the hard, grinding smash of Buck's low, upcoming blow to the belly and the thudding jab that bounced from his jaw like the blow of a mallet.

The big man moved back, dodging and weaving, a little clumsily, his hard eyes studying Buck as he moved in. Once again Buck stabbed to the guts and then to the jaw, dropping his right quickly to slam a blow over the heart. This time Bruce was ready. He had underestimated Buck a little, figuring on the man being worn thin by his experiences in the mine shaft. His left flicked out a little, just enough to unbalance Buck. The right smashed across Buck's guard, but Buck had danced back, weaving and bobbing. The blow had hardly touched flesh.

Bruce moved on steadily to meet two or three glancing blows, then he swung a rather ponderous right to the jaw. Three blows caught the big man like a rataplan and he smashed back hard on the ground, arms out-flung, wide open mouth leaking a little blood. He blinked his eyes and shook his head. Then he sat up, placed both hands on the ground and seemed to heave himself up like a clumsy jack-in-the-box. But he did not charge the smaller man like a maddened Cape buffalo. He raised his big fists and followed Buck slowly, drawing back a little now and then as blows missed by a hair or struck his arms, elbows or shoulders.

Buck drew back, chopping steadily at Bruce. His left foot turned on a stone. It was just enough advantage for Bruce. A straight left seemed to hold Buck steady and the right slammed in like a piston. Buck hit the ground and his breath wheezed from his throat. Bruce seemed to lift and waver in the clear air.

"Time, Mister Ruffin," said the big man.

Buck shook his head. He had not seen the blow that had grounded him. He spat out a little blood then heaved himself to his feet. Bruce rushed him, slamming hard rights and lefts with full power, blood flicking from his loose mouth, his breath coming hard and heavy, for with all his weight and strength, the big man was soft in the guts. A left sank into Buck's lean midriff and a partly deflected right uppercut slammed his head back against a timber upright of the mine structure. He fell heavily to one side. Bruce grinned, and Buck knew the big man had used the upright to his advantage. If the uppercut had struck fully and cleanly, the upright just might have caved in the back of Buck's head.

"Let him alone, Mason!" cried Edith. "The man is in no condition to fight you!"

Bruce spat and drew in a deep breath. He looked coldly down at Buck. "It was *his* idea. Get up so I can finish you off, Ruffin."

Buck obliged. He was driven from one end of the area back to the other, then obliged with a return trip, blocking about every second blow, taking a hammering at ribs and belly. Then Bruce closed in, a little too eager for the kill. He met a left to his loose mouth.

A tooth snapped. He shook his head in pain and anger, giving Buck just enough time to drive in a short and powerful jab that grounded Bruce in a litter of broken glass.

Buck stepped back. He'd hardly last another round like the last one. His legs ached and were a little rubbery. His mouth was salty with blood. His eyes were not in true focus.

Anger took over within Mason Bruce. He leaped to his feet and charged. They met toe to toe, the weight of Bruce holding them, as opposed to the hate and wiry strength of Buck. Bruce was taking too much punishment. Not enough to fell him, but enough to cut him up badly. He fell against the side of a shack and went down on his knees. His hand struck the discarded pick handle and in an instant he was up on his feet, smashing toward Buck with the flailing pick handle. Buck took one savage blow across the forearm. It was no time for the Marquess of Queensberry to check his book of rules and regulations. Buck went under the pick handle, met the big man chest to chest, rammed a knee up into his groin and as his head came down, Buck butted upward with his hard Ruffin skull, catching Bruce flush on his meaty chin. Bruce staggered backward, screaming in agony. He dropped the pick handle. Buck drove forward. From some deep wellspring of endurance, he brought up the power he needed to finish the job. Half a dozen blows, not scientific, but more than effective, struck Bruce like the slugs from a Gatling gun and smashed him back against the thin boarding of the shack. A board cracked and Bruce fell back into the shack with blood streaming from nose and mouth, big hands upheld in defense, abject fear in his pleading voice. "Enough! Enough! Enough! Let me alone! I've had enough!"

Buck staggered a little as he walked to where Bruce

had dropped his six-shooter. He picked it up and looked bloodily at the white-faced young woman. He couldn't resist it. "Did I underestimate him?" he said harshly.

"I find it hard to believe."

Buck looked at the wreckage he had made of the big man. Bruce was still sobbing and groaning. "Mister Bruce," Buck said, "I *am* a lawman, not a saddle tramp wearing a stolen star. By *helping* me down that shaft, you interfered with my duty. I'll give you time to restore yourself. I want my weapons, my star, coat, hat, boots and those search warrants." Buck cocked the pistol. "Another thing." He looked at Edith. "Just what are you two doing here in Lodestar? I want no more ignoring of my questions. What is this overlay business? What are you looking for?"

"We don't have to tell him a thing," spluttered Bruce.

Buck fired. The slug slapped through the thin boarding of the shaft a foot from where Bruce lay. The smoke drifted down the slope and the echo of the shot raced itself down the valley to die away muttering in the hazy distance.

"Tell him, Edie!" said Bruce. His face was white as flour beneath the blood that stained it.

"I told you my father was Major Young," she said quietly. "He owned a large interest in the Silver Belle here in Lodestar during the boom days. When the mines began to flood he refused to believe they could not be pumped out. He used every dollar he had to buy out his partners and get more powerful pumps. It was no use. He lost everything. He left Lodestar a broken man, but he always believed the mines would eventually be pumped out. When he became an invalid some years ago he could not travel. None of his friends or relatives had the heart to tell him Lodestar was a ghost town. He talked constantly of the old days."

Mason Bruce crawled from the shack and began to wipe the blood from his face. "All the old man would talk about was something of value still here in Lodestar. *I* never really believed the old windbag. I only came with Edie to protect her."

"I'll bet," said Buck dryly. He looked at Edith. "Go on, ma'am."

She shrugged. "He kept a detailed map of Lodestar hidden somewhere in the house. I had seen it years ago, but I didn't know where it was. I had almost forgotten it. He became weaker and weaker. He began to talk of coming back to Lodestar. It was hopeless for him, of course." Her voice broke a little.

"I think he was out of his mind," said Bruce.

Edith Young looked at her fiancé. "I'm beginning to learn a great many things about you," she said coldly.

He walked toward the empty water container and looked into it. "Dry as a bone," he said. "Without water it won't make any difference if there is a treasure here or not."

"Treasure?" said Buck. He couldn't help but grin. "Hidden maps. Overlays. Compass bearings. A ghost town. What next? I think I've heard everything now."

Edith Young bit her lip. "Why should my father lie to me?"

"He was loco," snapped Mason Bruce. He blanched a little as he saw the look on Buck's face.

"Some weeks ago," said the girl, "four men came into our area back in Utah. No one seemed to know who they were. Several times I was sure they were watching our house. My father became increasingly nervous. He gave me this overlay." She took it from her pocket and held it up. "He meant to tell me where the map was hidden. He never had a chance. Two of those four men broke into the house when I was gone. My father was still alive when I returned. They had tortured him so badly that he was almost dead when I found him..." She closed her eyes and looked away.

Bruce leaned against a post. "They got the map all

right. But Edie had the overlay. The four of them pulled leather out of Utah, heading south at first. We thought they might be just throwing anyone off the trail. We decided to try and get to Lodestar first and see what we could do."

"We?" said Edith a little bitterly. "It was your idea, Mason. I can see it all now. I should have known better."

"With all that silver lying around loose you didn't want to come?" Bruce laughed. "Yeah..."

Edith shrugged. "I didn't want to stay at home. The memories were too strong. Mason said we could come and get the treasure, then go to California and buy a ranch. It sounded good enough to me. But the overlay tells us nothing. The map and the overlay must be used together."

"And Deeth, Scheel, Yering and Stinger have the map?" said Buck.

"Yes."

Buck rubbed his battered jaw. "They came through my part of the country. Killed a stage coach driver and his passenger. Tried to make it look as though Paiutes had done the bloody work. Sheriff Ward sent me after them."

"Alone?" said Bruce sarcastically. "The rough, tough, singlehanded lawman. The man behind the star. You make me sick."

Buck eyed the big man. "They killed one of my posse east of Dixie Springs, and wounded two others. I had to leave two men behind to take care of them. I came on alone. They killed my horse. I ended up here." He smiled wryly. "I thought they were heading for the California border."

Bruce's eyes narrowed. "You mean you think they might come here?"

"*Quién sabe?* Those four diamondbacks would trail a kid to a candy store to take a nickel from his sweaty little hand."

"You think they really believe in that map?"

Buck smiled. "You did, Mister Bruce. *You* did..."

"All I'm concerned about now is getting out of this hellhole and to blazes with the treasure, if there is any." Bruce looked bitterly at Edith. "You and your crazy old man! Treasure, eh? It was all in his head."

"Mister Bruce," said Buck. "I want you to round up my gear. Pronto!"

The big man walked to the nearest pile of broken timbers and pulled out Buck's things. Buck buckled on his gunbelt, pulled on his boots and placed his hat on his burning head. "Now the warrants," he said.

"Mason placed them and your guns in one of the buildings near the bank," said Edith. "They're safe enough, Buck."

"Now what?" said the big man. "We'll need water."

"Maybe you want me to go down the shaft after more?" said Buck sarcastically. "This time you'd make sure, wouldn't you?"

Bruce paled a little. "It was an accident, Ruffin. I swear it!"

"I'll never believe that whopper," said Buck.

"I got no reason to kill you, Ruffin!" protested Bruce.

"No?"

Bruce could not meet Buck's level gaze. He turned away. "We still need water," he said sourly.

"I have water," said Buck, "but just to make sure you don't pull any tricks, I'm going to ration it out to you, big man, like feeding milk to a baby. When you cry, or start kicking, I cut it off. Understand?"

"Go to hell!" snapped Bruce. He began to walk down the slope toward the town.

Buck looked at the girl. She came closer to him. "It was really an accident, Buck," she said. "Please believe me."

He looked down at her. "I believe you, Edith. I can't believe him. How did you ever get mixed up with a four-flusher like him?"

She looked away from him. "My father had a saying that you never really knew a man until you had camped with him, went to sea, or to war with him. I guess that is true about Mason. Back home he was the soul of kindness. He helped us out whenever we needed help, and was very good to my father. It wasn't until we were lost in the desert that I began to suspect that Mason Bruce, for all his size and strength, wasn't very much of a man after all."

"Size can be a fooler," said Buck. He walked beneath the mine structure and took out one of his cached water cans. One a day would have to do the three of them. He could always go back into the drift and follow it to the shaft where the water was, but there was no heart in him for doing that, no more than there was in going down the shaft itself. A man could die quickly either way, by a fall, or beneath tons of collapsed earth. As a last resort he'd do it. Meanwhile the secret of the drift was his, as well as the hidden store of water, and he meant to keep it that way.

They followed the big man down to the town. Mason Bruce brought out Buck's guns and the warrants and handed them to him, then walked into the bank building. They heard his big feet grating on the rear stairway. Edith Young looked up at the second story of the bank. "He'll never forgive you for beating him," she said quietly.

"I almost didn't," said Buck dryly. "I was lucky."

"Be careful with him from now on. Buck. There is a vindictive streak in him."

Buck grinned. "Matches mine, I guess. Don't worry."

She stepped into the shade of the building and looked up the heat shimmering slopes toward the mines. "I suppose, as long as we are here, we might as well continue looking for the treasure cache."

"Waste of time," said Buck. He rolled a cigarette. "Let me see that overlay."

She shot a quick suspicious look at him.

Buck grinned again. "Listen, Edith," he said, "I'm not interested in phony silver caches, or lost treasures. So happens I have a few beat up old maps and charts in my room back in Piute. Not even worth the paper they are drawn on."

She handed him the overlay. He squatted on his heels and studied it, then the slopes above them. There were plenty of directions on the overlay, and from what Buck could judge, the two treasure seekers had been quite right in searching the gulch, for the compass bearings on the overlay indicated the gulch.

"You see?" she said. "There isn't much doubt but what the cache is in the area of the gulch." She placed a slender finger on a sunburst marking on the overlay. "There are two mine entrances up there, quite a bit of rusted machinery, tailings dumps and at least a score of old buildings. But the overlay was made in such a manner, that it must fit the map exactly."

"Maybe another map would help," suggested Buck.

She shook her head. "My father told me the map that he made, *must* be used with this overlay."

"Great, oh, great!" Buck stood up. He glanced up the slopes. "You could search for months up there and never find a cache. You'd have to move tons of junk and earth in the search. Between me and you, Edith, I'd forget the whole thing."

She looked up at him. "But what about those four men who killed my father?"

Buck drew out his Colt and checked it. He slid it back into its sheath, then checked the Winchester. He flipped away his cigarette. "You might not be in luck, Edith, but maybe I am."

"What do you mean?"

He looked down at her and smiled, but there was no mirth in the smile. "If Deeth, Scheel, Yering and Stinger have that map, they'll be heading for Lodestar instead of the California border, won't they?" He tapped the warrants. "I'll be waiting for them, Edith."

She narrowed her eyes. "Alone?"

"Are you aiming to leave?"

"I don't see how I can without a horse."

He smiled. "They'll probably have horses, won't they?"

A coldness began to creep over her as she watched this lean lobo of a man.

Buck rolled another cigarette. "Each of those men is worth a thousand dollars to me. Dead or alive, ma'am. *Dead or alive...*"

Neither one of them saw the wide shoulders and big head of Mason Bruce drawn back from a second story window directly over their heads.

"Maybe they'll know we are here," said Edith.

"We're moving elsewhere," said Buck. "Pronto!"

There were many things to do in the heat of that day. Already the carcass of the dead horse was beginning to swell. Buck worked like a coolie, digging a hole to one side of the animal, then enlisting the grudging help of Mason Bruce to lever the carcass into the hole. They covered it with earth, then rocks and bricks, then erased all tracks in the basement.

"All that good meat gone," said Buck. "Wasted!"

"Who'd eat that carrion?" demanded Bruce.

"You might be eating worse than that before you're through," said Buck dryly.

He had selected a third floor room in one of the huge, skeleton-like mining structures, placed high on the slope, and from the windows a wide panorama of the heat-soaked valley could be seen. There was a covered way to retreat, so that they would not be seen in case they wanted to leave the structure. The water was still Buck's secret, and he had made sure that the hideout was close to the hidden entrance to the drift whereby water could be reached.

It was late afternoon by the time they were through and by the time they had finished eating the last of the ancient canned beans, it was dusk. Mason Bruce threw himself down to sleep. Buck had relieved the big man of his arms, and had made sure during the day that the big man was always in view. Buck had not forgotten Edith's warning about Bruce.

Far to the east the first suggestion of moon rise showed. Buck went downstairs to make sure they had left no traces of their presence about the mining structure, and in a few minutes Edith joined him. "There will be a fine moon tonight," she said.

"Enough to do a little treasure hunting?" he said.

She smiled. "Well, now that you mention it!"

"Come on," he said.

As they walked together toward the gulch, they were being watched again by Mason Bruce, and the look on his battered face would have made a demon feel uneasy.

CHAPTER SIX

Buck Ruffin shook his head. The moonlight flooded the gulch making the area almost as bright as the day. With the burning sun gone, the night had cooled to almost a pleasant temperature. Buck looked down at the overlay that he had spread out on a box, with the compass placed atop it. "There's so much iron and steel scattered around here, I doubt if this compass is giving true readings," he said to Edith.

She came close to him and studied the overlay. He looked down at her lovely hair, feeling the softness and the warmth of her beside him. She traced a line along the gulch. "As far as I can see, the sunburst marking should locate the cache just about in that group of buildings up the slope."

"Yeh," said Buck dryly. "Look at them."

It was as though a gigantic fist had smashed from the heavens and flattened the structures, both of wood and of rock.

"It would take days, maybe weeks to clear away that wreckage," said Buck. He looked down at her again. She pressed a finger against her soft, full lips, and eyed the destruction. She tilted her head to one side, then suddenly looked up into Buck's face. He could not help himself. He slid an arm around her and drew her close. For a moment she resisted, then slowly she slid her arms about his neck and her lips met his. They stood there for a moment, then their lips separated. She suddenly drew back and then walked away.

Buck followed her to the edge of the wreckage. "I'm sorry," he said quietly.

"Why?" she said. "Didn't you like it?"

"Yes, but that wasn't the point."

She turned, so close to him that her breasts pressed against his chest. "I liked it too," she said softly. "It doesn't matter *what* the point is."

He cupped her lovely face in his big hands and kissed her gently. "Maybe I've found the treasure," he said. There was no need to tell her what he meant, for from the look in her eyes, she felt the same way. He kissed her again and again. The wind picked up and blew the overlay along the gulch. Edith turned and looked at it. "Maybe we should just let it blow away," said Buck.

She drew away from him and walked to the overlay. She picked it up. "It seems a shame that we are so close to the cache and cannot find it."

He smiled. "We can always wait until the boys get here with the map."

She did not answer. She was looking past Buck, down the sloping trough of the gulch, toward the town. Her face was white and set. "That might be sooner than you think, Buck!"

Buck whirled, instinctively raising his rifle. To the right, at the edge of town, a plume of dust drifted off on the night wind. Four horsemen were riding slowly toward the town. It was too far to tell who they were. Buck motioned to Edith. She quickly joined him. Buck led the way down out of the gulch, keeping to cover, for the moonlight revealed every movement on the whitish earth about them.

"Do you think it is them?" asked Edith.

Buck stared down the slope. "Hard to tell. The tall one may be Deeth and the heavyset man next to him may be Scheel. Did you ever meet any of them?"

"Not socially," she said a little grimly. "But I'd know them well enough."

"Stay here," he said. He slipped quickly through some tangled brush, leaving no sound of his passage, like a lean hunting cat.

Once she thought she saw a shadow flit quickly across an open area, but she wasn't quite sure. She shivered a little. Buck Ruffin had an uncanny way of moving swiftly and noiselessly. Then she remembered his profession. *Manhunter...* Still, there were four of them against Buck, for Edith Young knew well enough now that Mason Bruce, for all his size of body and of mouth, had a yellow streak a foot wide down the middle of his broad and muscular back.

Buck slipped into an empty building and flattened himself against the wall at the front of it, peering out through a partially shattered window, thick with dust and cobwebs. Hoofs struck the hard earth and then he saw the four of them ride past. The lead rider turned in his saddle as his gray whinnied and it seemed to Buck that the man was looking directly at him, as though those hard gray eyes could penetrate dust and cobwebs, dirty glass and deep shadow to see clearly the face of the man standing there in the empty building. It was Hazen Deeth all right. There was no mistaking his lean, triangular face, set and cold in the silvery moonlight, almost like a death's head, and indeed, from the man's bloody record, it was a death's head to many, for Deeth's features had often been the last a murdered man had seen before the eternal sleep.

"What is it?" asked the man next to Deeth. It was Quin Scheel, thick of body and of head, redheaded and green-eyed, a killing machine without a human thought in his heavy body.

"Nothing, Quin," said the man in his flat metallic voice.

Buck caught a good look at the last two men. He had seen both of them at a distance, staring at him over rifle sights. Jack Yering was known to be a tinhorn gambler, and he affected gambler's attire, in black suiting and hat. His blond mustache was Mexican dandy style, and he surveyed the world with what he intended to be a cold and deadly look, Doc Holliday style, but from what Buck had heard of the man, he wasn't fit to empty out Holliday's chamber pot. For all that, Buck would have chosen a diamondback for a bunking partner rather than Jack Yering. The last of the deadly quartet was Buck's John Doe, the man known as Stinger. Medium sized, but with a tough and wiry look about him, carelessly smoking a cigarillo, cynically eyeing Lodestar. "Where are the girls, Deeth?" he called out. He laughed loudly and the echoes fled down the empty street.

"Shut up, you clown!" rapped out Deeth. "You want to be heard?"

"By who?" asked Quin Scheel. He spat into the thin dust. "Jeeesus! This is the end of the line for sure!"

Buck eased back, left the rear entrance of the building and drifted like a wraith from cover to cover until he got back to the girl. He nodded. "It's them all right. Deeth, Scheel, Yering, Stinger and Company."

"Conquest, Slaughter, Famine and Death," she said quietly. "The Four Horsemen of the Apocalypse."

He leaned back against a wall and rubbed his jaw. "Do you think Mister Bruce would give me a hand?"

"After what you did to him, Buck?"

"Well, he didn't exactly treat me like a member of the family."

"I wouldn't trust him, Buck."

"There's four thousand dollars in the saddle down

there," he said. "Mister Bruce is a man who likes the sound of silver eagles clinking together. Supposing I agree to split with him?"

She shrugged. "He might do it under those conditions."

"If Mister Bruce wants to get out of Lodestar alive, he'll have to agree to those conditions."

Buck led the way toward their hideout, and even as they crept through the shadowed ruins, they could see the four outlaws riding up the street that led to the gulch. Buck left Edith at the bottom of the stairway and swiftly ascended to the room where they had left Mason Bruce. The big man was asleep. Buck awakened him and bent close to the man's battered face. "Our four boys are here," he said. "Keep your voice low."

Bruce blanched. He sat bolt upright. "Where are they?" he asked shakily.

"Right now they're heading for the gulch."

"Maybe they'll find the cache!"

"I doubt it. Without the overlay, you could hardly pinpoint where the cache is. If there is such a thing."

Bruce stood up and peered from a window.

"Get back, you damned fool!" hissed Buck. "Any one of them can drive a rifle slug through you from where they are!"

Bruce jumped back. His left heel struck an empty can. It clattered across the floor and fell into the stair well. It clattered and bounced down the steps, sounding twice as loud because of the confinement of the stair well, and the echoes awoke against the side of the hill. Bruce dropped to the floor. Buck cursed under his breath. He glued his eyes to a crack in the side of the wall. He could see two of the outlaws, standing beside their horses at the mouth of the gulch, looking toward the structure where Buck and Bruce were.

"Get downstairs," said Buck. "Move quietly!"

Buck gathered their gear together and placed it in a

corner, covering it with trash. He glanced from the window as he finished. Two of the outlaws were moving on foot slowly toward the structure.

Buck fled silently down the rickety stairs. He reached the bottom and looked about for Edith and Mason but neither of them were to be seen. There was no time to speculate as to where they had gone. Buck vanished into a tangle of rusted wreckage, worked his way up a slope, then darted behind a huge shed and dropped flat, to belly along to the end of the shed and look down toward the area he had just vacated.

The two men were Yering and Stinger. They held their rifles ready as they eyed the gaunt structure. "Must'-a been a rat or something," said Stinger at last.

Yering shook his head. "I could have sworn I saw a man standing framed in that top center window up there."

Stinger spat. "Must'-a been a ghost then! Haw! This is a ghost town, ain't it?"

"A ghost doesn't make a racket like that," said the gambler. He surveyed the area. "Damned if I didn't feel like someone was watching us when we came into town."

"Like who? Hell, I ain't worried about ghosts, Jack. They can't hurt you."

Yering wet his thin lips. He turned and looked up the slopes, almost directly at the spot where Buck lay hidden. Buck did not breathe or blink. For a moment the gambler seemed to look directly at Buck. It was hardly possible that he did not see Buck.

A stone clattered high on the slopes beyond the structure. Yering jumped back. He raised his rifle and fired. The sound of the report echoed loudly against the hillside and seemed to boom through the emptiness. Smoke drifted down the slope.

Buck slid back. He looked up the slope. The hillside was stippled with rocks and brush, rusted iron, glory holes and warped lumber. There was no sign of life up there.

"Hell, Jack!" said Stinger. "You scairt the bejasus out'a me! Lemme know the next time you take a shot at a ghost! Haw!"

Yering levered a fresh round into his Winchester. "I don't like this damned place," he said.

Stinger lighted a cigarillo. "No?" he said. "Then why don't you pull leather out'a here?"

"With that cache hidden here? By God, we killed a man for that map! We killed a few more getting here! I'm in for my share, and don't you forget it!"

Stinger grinned. "Yeh. But if that lawman we left out in the desert gets back to his friends, mebbe they'll take a looksee here at Lodestar." Stinger looked up at the rusting framework in front of them. "By Godfrey, Jack, they wouldn't have far to go to get a readymade gallows. Haw!"

Yering cursed. He turned and walked off. Coming from the gulch were the other two men, leading four of the horses. Deeth glared at Yering. "What the hell was that shot for?"

"Jackie has been seeing and hearing ghosts," said Stinger. He blew out a cloud of smoke.

Yering grounded his rifle. "First I could have sworn I saw a man up in that structure, Deeth. Then we heard something like a can bouncing around. When we got here, we heard something up on that slope."

Hazen Deeth eyed the area. "By damn," he said thinly. "The next time I come into a ghost town, I'll hold both of you boys by your hot little hands, so you don't get scared so bad you fill your britches!"

Yering flushed. "I'm not afraid of any man, Deeth! Ghosts are different."

"Hear him!" crowed Stinger in vast delight.

Quin Scheel eyed the slopes and the gaunt structures. The dry night wind moaned softly through the brush and the old buildings. "Don't laugh, Stinger," he said in his deep voice. "They's lots of things we don't know about."

"You too?" Stinger slapped his thighs.

Hazen Deeth touched his mouth. "How much water do we have left?"

Scheel shrugged. "About half a gallon apiece."

"Any around here?"

"Ought to be, Haz."

"Yeh," said Yering, "but where?"

"Better find water before we do anything else," said Deeth.

The four of them walked back toward the town.

Buck shook his head. He had been so close to them he could mark their every feature, and he had liked none of what he had seen. Any one of the four was deadly dangerous, and together they might just spell disaster. He looked up the slope. It must have been Bruce and the girl who had made that noise up there.

He saw the four outlaws as they reached the main street and separated to hunt for water. He grinned. They'd have a damned dry hunt down there. Suddenly his eyes narrowed. He'd have to use every weapon he could against them. "Water!" he said. He smashed a fist into his other palm. Water was the key. There were half a dozen shafts that were still open, but the only one that held water was the one where Buck had almost died. The four outlaws would of course examine the shafts for water once they found out that the town held nothing but dust and decay. Water would certainly drive them to attempt the hazardous descent of the water filled shaft. They would know of only one way to get to the water, as did Edith Young and Mason Bruce. Buck was the only one who knew about the hidden, and almost equally dangerous drift that led to the water level in the shaft.

Buck slid down the slope and looked about the area for Edith and her fiancé. "Fiancé!" said Buck dryly. They had vanished completely. It gave him a slightly eerie feeling. He walked into the shaft entrance and looked about it. Pulling out a few props would probably cause a heavy fall from the roof, but it would take a team of good mules to pull those heavy props loose. A charge of powder would do a beautiful job of sealing the entrance, and Buck had had enough experience in such matters to be able to seal the entrance without filling the shaft. That too was out. No powder in the first place and the racket would awaken even the long sleepers in the weedy graveyard of Lodestar.

He walked outside and pulled himself up above the entrance. Masses of loose earth and detritus had slid down the slopes until they almost overhung the shaft entrance. He eased his way up past the material and looked down into the town, far below in the bright, revealing light of the moon. There was no sign of movement down there.

Buck picked up a shattered board and began to push against the loose material. It was hard work and the sweat burst from his pores before he felt a movement. He had just time to leap to one side and grip an upthrust timber balk before the earth and detritus slid with a soft, hissing rush over the lip above the entrance and poured steadily down until the slope seemed to be one surface, thoroughly concealing the entrance. But a thick wavering cloud of dust arose from the settling earth and hovered above the entrance. It was no time to stay and watch his work. Buck vanished up the slope, taking shelter in a roofless shack where he could watch the road that led up to the mining area. He stayed there until the dry wind had thoroughly dissipated the dust. There had been sign of life in the town. He wiped the mingled sweat of exertion and relief from his battered face. He took a chance, rolling and lighting a cigarette, squatting there in the ruins with his rifle across his thighs, watching the town, and wondering what had happened to Edith and Mason.

The safest thing for Buck to do was to stalk and kill

each of the four outlaws. He'd have to kill them. He had no facilities for holding them as prisoners, and such men knew the penalty they'd face if taken back to the authorities where they had committed their crimes. It wouldn't be easy to keep them as captives. Not for one man at least. He had fought against odds much of the time in the years he had been a lawman, but this time he was up against four of the toughest characters one could meet in a quartet of law breakers. He might get one or two of them, but the odds were they would get him before he got all of them.

Buck crushed out his cigarette butt. The reward would be paid for them, dead or alive. Killing them would be the easiest way to collect, if he ever had the chance of collecting. Manhunting was his business, but killing was not. He could not bring himself to kill that easily. Buck Ruffin wore the star.

The moon was on the wane when at last he left his hideout to drift like a shadow through the ruins and the dry rustling brush, and this time he was not hunting men, but a woman, the woman he now knew he loved. Even as he hunted, however, a lurking thought kept prying into his mind. Maybe she had gone willingly with Mason Bruce. Maybe she was hiding out with him. Maybe she had lied to Buck. There was no trust in Buck for Mason Bruce, but there had been for the girl. Now he wasn't sure. He knew if she loved him, he'd have to have faith in her, but the thought did not rest easily in his mind. Maybe she had been using him. Maybe she still loved that big slob. The thought was anathema to Buck. He spat dryly.

The valley was shrouded in the darkness of the after moon when at last he gave up the futile search. A single light showed in a building on the main street of Lodestar and he knew well enough who dared show light down there. He scanned the dark slopes to right and left of him, wondering to where Edith had vanished.

His last act was to walk up the gulch where the *treasure* was supposed to be hidden. He shook his head in the darkness. If there was any treasure in Lodestar, he was almost sure it would never be found by using the overlay and map left by Edith's father. The old boy must have been a little loco.

Buck found a new hideout. It was a large excavation that had been walled with heavy stone, roofed with heavy timbers that had been covered with a thick layer of earth, like a Civil War boomproof. His boots crushed something as he peered into the darkness of the interior. He knelt on one knee and saw what had once been a heavy hand-welded metal flask, now almost completely eaten away by rust and the corrosive action of the borax-laden wind of the valley. He stepped inside the low structure and lighted a match. The interior was like a catacomb, but it would make a good place to hide. He found a pile of tattered, dusty tarpaulins lying to one side, and on them he made his bed for the rest of the night.

His last thought as he drifted off to sleep, listening to the dry rustling voice of the desert wind as it swept across the hills, was of Edith Young.

Down in Lodestar the lone light winked out at last. Jack Yering was on guard. He stood outside the old saloon where he and his companions had made their quarters. He leaned back against the warped front wall of the saloon, watching the dark slopes high above the town, still able to see the gaunt and rusting structures etched against the night sky. The others could laugh at him, but he knew he had seen a man up there. He knew too that he had heard a sound on those slopes. There was an uneasiness in the man that night, an uneasiness that had given birth when they had killed the old man back in Utah for his map; an uneasiness that had grown steadily all the time they had worked their way across Nevada, sowing death, until they had reached Lodestar, and here the uneasiness was greatest of all.

The wind howled a little as it gained strength, as it always did at night, because of the displacement of the vast masses of heat-sluggish air hanging in the low valleys and depressions. Furnace winds. Winds of searing heat that could steal the breath and life from a man if they grew strong enough. *Winds of death*.

CHAPTER SEVEN

I n the darkness of the pre-dawn a shadowy figure moved noiselessly through the windswept streets of Lodestar. Tumbleweeds had rolled that night through the streets of the town, some of them racing on into the open country beyond the town, while others had banked up against buildings and fences in great tangled masses. It had been a noisy brawling night. Old glass had shattered. Warped shutters had been ripped free from rusted fastenings. Galvanized sheeting had been torn from several of the old mining buildings and had gone clattering and rattling down the slopes to batter against some of the buildings. A sagging shed had fully collapsed and the wind had strewn the sun silvered timbers across the main street. Buck Ruffin worked his way through a narrow gap between two buildings not far from the saloon where the four outlaws had made their quarters.

The saloon seemed quiet enough. Buck wet his dry lips and studied the building. With one gutty man to back him, he'd be able to pen them up inside the saloon. There was precious little profit in thinking about that. He worked his way back through the space between the buildings and walked quickly and silently along the rear of the building row until he could cut across the street and come in toward the rear of the old saloon. As he passed the livery stable where he had slept his first night in Lodestar a horse whinnied suddenly and the sound made him start. Cold sweat trickled down his sides as he darted into cover. He had forgotten that the four outlaws had kept their horses near them.

Buck eased into a sagging shed and peered through a crack. Four horses. If he could get at those mounts he'd be able to leave Lodestar and get to where he could swear in possemen. His quarry would hardly take a chance on leaving Lodestar to face on foot the perils of the desert without water. It would almost be like keeping them on a desert island, a sort of Nevada Devil's Island, until he could come back for them.

The wind shifted. Hard gravel slashed at the side of the shed, shaking it a little. Buck felt thirst clawing at his throat. He touched his dry lips with his tongue. It would be easy enough for him to up stakes and pull foot. He knew he'd make it to civilization and help. Even if they were dead of thirst when he returned it didn't really matter. It would save the posse or a jury the trouble of finishing them off. But what of Edith Young? Buck didn't give a plugged nickel for Mason Bruce. The big man would give short enough shrift to Buck Ruffin if *he* had the chance.

He studied the rear of the saloon. The back door had been closed against the wind and the rear windows had been cross barred with wood slats nailed firmly to the frames, as though the departing owner had fully intended to come back some day to Lodestar if the mines opened again.

Buck climbed through a rear window in the shed and padded along behind a collapsed warehouse until he could see the side and rear of the stable. As he moved he again heard the plaintive whinnying of a horse, and then he could hear all of them whinnying. Thirst was attacking them and their masters had hardly enough water to keep themselves alive. His heart went out to the dumb beasts. He was the only one who could give them water, but if he tried to free them from the stable and get them to water he'd forfeit his own life.

He was about to start for the main street when suddenly the rear door of the saloon swung open, was caught by the wind and slammed hard against the side of the building. Buck froze against the side of the warehouse. He could not see the open doorway of the saloon. He started to move toward the rear of the warehouse. The horses were whinnying in chorus now. It was then that he sensed, rather than heard, the slow movement along the alleyway between the warehouse and the rear of the livery stable. Buck flattened himself again against the side of the warehouse with nothing but a narrow vertical beam between him and the view of anyone in the alleyway. He pressed back hard, looking sideways through a narrow crack between the beam and the side of the warehouse. A man was standing in the alleyway, not twenty feet from Buck, looking at the rear of the livery stable. He recognized the heavily muscled and tremendously wide shoulders and back of Quin Scheel.

Scheel's head turned from side to side as he looked up and down the alleyway. He held a Winchester in one meaty hand. Then he reached for the rear sliding door of the stable and as he slid the door back on its dirt clogged and rusted track, Buck took advantage of the noise to run back behind the warehouse. As he did so he kicked a stone hard against the side of a large tin container lying on the ground. The contact of stone against metal sounded like a pistol shot.

Quin Scheel whirled. His small eyes narrowed. He stepped back inside the stable and looked quickly about. Then he peered along the side of the warehouse. By God the wind didn't have enough strength to hurl a stone that hard against the container! The big man stepped out into the alleyway and walked slowly toward the rear of the warehouse, Winchester cocked and ready in his hands, eyes darting suspiciously from side to side. He paused beside the vertical beam. There was an animal awareness in Quin Scheel. No brains, but plenty of quick suspicious alertness for impending danger. When other men depended on brains, Scheel depended on his senses. They hadn't failed him yet.

Buck eased back into the warehouse through a wide gap in the wall. He drew in a deep breath. Then he heard the soft, furtive movements alongside the building, a few feet from him. He raised his head and waited. Something grated on the ground behind the warehouse and Buck almost jumped back as he saw Scheel's broad back not a yard from him, blocking the gap. It was getting close to dawn and already the darkness was shaded with gray in the east.

Buck hardly dared to breathe. Scheel's head turned from side to side on its short, thick neck. Then he stopped turning his head. For a long moment he stood there, listening and waiting. Buck shifted a little. A stick cracked beneath his right boot sole. Scheel moved, starting to turn his head, but Buck moved a fraction of a second before Scheel did. Buck stepped in close, swung up his Winchester and drove the metal shod butt hard against the back of Scheel's head. Scheel grunted. His breath rasped out of him. He staggered forward. "Deeth!" he yelled hoarsely.

Buck stepped into the gap and struck again, hard and viciously. Scheel went down on his knees and tried to turn. Any ordinary man would have been unconscious after the first blow. Once more Buck struck the big man and he fell face downward on the hard ground to lie still. Buck heard a man shout in the alleyway. He stepped back into the warehouse and picked up a heavy plank, studded with rusted nails, that had fallen from the side of the building. He stepped outside again and dropped the plank across the broad back of Quin Scheel. Boots grated on the ground alongside the warehouse. Buck stepped inside again and darted toward the front of the warehouse, carefully avoiding fallen wood and littered junk, until he reached the front of the building. He looked back to see a man standing over Quin Scheel. It was Hazen Deeth. Buck peered through a crack and saw Jack Yering and Stinger running toward the livery stable.

"Back here!" yelled Deeth.

The two men ran toward the rear of the warehouse.

Buck stepped into the alleyway and darted across to the rear of the saloon. He jumped inside and looked about. It was just light enough to see the blankets on the floor and the scattered gear and saddles. There were four large canteens hanging from a wall hook. He quickly raised each one of them in turn. Two of them were almost empty, while the other two seemed to be about half full. He yanked the stopper out of one of them and stepped behind the long dusty bar to pour the contents down the old sink. The precious fluid gurgled down the dirt clogged drainpipe. He hung the canteen on the hook and reached for the other one that held the most water. Just as he did so he heard argumentative voices in the alleyway. There was no time to leave the saloon. He darted behind the bar and ran up to the far end where a cabinet gaped open, concealing him in case anyone looked along the back of the bar from the rear end. He crouched behind it with ready Winchester just as they came into the rear door of the saloon.

"Wasn't no damned beam that hit me!" roared Quin Scheel.

"It was lying on top of you, Quin," said Hazen Deeth.

"Must-a been one helluva wallop to drop an ox like you," said Stinger.

"Dammit!" yelled Scheel. "You think that blasted beam hit me three times! *Three* times I tell you!"

"I gotta admit it would take three good wallops to lay

you flat," jeered Stinger, "but the wind couldn't have done it!"

"I tell you I was hit three times!"

"How do we know it was the wind?" said Yering quietly.

"What do you mean?" demanded Deeth.

"I still say I saw a man up there in one of those buildings, Deeth."

"Here we go again," said Stinger.

"Let me take a look at your head, Quin," said Deeth.

Buck drew in a breath. He crouched further back into his place of concealment. If they found him there would be one devil of a shooting scrape.

"Ain't there three lumps?" said Scheel.

"Hard to say, Quin," replied Deeth. "Your hat and the thickness of your hair blunted the blows, if they *were* blows."

"The thickness of his head you mean," said Stinger. He laughed and slapped his thighs.

"One a these days," promised Scheel. "One a these days I'm gonna tear out that little man's tongue and stuff it down his laughing throat. Get me some water, Haz."

Feet grated on the floor. There was a pause. "Your canteen *is* empty, Quin," said Deeth quietly.

"What the hell you talkin' about!" roared Scheel. "I had it morn' half full last night! By God! I..." His voice trailed off. Feet grated again. Then suddenly the empty canteen struck the wall behind the end of the bar and clattered to the floor. "By God! It *is* empty!"

"You sure you didn't empty it last night?" asked Deeth.

"I was last on guard," replied the big man. "Took a little swallow afore I went outside. The thing was mor'n' half full like I said. Who drunk it! Who took it?"

A stopper popped a little as it was withdrawn from another canteen, then Hazen Deeth spoke. "This is mine, Quin. It's still half full."

"I didn't touch it!" snapped Yering.

"Me neither!" said Stinger.

"Yeah," snarled Scheel. "Nobody took my water! Nobody slammed me three times on the skull! Just the four of us in this town, eh?"

"No need to get so damned excited about it, Quin," said Deeth. "You might have been mistaken about the water. You could be wrong about being hit three times."

"I know what I know!" roared the big man. A fist smashed down on the bar and dust rose from the surface of the mahogany and drifted thinly down on Buck. He had to thrust a finger beneath his nose to keep from sneezing.

"Damned queer," said Jack Yering. "I tell you, Haz, there's something queer about this town."

"Ghosts," said Stinger in great delight. "Hawww!"

"One of these days," said the gambler in a low voice, "you might just die laughing, Stinger."

There was another pause, then Stinger spoke in a different voice. "Meaning *what*, Jack?"

"Don't mistake my superstition for fear."

"Listen to him," said Stinger in a low hard voice. "Talking like a school teacher again."

"That's enough out of both of you," rasped Deeth. "I want no fighting here!"

"You the boss man?" asked Stinger.

Buck could almost feel the tension. His legs were beginning to ache from his cramped position but he didn't dare move a fraction.

"You saying I'm *not?*" asked Deeth in his flat metallic voice.

"We're all in this together, equal shares," said Stinger. "We take all the risks, stand the chance of walking up Ladder Street and down Rope Lane for them killings we done. Share and share alike on the risks: share and share alike on the take."

"It was my idea to hit old man Young for the map," said Deeth.

Stinger laughed dryly. "For a map that ain't worth a piece of outhouse paper from what I can see."

"Maybe you want out of the deal, eh?" said Scheel.

"I ain't talking to you, Quin," said Stinger.

"Well, you'll listen! Haz thought up this deal. Without him we'd be sitting back in Utah with our hands on our butts wondering what the hell we was gonna do next. Well, I'm with Haz. What about you, Jack?"

"Count me in," said the gambler.

"Stinger?" said Deeth.

There was no answer.

"Stinger?" said Deeth once more.

"All right, dammit! Let's get straightened out on this water thing. Them horses won't likely live another twenty-four hours without water. I ain't gonna let my horse die of thirst."

"You're likely to die of thirst yourself," said Yering, "if we don't find water."

"I'd like to know which of you jaspers stole my water," growled Scheel.

"We'll split up the water," said Deeth. "Equal shares. Like Stinger said: equal shares on the risks; equal shares on the take. Any arguments on the water?"

No one spoke up.

Buck heard water gurgling from a canteen. Boots creaked on the grated floorboards behind the bar and the empty canteen was picked up.

Deeth spoke up. "We'll go up to the mine area now that it's light outside. We'll search for water first. In pairs."

"Why pairs?" said Stinger. "Ain't no one up there, Deeth."

"How do we know for sure?"

Buck listened to them leave the saloon. He waited a few minutes, then stood up, gratefully stretching his muscles. It had been too close to suit him. He had learned plenty though. The best way to attack an enemy is to learn his weaknesses first. Deeth knew they'd have to have a leader or their efforts would be wasted because of lack of cooperation between them. He had taken over that leadership, but he was dealing with tough minded, highly individualistic and merciless men. Deeth was likely the most dangerous, as well as the most intelligent of the four of them. Quin Scheel's mind was nothing to fear, but his massive strength certainly was. Jack Yering was no tenderfoot by far, but the man seemed to have an inherent fear of the unknown. On the opposite side of the ledger, Stinger had no fear whatsoever of the unknown, but his weakness might be in his cynical attitude and his dislike of authority. Buck grinned. He was thinking like a professor of psychology.

He walked to the front of the saloon just in time to see the four of them pass from sight beyond the bank building on the street that led toward the mines. The first thing he did was to check their saddlebags. From one of them he removed half a dozen boxes of .44/40 cartridges, standard for rifle and pistol both. It wasn't likely that the four of them would need more than the cartridges now contained in their rifles, pistols and cartridge belts, but Buck would take no chances. The cartridges also fit his rifle and pistol. He stuffed them into his pockets. There wasn't much else of value to him in the other saddlebags except food, but he did not dare take any of that. They'd miss that as they had the water. He did take a good long drink out of a bottle of rye he found in one of the bags.

Buck left the saloon in the watery light of dawn and walked to the stable. The horses whinnied as he walked into the stable. He eyed them thoughtfully. It would be a cinch to take them from the stable while the four outlaws were hunting for water, but there was no place he could conceal them, nor could he free them, for he'd probably need them to escape from Lodestar. *If* he managed to take care of Deeth, Scheel, Yering and Stinger. "Yeh," he said dryly.

He closed the door behind him and walked to the south end of the town, keeping in the shelter of the alleyway. The sun was tipping the eastern range when he reached the last building on the street. He cut through its echoing emptiness, scouted the street with wary eyes, then ran across to the end building on the other side of the street. The night wind had died away and a deathly stillness hung over Lodestar. It was almost like it had been when he had arrived there from the desert.

He was halfway up the slopes, keeping under cover, and moving slowly when he remembered that someone else would be needing water that day. Edith Young had no water, and no way of getting any unless Buck saw to it that she was supplied. That put a far different complexion on things. It was bad enough that the horses were suffering from lack of water, but he could not bear the thought of Edith suffering, even if she might possibly have turned against him.

He lay belly flat in the brush watching the area where he had cached his water. No one was in sight, but something held him back. Foot by foot he studied the slopes. Once he thought he heard the distant sound of voices but he wasn't sure.

The sun was beating mercilessly on his back when he made his move toward the cache. No one could live long under that sun without water. Even Buck was beginning to feel the lack of it. Now he regretted pouring Quin Scheel's water down the bar drain. Sweat worked its way down his face and he could taste the salt of it upon his dry lips.

He stood up and walked in a crouching position until he gained the shelter of one of the towering mine structures.

He reached a place where he had left a can and felt

about amidst the rubble for it. His hand touched the metal and he drew out the full can. He raised it to his lips.

"Just hold it there, Ruffin," said the voice behind him. "Don't drop it!"

Buck slowly lowered the can. It was the voice of Mason Bruce.

"Outsmarted you, eh, Ruffin?" sneered Bruce. "By Godfrey, I had an idea you'd come sneaking back up here for water." Boots grated on the ground. "Put down the can, easy-like."

Buck obeyed. He saw Mason's hand reach out and pick up Buck's Winchester. A moment later he felt his Colt get pulled swiftly from its sheath.

"Turn around now," said Bruce.

Buck turned to see Bruce holding a cocked Colt at Buck's belly level. Buck had taken Bruce's weapons from him and concealed them, but he had not taken Edith's six-gun from her. He recognized it now because of the barrel engraving and the ivory butt grips. "Where are they?" asked the big man.

"Somewhere around here. If you don't want to be seen we'd better get under cover."

"Where are their horses?"

"In the old livery stable."

"Where's the rest of the water?"

"Here and there."

"Get it."

Buck retrieved another of the cans. There was no chance to jump the big man, and even if he did, the noise of the fighting would probably bring the outlaws to the scene.

There was a speculative look on Bruce's battered face. "You sure this is all the water?"

"Yes."

The man grinned. "There's more down the shaft."

Buck jerked his head toward the entrance. "Take a look, Bruce."

The man's face fell as he saw the earth that sealed the shaft entrance. "By Godfrey! Take a man days to dig through that fall!" He turned quickly and looked at Buck. "What do you know about it, eh?"

"You think I'm loco enough to cut off the only water supply in this whole valley, Bruce?"

Bruce's pale eyes narrowed. "You're loco, but you ain't *that* loco." He wet his lips. "On the other hand, it might be just like you to seal up the entrance to fool us, and you knowing all the time where other water is."

Buck looked along the slope. "While we stand out here like two jackasses, those four buzzards just might spot us, Big Man. Right now they don't know for sure if anyone else is around here. So help, Bruce! If they *do* find out the two of us will live just long enough to take one last breath. You know what they did to Major Young."

"Stop bluffing, Ruffin."

"All right! Forget about us! But they won't kill Edith. Not right away anyway. Can you get *that* through your thick head?"

Bruce hesitated. "All right," he said at last. "Walk south along the slope. Take the water cans."

Buck walked ahead of the big man. He wouldn't have put it past Bruce to kill him by a shot in the back. There wasn't any doubt in Buck's mind that Bruce had meant to do away with him in that mining shaft. But now a shot would alert Deeth, Scheel, Yering, Stinger and Company. Mason Bruce wasn't that big a fool.

"Turn right," said Bruce.

Buck saw a sagging structure, wooden framed, sheeted with galvanized metal. He walked into it and looked about. He had hoped to see Edith, but there was no sign of her.

"Go behind that partition," commanded Bruce.

Buck did as he was told. He faced a blank wall.

Something creaked. Buck looked over his shoulder to see Bruce standing beside an open trapdoor. Cool air swirled up. Buck could see a ladder descending into the depths. Bruce jerked his head. Buck walked to the trapdoor, placed the water cans at the edge of it. then got down on the ladder. He picked up the cans and felt his way carefully down to the ground at the foot of the ladder.

"Get back," said Bruce. He came slowly down the ladder, closing the trapdoor above him. A moment later he snapped a match on his thumbnail. He lighted a candle standing on a shelf. "Walk," he said. He jerked his head toward a tunnel entrance.

Buck walked ahead, half feeling his way, for the flickering light was hardly enough to show the way. They walked a good fifty yards before Bruce fold Buck to stop. Buck narrowed his eyes. Noises echoed along the tunnel.

"Put down the cans," said Bruce.

Buck did as he was told to do. There was no sign of Edith in that tunnel. A cold feeling came over him.

"Turn around," said Bruce.

Buck turned and saw the pale eyes of the man fixed on him. The gun hammer clicked back crisply. "How do you want it, Mister Ruffin?" said Bruce quietly. "Head or belly?"

"Why kill me?" asked Buck.

Bruce was silent for a minute. "You're in the way, Ruffin."

"I don't want your hidden treasure, Bruce."

"It isn't that, Ruffin. It's Edith."

"She means nothing to me."

Bruce spat at Buck's feet. "Lying ain't going to get you out of this hole, Mister Ruffin. Nice and quiet down here, ain't it? Found it myself. Take a good man outside to hear a shot fired down here, wouldn't it?"

"Does Edith know about this?"

"Yes."

"Now you're lying, Bruce."

A curiously lopsided grin came over Bruce's battered face. "What difference does it make to you?"

He was right. It made no difference. Bruce could do away with him neatly, as he had tried to do in the shaft. Edith probably didn't know what Bruce was up to. One shot would silence Buck forever. Trust Bruce to dispose of the stiffening body so that it would never be found until Judgement Day. He'd have the girl then, and perhaps the treasure, though Edith would have been treasure enough for Buck Ruffin, not that it mattered now.

"You'll need more water to get out of Lodestar," said Buck.

Bruce looked down at the cans. "There's enough there."

"Not for a man and woman afoot, Bruce."

The pale eyes flickered a little.

"Those four jaspers have left their horses down in town. A good man could slip down there and get the horses, but they'd need a lot of water. They won't live much longer without it."

"Go on."

"Supposing I show you how to get more water, then help you get the horses? You could take two of them and leave me one. My job is to get those four outlaws. If I can get back to civilization, I can bring back a posse for them. They won't leave here and chance the desert without horses."

"I can get the horses by myself."

"Sure, but not the water."

"By Godfrey I can sweat the location of it out of you, Ruffin!"

"Try it," said Buck softly.

Their eyes clashed. Bruce was yellow. He wouldn't have the guts to get those horses alone. He wet his lips. "All right," he said. "But I'll keep you covered every inch of the way. You make one false move, Ruffin, and you'll die with a bullet in the back. Get it?"

Buck nodded.

"Leave that water here. Walk to the ladder."

Buck walked ahead of the big man. At the foot of the ladder, he was told to cross his wrists behind him. Swiftly Bruce bound Buck's wrists together, viciously drawing the rope as tightly as he could. "*Now,* you smart bastard," he crowed. "You can't do a damned thing! Get up that ladder, Lawman!"

Buck started up. He placed his head against the bottom of the trapdoor to push it up. He struggled a bit. "Too heavy," he said. "Give me a hand."

He felt Bruce's weight on the ladder. Then he leaned forward, resting his chest against the rungs. He suddenly raised a leg, drew it up and smashed it down again with the full power of his lean, hard muscles. The hooked heel struck solidly against flesh. Buck dropped from the ladder as Bruce gasped and choked. Buck's knees struck Bruce on the chest, driving him backward so that he sprawled flat on the tunnel floor. The big man tried to raise his head. A boot heel landed solidly alongside his fleshy left jowl and he lay back quietly with a twin runnel of blood leaking from his nose.

Buck leaned weakly back against the ladder. It had been a close thing. He wondered how much more of this a man could take. He grinned a little. "You always wanted to be a lawman, Ruffin," he said. He walked to a prop and found a headless spike thrusting through the wood. He worked quickly, sawing the rope against it, gritting his teeth as the rusted metal tore raggedly into his flesh. Then a strand parted. He heard Bruce move. He sawed faster, ignoring the raw searing pain of it. Another strand parted. Bruce raised his head and stared wildly at Buck. He pushed his hands down on the floor and tried to get up. Cold sweat mingled with the blood on Buck's hands. Bruce would never again be talked out of killing him.

Bruce forced himself up to his knees, drooling blood and saliva. Then he started up again. The last strand parted. Bruce made a driving, bull-like rush at Buck. Buck leaped up and raised both feet, driving them out. Both boot heels struck this time on the top of Bruce's head, driving him back against the tunnel wall. He sagged down to the floor and lay still once more. Buck picked up the Colt. He wiped the sweat from his eyes. "One of these days, Big Man," he said thoughtfully to the unconscious man, "I might just have to kill you..."

CHAPTER EIGHT

Buck straightened up after he'd finished lashing Mason Bruce's wrists together. "Turnabout, Brucie," he said with a grin.

Something thudded on the flooring above the tunnel. Buck's left hand instantly closed over the candle flame and he picked up his rifle. The smell of the extinguished candle hung thickly in the tunnel. Buck raised his head and listened. The thudding sound came to him again, and then he heard the muffled sound of voices. He knew well enough who it was. Edith Young was not quite the type to talk to herself.

Feet scraped on the sagging trapdoor above the tunnel. Dirt pattered down into the tunnel. Buck leaned his rifle against the wall and gripped Mason Bruce under the arms. He dragged the big man along the tunnel in the pitch blackness, hoping those in the building couldn't hear the noise. Fifty yards up the tunnel Buck's left foot struck something that fell with a clattering noise. Something gushed on the floor. He had forgotten that the water cans had been left in the tunnel. He dropped Bruce and felt for his own Colt. He cocked it and walked silently back through the darkness to the area below the building. He waited, smelling the greasy smoke of the candle. If they opened that trapdoor they'd be sure to notice it.

The sound of voices came again. Buck pocketed the candle. He picked up his rifle and looked up toward the unseen trapdoor. Feet scuffled on the floor. He faded back into the tunnel like a ghost as the trapdoor was flung violently open and daylight flooded down into the tunnel.

"What do you see, Quin?" asked Hazen Deeth.

"Nothing but a ladder, Haz."

"Anything down there?"

Scheel laughed. "That's Yering again. Ain't nothing down there but a bad smell."

Feet grated on the flooring. Buck drifted further back. The tunnel was not a straight one. There were enough shallow turns in it to conceal anyone far enough up the tunnel if a light was shown into it from the area below the building. He could clearly hear them talking.

"Damn it, Yering," said Deeth. "You've been seeing too many things to suit me!"

"I tell you I saw two men come in here."

"You see who they were?"

"Too far away."

"Yeh," said the sarcastic voice of Stinger. "So was the jasper you said you seen in that mine building."

"I saw two men come in here I tell you! And I still don't believe Quin was knocked out by a falling plank!"

"Sure smells bad down there," said Scheel. "Mine gas, eh?"

There was a moment's pause, then Jack Yering spoke. "That smells like candle grease to me, Haz."

"Haw! Haw! Haw!" roared Stinger. "Now he's got ghosts lighting candles to see their way along a tunnel! Haw! Haw! Haw!"

Feet shuffled. "Wait," said Deeth. "It *does* smell like candle grease."

Buck moved back to where he had left Bruce. The man moved a little, but no sound came through the solid gag Buck had shoved into his big mouth. Buck dragged the heavy weight of the man further up the tunnel, expecting any minute to see a light down the tunnel. He felt about with his hands. He had reached a sort of wide area in the tunnel. He rolled Bruce to one side, then padded back to the next turn. He caught the vague movement of light down the tunnel. Buck raised his rifle.

Boots grated on the tunnel floor. Then Buck heard hard breathing. He eased back the rifle hammer to full cock.

Minutes ticked past. Then the grating sound came again. It stopped. Something struck metal. "Well I'll be double-damned," said Stinger. "Haz, this is a full can of water. An empty one lying beside it."

"So? Could have been down here a long time, Stinger."

"Haz, this is *fresh* water and the floor is all wet under the empty one," said Stinger quietly.

Buck hardly dared breathe. If they came at him he'd have to shoot. He would get one' of them, perhaps both of them, but the other two would probably escape, and if they knew he was down there armed, they'd make sure he'd never get out of that tunnel.

Time seemed to congeal in that dark tunnel. The light flickered uncertainly. Then feet grated a little. The light moved back until Buck could see none of it. He could still hear movements in the area below the building.

"What's the matter with you hombres?" demanded Quin Scheel.

"Shut up, Quin!" snapped Deeth.

"You see anything?" asked Jack Yering.

"No!" snapped Stinger. "Shut up!"

"You *did* see something!" said Yering triumphantly.

"Damn you! Shut up, Yering!" rasped Deeth. "Pass that water can up, Stinger."

Metal bumped against wood. It was too quiet to suit Buck. He wet his cracked lips and bent his head forward. The light was completely gone now. Feet grated on wood. The trapdoor crashed shut. He padded forward. A moment later something heavy fell atop the door. Feet scuffled. "Now you sonofabitch," came the muffled voice of Hazen Deeth, "whoever you are, flesh or the devil, let's see you get out of there!" He laughed metallically.

Buck wiped the sweat from his face. He cursed his stupidity in leaving the water cans behind him. On the other hand, if they had not found the cans they might have come on, to a deadly fight in the darkness of the tunnel.

The voices were now too muffled for Buck to distinguish anything they were saying. There was no use trying the trapdoor. They had it well blocked, and even if he could have forced it up he'd probably find himself staring into the black ring of a gun muzzle. He leaned weakly against the side of the tunnel.

It was deathly quiet now. Not a sound came from the building above the tunnel. Buck walked back into the tunnel and lighted the candle. He walked back to Mason Bruce. The light reflected from the wide, staring eyes of the big man, mingled fear and hate in them.

Buck walked past Bruce and along the tunnel. His luck in escaping from the water shaft had been phenomenal. He couldn't again expect such a break. If he could not find another way out of the tunnel he'd have to try and shoot his way out. He might as well save the time and effort doing that. It would be much simpler to shove his gun muzzle into his mouth and press the trigger.

He walked for five minutes and then suddenly around a sharp turn he faced a mass of fallen earth through which shattered pit props thrust their heads. There was no way he could tell how big the fall was. He had no way of digging through it but with his bare hands. The air here was a little bad. The candle light flickered uncertainly for lack of oxygen. If enough air did not leak into the tunnel around the tightly fitting edges of the trapdoor, he wouldn't have to worry about committing suicide. Lack of air would force him up into the building to face the flaming guns of the four outlaws. He walked back to Mason Bruce and pulled the soggy gag from his mouth. He swiftly told the man what had happened. There was rank and sickening fear in Bruce's eyes when Buck finished.

Buck stood up. He rolled two cigarettes. He thrust one into Bruce's mouth. He lighted them. Bruce spoke around the cigarette. "You'll exhaust what little air we got!"

Buck smiled thinly. "What difference does it make, Bruce? We can't stay down here."

"So?"

Buck glanced at his rifle. "We've got two Colts and a Winchester."

"So?"

Buck looked upward. "We'll have to try and get up through that trapdoor."

"With them up there? You loco? Count me out, *Mister* Lawman!"

"You figure I'll go alone then?"

"You're loco enough to try it."

"Two of us would have a better chance."

Bruce laughed softly. "All alone again, eh, Ruffin? Face it like a little man. Go on, get your head blowed off."

Buck shrugged. "O.K., Big Man. I can't win sitting down here waiting to die. I'd rather die fighting."

"Hear! Hear!" jeered Bruce.

Buck looked down at him. "Either way you lose, Bruce."

"What do you mean?"

"If they kill me, they'll kill you as well. If they don't

kill me I don't have to come back here for you, Bruce. After all you did try to kill me twice."

Bruce stared at Buck. "You wouldn't!"

"Try me," said Buck quietly.

"There's four of them up there! Killers! We wouldn't have a chance!"

Buck blew a smoke ring. "Remember something else, Bruce. Edith is out there somewhere all alone."

"She can take care of herself!"

Buck leaned back against the side of the tunnel. "I figured you'd say that. Well, I mean to make a try to get out of here. If I make it, Brace, you can be damned sure I'm not going to bother coming back here for you." Buck leaned over casually and picked up his rifle, then he quickly snuffed out the candle, plunging the tunnel into darkness. He began to feel his way toward the area below the trapdoor. A muffled sob came through the darkness. Buck kept on.

"Ruffin! Ruffin! For God's sake don't leave me here to die! I'll go with you! Ruffin! Can you hear me!"

Buck stopped and turned.

"Ruffin!" shrieked Bruce.

Buck walked back and relighted the candle. Without a word he untied the big man. Bruce was shaking like an autumn leaf ready to fall. Cold sweat beaded his taut face. Buck pulled him to his feet. He handed him Edith Young's engraved Colt. "Go on," he said.

Bruce looked down at the weapon and then at Buck and what he saw in those eyes was enough to make him walk toward the trapdoor area. Even a cornered rat will fight to the death. They stood in the darkness beneath the flooring, straining their ears to hear a sound of voice or movement, but there was none. Buck was puzzled.

"What do you think?" whispered Mason Bruce.

"Beats the hell out of me," admitted Buck. He shoved back his hat. It was getting a little too thick of air in the tunnel to suit him. "Maybe they're sure no one can push up that trapdoor. They need water badly."

"They got water!"

"Not enough for tomorrow, and besides, if they don't water those horses, the horses will surely die. They don't want to leave Lodestar on foot, Bruce,"

"Yeh," said the big man slowly, "I never thought of that."

"You want to risk trying the door?"

Bruce paused. "You win," he said at last. His breathing was getting erratic, as though he could not get quite enough air into his large lungs.

"Go ahead then."

"Me first?"

Buck cocked his pistol. "You first, Muscles."

Bruce worked his way up the ladder. There was a moment's pause, then Buck heard the ladder creak with the weight of Bruce as he shoved up on the door. There was no welcoming rush of air or line of daylight. Once again the big man tried. "No use," he said wearily. "No wonder they pulled foot. Can't get this door up, Ruffin." A note of panic crept into his voice.

"Give me your pistol." Buck took it from Brace's shaking hand and placed all weapons on the floor. He worked his way up beside the big man. Together they pushed against the bottom of the door, gaining about an inch of lift until the door sank down again. Sweat trickled down Buck's face and body.

"Now what?" asked Bruce.

"Stay here." Buck climbed down the ladder and found a wedge-shaped piece of rock on the floor of the tunnel. He carried it up the ladder. Once again they heaved and as the door raised a little Buck managed to work the thin side of the rock into the narrow gap. The two of them went down the ladder and dropped on the floor, breathing harshly. But the air was a little fresher.

"They must have dumped the whole shed atop that door," said Bruce.

Buck sat up and rested his back against the side of the tunnel. His mind teemed with ideas to get that door up so that they could escape, but none of them were practical. There wasn't a tool in the tunnel, nothing that could be used to force up that heavy door, fully weighted from above.

"Hopeless," said Bruce at last.

The exertion and the foul air were hardly conducive to clear thinking. Buck lighted the candle and picked up his weapons. He walked back into the tunnel and studied the fall that closed the tunnel. From his memory of the terrain above the tunnel he knew had been driven into the side of the slope and the further in it went, the thicker, of course, became the roof overhead. Even if he dug through the fall it was hardly likely he'd find a way out. More tunnels and more falls, and worst of all, no air.

He walked back to the ladder and examined the ceiling of the tunnel. The building had been placed firmly on the ground rather than on beams across the top of the tunnel, and the only place where the rock and earth had been dug away was where the thick wooden collar of the trapdoor rested.

Buck took out his Barlow knife and opened it. He climbed the ladder and began to cut away at the hard wood. Even as he worked he knew it was hopeless. Sweat half blinded him as he sawed and whittled away, working up red spots on his hand that would soon enough develop into blisters.

"Hopeless," said Bruce hollowly.

Sure it was hopeless, but Buck Ruffin couldn't sit and cry about it. He wasn't built that way, and the longer he worked the more his determination mounted to get out of that hole of death. He attacked the wood with his renewed strength and then there was a sharp snap and the blade of his knife clinked on the hard floor of the tunnel. He stood there on the ladder feeling the sweat running down his body, still gripping the bladeless knife in his hand.

"You see?" said the hollow voice from below.

"You have a knife?"

"No."

Buck came down the ladder and unloaded his rifle. He climbed the ladder again and thrust the barrel of the Winchester into the gap between the flooring and the trapdoor, working it through until he could get a good purchase on it. He heaved and pried with all his strength. Something began to give just a little. He heaved and pulled with his breath harsh and burning in his throat until something gave again. He pulled back the rifle to get a new purchase. The barrel was badly bent. The rifle had been giving, not the trapdoor or the wooden collar of it. He slid down the ladder and threw the rifle into a corner.

"See?" said Bruce.

"Shut up!" Buck wiped the sweat from his face.

"Hopeless."

"We're still alive, aren't we?" demanded Buck.

"For how long?"

Buck spat dryly. He needed water after losing all that sweat. He had no idea of what time it was. In the dimly-lighted tunnel daylight or darkness made no difference'. He snuffed out the candle. Exertion would only exhaust him still further and use up too much air. He closed his eyes, trying to think clearly.

A big hand closed over Buck's mouth and he awoke with a start, fighting for air. "Quiet!" hissed Bruce. Buck could smell the sour sweat of the big man. Bruce withdrew his hand. "Listen!"

Buck looked up. He could no longer see the narrow line of light along the side of the trapdoor. It must be dark outside. He probably had slept for hours.

Something was moving about overhead. Buck felt for

his pistol. He stood up and stared at the darkness above his head as though trying to bore through it. Something rattled. "Buck?" came the soft, low voice.

He closed his eyes in sheer relief. "Edith?" he said hoarsely.

"Thank God! I was afraid to come near here during daylight."

"Where are they?"

"Down in the town."

"Can you move that stuff from atop the trapdoor?"

"I'll try, Buck. I will! I must!"

"I'm down here too, Edie," said Bruce coldly.

There was no answer from the girl. Metal scraped on the trapdoor, and dirt pattered down on the two men below. They could hear her hard breathing. "Buck?" she said at last.

"Yes?"

"Try to lift up."

Buck worked up the ladder and pressed his shoulders and back against the under surface of the door. He heaved upward until his muscles seemed to crack. Something heavy slid gratingly from the upper surface of the door and the door rose upward, admitting a flood of fresh air that almost made Buck dizzy. He forced his way up the last rungs of the ladder and his hands felt her slim waist. He could not help himself. He drew her close and kissed her. A heavy body brushed against him from behind as Bruce came up into the room, drawing in great lungfuls of the fresh dry air.

"We'd better get out of here," said Edith. They've been hunting for water all day. I hid up in the hills. I wasn't sure where you had gone to. I thought I had seen you and Mason come in here, but the view was blocked by brush. I didn't know what to do."

He passed a hand across her hair and kissed her again, completely oblivious of Mason Bruce and the fact that Edith Young had promised herself to the big man. At last

Buck stepped back. He looked about for Bruce. "Bruce?" he said.

There was no answer. Buck walked quickly to the front door of the building. "Bruce?"

No answer.

Edith came up beside Buck. "Look," she said quickly. "Isn't that Mason?"

Buck could see the big dim figure going down the slope toward the town, and then Bruce vanished behind a building. "Let's get out of here," he said quickly. "He's not going down there for our good, Edith. I have a feeling he's going down there to make a deal with our four friends!" He led the girl up the slope behind the building into the darkness.

Her hand was warm within his. Warm and trusting, thought Buck grimly. He looked at her. "Are you thirsty? Come to think of it, that's rather a stupid question, isn't it?"

"Yes, I am thirsty," she said. "But there's no use crying about it, is there? I'm happy enough that I found you, Buck. I just can't let you go down that awful shaft again."

He stopped near the shaft entrance and pointed to the fall he had engineered. He felt her hand tighten within his. He drew her close. "I had to do it," he said.

"It's like a death sentence."

He shook his head. "Follow me, Edith," he said quietly. He picked up some empty cans from the litter near the shaft and led her down into the deep hole where the narrow entrance to the drift was concealed. He looked at her. "This is how I escaped when *Mister* Bruce tried to kill me. It leads down into a dangerous drift, and from there to the water shaft. I'll have to risk it again, Edith."

She shook her head. "Not on your life, Buck. I'm not letting you risk your life alone. I'm going along."

He looked down at her. "You might not get out of there, Edith. Ever..."

She smiled. "I'll be with you," she said quietly. "That's enough for me, Buck. Where you go, I go."

He kissed her and slid down into the hole, holding up his arms to help her. She came to his arms almost like a bride.

CHAPTER NINE

They sat together in the dim, flickering light of the candle, with the deep dark hole of the shaft beyond them, sipping the cold clear water as though it was nectar. Edith shivered a little.

"Every time I think of you regaining consciousness down there in the darkness I get sick, Buck."

He grinned. "Imagine how I must have felt."

She placed a hand against his face. "I know now that Mason tried to kill you. He hates you, Buck."

"With good reason," said Buck.

"Do you really think he has gone to them?"

Buck slowly rolled a cigarette and lighted it. He blew a ring of the smoke out toward the shaft.

"Twice he tried to kill me and failed. He knows now that you love me instead of him. That alone would be cause enough for him to go to them, for revenge, if nothing else."

"But how could he deal with them?"

Buck looked upward. "They don't know there is water in this shaft, but he does. If he agrees to show them where the water is, they may agree to count him in on the treasure, if they can find it. It just might be that Mister Bruce has outsmarted himself."

"What do you mean?"

He looked at her. "Do you think they'd cut a fool like him in on *anything?*" Sure, they'll agree to anything for water. Once he shows them where the water is..."

She paled. "And he knows I have the overlay, Buck. If he tells them that they'll turn over every rock in this valley looking for us."

He nodded. "If they find this water they'll find us if we try to keep them from it. This is the only source of water in the valley as far as we know. They'll do anything for water and for that hidden treasure."

"I wish I had never listened to Mason," she cried. "I don't want any treasure, Buck. I just want you and the happiness we can find for ourselves in the future."

He drew her close and kissed her. She rested her head on his shoulder and watched the candle light with her lovely eyes. "Strange, isn't it, that we really know so little about each other, but we know we love each other. How do such things happen, Buck?"

He shrugged. "*Quién sabe?* I don't question it, Edith. It's wonderful enough for me. A miracle perhaps. Why question it at all?"

She raised her lips to his. As he drew her close and kissed her something splashed in the water below the lip of the drift. He drew his head back. Gravel pattered down into the water. Buck crawled to the mouth of the drift and craned his neck to look upward. He could see nothing. Suddenly a stone glanced from his shoulder and splashed into the water. He jerked his head inside the drift just as a mass of stones and dirt cascaded down into the shaft, rattling against the timbered sides and splashing loudly in the dark waters.

"What is it?" she asked quickly.

He reached over and snuffed out the candle. "I think Mister Bruce has shown the boys where the water is, Edith." His words were echoed by another fall of material from high above them. Buck drew his Colt and checked the loads in the darkness. The crisp metallic sound of the spinning cylinder sounded inordinately loud in the stillness.

"What can we do, Buck?" she asked.

"We can't let them get water."

"That won't be easy to do."

"No," he said. He slid an arm about her shoulders. "There might be some killing, Edith. It has to be."

She was silent for a few moments and then she spoke up. "I won't mind killing. They killed my father, didn't they?"

Buck kissed her. He stood up and listened to the harsh scrabbling echoing down the shaft. A man and a woman, with one Colt between them, against five hard cases, well-armed and determined, with water the lure and the goal. Water was the key. He flogged his tired mind. It really didn't matter to him about the treasure, for he had never believed in the story. It didn't really matter to him that he was sworn to bring them in, dead or alive. What mattered now was Edith Young. What else can matter beyond the woman you love and who loves you? *That* is the world. Nothing else matters. *Nothing...*

There was another heavy fall of earth. If the fools didn't watch out they might just plug the shaft so that no one could get water. Then Buck heard the faint sound of voices high above them echoing eerily down the deep shaft. A stone dropped into the water. The indistinguishable voices arose excitedly. They were hard up for water. Water was their treasure now.

"Edith?" said Buck.

"Yes?"

"We can't let them get water," he said again.

"No."

"If anything happens, you get down to the livery stable and take their horses. It's better than waiting around for them to get you."

"What do you mean?"

He passed a hand over her soft hair. "Go back," he said firmly. "Stay under cover. I hid Mason's guns in a first floor room of that structure we planned for our hideout. Beneath some boards leaning against the rear wall. I wish to God I had thought to get them before we came in here. When you leave, get those guns. Don't hesitate to shoot to kill if they come after you. Do you understand?"

"I understand this, Buck: I'm *not* leaving this drift! For better or for worse I'll stay by your side. I'm not leaving you, Buck!"

He closed her mouth with a kiss.

The voices sounded louder now as though they had cleared the shaft entrance. Tin rattled high above the two listeners in the drift. Then it sounded closer. Buck walked to the very edge of the drift. He risked a glance upward. Moonlight was shining into the shaft entrance and in the vague light he could see a bucket being lowered into the shaft. As it drew abreast of the drift and swung toward him he gripped the rope by which it had been lowered and swiftly made a few turns in it around a rusted spike sticking out from a prop. He drew back as he felt the line tighten. A bitter curse floated in the echoing air of the shaft. Again and again the rope was tugged until suddenly it snapped. Buck let the bucket fall. The rope was swiftly drawn up the tunnel to the accompaniment of salty curses. Buck grinned.

Down came another container, swinging back and forth, banging loudly against the sides of the shaft. Buck waited his chance. He gripped the rope as it drew close and snubbed it about the spike. Again the rope was tugged and tugged. It began to slip upward as it was pulled. Buck grabbed for it and pulled it a little too hard. Dirt poured down the shaft. There was a thin scream that echoed eerily and a man shot past the mouth of the drift futilely clawing the air. He struck the side of the shaft and then plunged to the bottom with a great splash of water. Then it was quiet again in the tunnel except for the lapping of the waters and the faint pattering of earth down the sides of the shaft.

"Jack?" yelled Hazen Deeth.

"Jack... Jack... Jack..." echoed the shaft.

Buck looked down. He could just make out a faint reflection on the water. There was no sign of Jack Yering. Buck leaned back against the side of the drift. The linked lariats they had been using to lower the bucket had fallen to the bottom with Jack Yering.

Edith came close. "Is he gone?" she whispered.

"Yes. But the rope fell too."

"Maybe they'll give up."

"No. They'll have to send a man down now." There was no need to talk further. They both knew that if a man came down he would have to pass the mouth of the drift. If he saw them, it would be all up. If he didn't see them, he might get the water, and Buck could not allow that. There was always the chance he might fall as Jack Yering had done.

The muttered sound of voices came down the shaft. The voices rose in pitch. "By God Bruce," said Hazen Deeth, "you said you knew where water was! We've got no way of getting it now un'ess a man goes down for it."

"I'm too heavy!" cried Mason Bruce. "You don't know those ladders! The whole shaft is crumbling! I'm not the one to go! Send someone else!"

"Listen to him," said Stinger. "Haw! Haw! Send someone else. Get on that damned ladder, Bruce!"

"No!"

There was the sharp sound of a blow. Dirt pattered down the shaft. Then a curious, dry sobbing noise came down to the two people in the drift. Buck slid his arm around Edith's shoulders. They could hear feet striking the rotting wooden ladder rungs. Metal banged against wood. Buck knew that ladder all too well. Bruce outweighed him by at least thirty pounds, and Buck's weight had almost been too much for the dangerous descent of the ladder. But there was no pity in him for Mason Bruce.

"What if he sees us?" whispered Edith.

"Go back into the drift," said Buck.

"What are you going to do?"

"Go back into the drift!"

She obeyed. She knew the ground rules of the deadly game they were playing. Kill or be killed. There were no alternatives.

Buck crouched at the side of the drift behind a prop. So far they did not know that Jack Yering had not died accidently. If Mason Bruce was to die by Buck's hand as well, it must be concealed from those above.

The dry sobbing of the big man came eerily down the shaft. Buck unsheathed his Colt and held it ready. He could not fire, but a pistol barrel laid neatly over an ear could do the job if he had the chance.

The big man was about level with the drift above the one in which death, in the guise of Buck Ruffin, waited for Mason Bruce. Bruce's harsh breathing seemed louder and louder, for fear was riding his back like the Old Man of the Sea. Despite his great size and strength fear had always been a close companion to Mason Bruce.

Bruce was working down the ladder just above the drift where Buck waited. It was one above the drift in which Buck had remained while he bailed up the water. The ladder on which Bruce now stood did not reach to the drift where Buck waited. Feet struck the side of the shaft. Then Buck saw Bruce's heavy legs swinging in front of him and before he could jump back, those great legs swung inward and the feet struck Buck on the chest, smashing him back into the drift. He dropped his Colt. "What the hell!" said Bruce. Then he landed heavily at the very lip of the drift.

There was no time to waste. Buck came up off the ground and hit Bruce with a hard driving shoulder, smashing the man back against a pit prop. "Look out!" screamed Bruce as though to warn his erstwhile companions. "It's..." Buck's hands closed on Bruce's corded throat and begin to squeeze the life from him.

There was a tremendous vitality in the huge body of Mason Bruce but Buck Ruffin was fighting for his life and the life of the woman he loved. A knee smashed against the side of Buck's groin and he sickened in pain. Great hands clawed desperately at his face. Blood dripped from his nose after a savage blow. Bruce's feet danced on the rim of the drift. He pawed for something to hold onto. Dirt splashed into the water below the drift mouth.

"Bruce!" yelled Deeth. "Answer me! Bruce?"

Bruce's feet slipped and he fell pulling Buck toward him, but a pair of slim arms wrapped themselves about Buck's waist. Buck released his hold on Bruce's throat. His foot slipped and for one sickening moment he thought he was going to follow Bruce. His outflung hand caught the rusted spike in the pit prop and he swung out into the shaft with his feet driving hard for a hold just as Bruce's voice rose in a shrieking scream, followed by a huge splashing. Once more the big man screamed and then he sank, followed by a gurgling sound and then nothing but the quick lapping of the black waters against the shaft sides.

Buck dropped to the drift floor with his breath rasping in his throat. Edith kept her arms about him. Her body shook. Buck pressed his bleeding face against the coolness of the drift floor.

"That took care of the big clown," said Stinger far above.

"Yeh," said Quin Scheel. "It took care of the water too. Stinger, you're the smallest of us. You go down."

"You go to hell!"

"We've got to get water, Stinger," said Deeth.

"Then go get it yourself! I ain't going down into that death hole!"

"All right! Let's scout around for more rope, wire cable, chain or anything else. We've got to have water!"

Buck sat up. He felt about for his Colt. His questing hands did not touch the metal of the six-shooter. He raised his head. The shaft was quiet. He risked lighting the candle stub. The gun was gone. He knew well enough what had happened to it. It had joined the stiffening bodies of Jack Yering and Mason Bruce deep beneath the water of the shaft. He looked at Edith. "What next?" he said with a crooked smile.

"Maybe we can stay hidden until they leave."

"You forget they know you're around here somewhere and that you have the overlay. Bruce would have told them that to get himself in solid with them."

"You haven't a chance against them, Buck."

"We've done all right so far," he said quietly, but for all his bravado he knew she was right. He had to have weapons and the only weapons he could get were those hidden in the mining structure. To get them he'd have to leave the drift and emerge into full moonlight. If they saw him before he reached the weapons...

There was something else too that was added to the hazards already piling up against them. It might not be too long before the water supply in the shaft would be impossible to drink. Perhaps the water was cold enough to preserve the bodies but if it wasn't...

Buck helped her to her feet. "You can stay in the drift," he said.

"No!"

"A little while back I couldn't get you to leave it."

She kissed him. "Remember what I said before we came into the drift? Where you go, I go."

He took her by the hand and walked up the drift with the stub of candle casting a flickering uncertain light about them.

She waited at the foot of the earth fall just below the narrow hole at the end of the drift. Buck wormed his way out of the hole, cursing the bright moonlight that flooded the valley. He could hear the distant murmuring of the furnace winds of the desert night. There were no other sounds to be heard.

Buck bellied up to the lip of the deep hole at the bottom of which was the way into the drift. He lay flat at the edge of the hole with his head concealed by a tuft of dry brush. He studied the cluttered terrain foot by foot. His vision was cut off by the many buildings, mining structures, rusting machinery and piles of earth stippled with sparse brush. What lay behind them? Three hard cases, well skilled in peddling death, desperate and well-armed. He shook his head. He slid down into the hole and spoke softly. "Stay here while I scout about. If anything happens to me, stay in the drift." He could see her white face in the dark hole. She nodded bravely.

Buck worked his way out of the big hole and crawled like a gecko lizard from rock to earth pile until he could lie flat against a mass of rusted machinery on a slope above the structure where he had left Bruce's weapons. There was no sight or sound of the three outlaws. The wind was rising, drifting a skein of fine gray dust toward the town. A tumbleweed rolled slowly along a street. A loose shutter thudded against the side of a building.

Buck stood up, then darted swiftly and silently to the next building. Every nerve within him seemed to cry out to get to those weapons as quickly as he could, but he held a tight check rein on them. One mistake would be his last mistake. To him, it mattered not that he might die under their smoking guns. It was Edith that mattered most.

He reached the slope directly below the structure.

He couldn't hold himself back. He moved quickly toward the building.

"Hey, Deeth!" cried out Quin Scheel. "I found some old rope in here!"

The voice came from almost directly above Buck. In

the very building where he had hidden Bruce's guns. He was in full view, bathed in the clear moonlight, of anyone who might casually look out of one of those windows above him. He sprinted toward the building and pressed himself flat against it. The galvanized sheathing of the building had bellied out a little from tearing away from its fastenings. He stood there nakedly in view of anyone who would look toward the structure.

Feet grated on the littered wooden flooring in one of the rooms of the structure. "I could have sworn I saw something move down there," said Quin Scheel. His voice came from directly above Buck and he knew the big man was looking out of a window.

"Haw! Haw! Haw!" laughed Stinger. "Now he's doing it too! Haw! Haw! Haw!" His voice echoed through the empty rooms.

"Shut up, you!" said Scheel. "I'm beginning to think maybe Jack was right. I still ain't convinced I was clobbered by a board down there this morning. Besides, who was down in that tunnel under that old shed? Was it mice who put them water cans there?"

"Haw! Haw! Haw!" roared Stinger in vast delight.

"He's got something there, Stinger," said the flat, metallic voice of Hazen Deeth. "Before Bruce fell into the water he said something that has been puzzling me ever since."

"Like what?" asked Stinger.

"Look out! It's..."

"What the hell does that mean?"

"I think he seen *something*, or *somebody* down there," said Quin Scheel.

"Bruce told us the woman and Ruffin, the deputy-sheriff, were around here somewhere," said Deeth quietly. "Maybe we made a mistake in rushing to get that water. Maybe we should have hunted them down first."

"Let's go," said Scheel.

Feet grated on the stairs inside the building. Buck

waited until they reached the bottom floor, then he vanished around the back of the building like a lean shadow. He heard their booted feet striking the hard earth. Buck circled the building to keep it between him and them. He heard their voices fade away. The wind was rising now, swiftly and steadily. It promised to be a rough night in Lodestar, in more ways than one.

He found the guns and armed himself, then hurried upstairs to peer through the shifting veils of thin dust that had begun to fill the night air. There was no sign of the three outlaws. He left the building and worked his way slowly and carefully to where he had left Edith. He whistled softly and heard her reply. He slid down into the hole. She came out to meet him bringing their water supply. This time Buck would take no chances. He wanted to get Edith to a safe hideout. After that he'd have to stalk those three to their deaths. It would be the only way.

He led her by covered ways past the mining structures and up to the far end of the gully. The gully was empty of life. He led her to the place he had holed up in the night before. The large, roofed excavation was like a small fortress. With water enough a man could hold out for a short siege. She entered the dark interior and sat down on a box. He passed a reassuring hand over her soft hair. "We'll be safe enough here." he said.

A gun cracked flatly from across the gully and the bullet whipped through the doorway and smashed against a timber upright. The echo of the shot slammed back and forth in the moonlighted gully, then died away. It was as quiet as before, except for the keening of the night wind.

CHAPTER TEN

Buck Ruffin stood well back within the low arched doorway of the stone building in which he and Edith had been so neatly trapped. He held the rifle in his big hands, ready for a snap shot, but he knew well enough they would not expose themselves. Why should they? No one could walk out of that doorway into bright moonlight and escape being wounded or killed. Even after dark it would hardly be possible to escape, for they'd move in when the moonlight was gone, so close they could hardly miss seeing or hearing anyone.

"Ruffin!" called out Hazen Deeth from one side of the building. "You haven't got a chance! Come outside and throw down your guns! The woman comes with you!"

"What do you want?" called out Buck, stalling for time, hoping one of them would expose himself.

Deeth laughed. "What do we want? Cut the stalling, Ruffin. You've got the overlay for Young's map of this place. Turn it over to us and we'll let you go free."

Buck could not see a one of them. "What guarantee do we have of that?" he called out. He darted toward the inside wall of the building closest to where he gauged Deeth to be hiding. He looked about for a possible loophole.

"You'll have to take your chances on that," said Deeth.

It was no use. There was no possible way to get a shot at the man. "Supposing we let you have the overlay, Deeth. You can look for your treasure and leave us alone. I'm not turning over my guns to such as you."

Minutes drifted past. "We can come in and get you, Ruffin," called out Deeth at last.

"Try it."

"Ain't *he* the tough one?" jeered Stinger.

It was as though the voices came from disembodied spirits. There was no sense in wasting a shot at them, and even if he did, they'd fire instantly at the flash of his gun.

Buck walked over to the girl. "What do you think?"

"Give them the overlay, Buck."

"You think that would make any difference to them? They know I have warrants for them. If I ever get out of here they'll know I'll track them down eventually. No, they'll have to kill me, Edith. They'll kill you too if they can, after they are done with you."

"Are they as bad as all that?"

He nodded. "Worse, Edith." He handed her the rifle. "Watch for them. Don't shoot unless they rush the place, which isn't likely." He walked into the thick darkness at the rear of the long, low structure. The way was cluttered with shattered boxes, scrap lumber and other odds and ends. He clambered over a pile of earth and came face to face with heavy boarding that ran from one side of the structure to the other, but he was quite sure it could not be the end wall of the place. He felt along the heavy timbers, but there was no opening in them. Just a heavy flat expanse of well-preserved timbers.

"You can't stay in there forever, Ruffin!" yelled Scheel.

"Just send out the filly with the overlay, and you can stay in there as long as you like, Lawman!" yelled Stinger. "Haw! Haw! Haw!"

There was an iron bar lying in the clutter. Buck

picked it up and set to work on the end timber, prying hard against the stone wall.

A gun cracked and the bullet whipped through the doorway and struck the timber a foot away from Buck. The impetus of the shot gave him the strength to work the timber loose. He pried loose the next one. It made a gap big enough for him to get through and his heart sank as he lighted the candle, for just beyond the timber walling was nothing more than heaped rock and earth as far back as he could see, filling the structure from one side to the other and from floor to ceiling. It would take days to dig through such a mass.

Buck leaned against the thick timbering. Why would they have walled off nothing but dirt and rock? He peered closely at the pile. Something was protruding from it. He touched it and found it to be metal. He moved closer to it, then began to push away the covering earth with his hand until he could see part of a heavy iron flask. He narrowed his eyes. He remembered the first time he had come to this place, for he had stepped on the rusted remains of just such a hand-welded flask lying outside the doorway.

A gun flatted off and the slug screamed thinly from the stone of the building. A second bullet sped through the doorway and thudded into the timber.

"Buck?" said Edith softly.

"I'm all right. Stay behind the front wall."

Buck hefted the flask in the pile of earth. It weighed all of seventy-five pounds. Swiftly he worked along the pile, unearthing the necks of more and more of the flasks, testing one now and then for weight. They were all full. There must be at least a hundred of the flasks, perhaps more beneath the concealing earth. He wiped the sweat from his face, then carefully covered up the flasks he had exposed. He went back to the place where he had removed the end timbers, squirmed through, then snuffed out the candle. He replaced the timbers and wedged them into place with scraps of iron and wood.

Buck kept close to the wall and reached Edith. "What were you doing back there?" she asked.

"Never mind," he said quickly. "Do you have the overlay?"

"Of course."

"Let me have it."

"Why?"

"I'm going to try to make a deal with them."

"You know they won't make deals. Buck."

"We're in no position to argue right now, Edith."

She reached inside her shirt and withdrew the overlay. He took it, feeling the warmth of her body held in the paper. "No matter what I say, Edith," he said quietly, "you must believe in me."

"I do, Buck."

"Good!" He walked to the door and kept well back. The moon was still shining brightly. The wind swept grit and pebbles down the gully. "Deeth!" he called out.

"What do you want, Ruffin?"

"I'll make a deal with you."

"Shoot!"

"I'd like to," said Buck grimly. "I'll give you the overlay if you let us alone."

"I don't trust you with those guns in your hands. Ruffin."

Buck laughed softly. "You don't trust me with guns in my hands! No, I keep the guns, you get the overlay. Is it a deal?"

Deeth did not answer, but in "a moment or two Buck heard the faint muttering of voices. "Better'n trying to rush that damned lobo," came the voice of Quin Scheel. The muttering continued.

Buck tried to spot where they were but the constant rushing sound of the rising wind made it impossible to tell.

"Ruffin!" came the flat voice of Deeth. "We agree. Keep the guns. We'll take the overlay."

Buck glanced back at the girl. "They figure they'll keep us trapped in here and look for the treasure cache."

"They said they'd let us go."

Buck shook his head. "Never, Edith. With us out of the way and the treasure in their hands, they'll have a free ticket to California." He placed an arm against the stone wall and rested his head on his forearm. His head was aching and his body was beaten and tired. It was increasingly harder to think and the moaning desert wind that swept across the town was hardly helping. There is a madness that comes with the desert wind. Men have suddenly killed old partners over some trivial argument when unbalanced by the swirling, cutting edge of the desert wind. Tired as he felt, of brain and body his strength began to rise a little, whipped on by his hatred of those three killers outside.

"How long you figure we're going to wait out here?" yelled Stinger angrily. "This wind is plain hell!"

Buck walked to the girl and drew her close. "I'm going to let them have the overlay now. It will be touch and go, Edith. I know you can handle a gun and I'll need all the help I can get. If I can get away from this trap I may be able to fight them on more equal terms. It isn't likely they'll rush you in here once they have the overlay. They're not like soldiers ordered to charge a strong point against odds. All they want is that treasure and not one of the three of them would sacrifice himself for the good of the others."

"What do you want me to do?" she asked. She knew the odds well enough. She knew if this big man was killed trying to save her, her fate at their hands would be just more than a quick death to shut her mouth forever. The death would come afterward, and it might be by that time she'd more than welcome it. Still, if anything happened to him they'd have to rush her if they really wanted her. There were six rounds in the Colt, five for them and one for her if it came to such a showdown.

Buck passed a hand over her soft hair. "I'll have to take a long chance. In a split second I can make a break or get shot down. The only thing you can do is to wait here. Help me if you can but only when the chips are really down. If I get away you'll have to sit it out."

"We'll make it yet. Buck," she said.

He grinned. "There speaks the strong heart. Give me the rifle." He handed her the six-gun. She stepped back and checked it expertly. Buck held the cocked rifle in his right hand and the overlay in his left. The outside world was a weird one engendered by the moonlight and the swirling dust, creating uncertain vision and the hazards of getting one's eyes filled with the blow-dust.

"Gawd dammit, Ruffin!" roared Quin Scheel. "Get out here!"

"You giving the orders now?" yelled back Buck. He had Scheel spotted now. "I thought Deeth was the head man!"

"Haw! Haw!" laughed Stinger.

Buck wasn't quite sure where Deeth was. He was too shrewd to give his position away. Maybe he was even hoping the other two would get a slug in them. It would be his way.

"Now, Edith," he said quietly. He flung a quick smile at her. He stepped outside and looked to the place where he thought Quin Scheel was hiding. He let the overlay go and the wind sailed it toward the earth mounds across the street from the building. The white sheet was plain to be seen. It rose in an updraft almost directly over Scheel's position.

"Grab it?" yelled Stinger.

That's just what Quin Scheel attempted to do. His big bulk rose like some prehistoric monster from the slime, working with just a little more brainpower than that of a dinosaur. He pawed frantically for the overlay. Buck darted to the side of the building and raised the Winchester. It cracked flatly. Quin Scheel grunted. Again the Winchester spat flame and smoke and the second forty-four slug caught the big man in the belly. The overlay sailed serenely past the man as he staggered backward. Then Quin Scheel's mouth opened to spew out a flood of blood, black in the bright moonlight. He fell heavily with his big fingers trying to dig into the stony ground. "Haz!" he yelled thickly. "Stinger!"

Two dim figures darted through the swirling dust and sand, past the dying man, racing into the distance after that elusive piece of paper.

"Edith!" barked Buck. "Now!"

She left the building and followed him down the gully in the opposite direction from where the two outlaws were performing their hare and hounds act through the moonlight. Behind them, on the ground, Quin Scheel stared up at the moon with eyes that did not see.

"The horses," said Buck. "We've got to move them."

They ran down the long slope. Now and then Buck darted a look behind them but there was no sight of the two outlaws. They reached the main street. Edith went into the stable and the whinnying of the thirsty horses brought tears to her eyes as she untethered them and led them out into the alleyway. Buck kept guard between Edith and the horses as she led them down the long alleyway buffeted by dust and wind. "They'll just have to have water, Buck," she said.

Buck looked up the slopes, now vague and unreal, half hidden by the whirling veils of dust. Instinct was strong within him to take the horses and Edith and make a break through to the south or west to reach water and help. Two of his quarry were dead. The warrants had been written for four of them. *Dead or alive...*

Buck led the way to the southern end of the town. Here a long warehouse had collapsed, leaving a right angled junction of the standing wall and the roof. Sand had piled high up on the roof and the wind was driving toward it across the town, so it wasn't likely the whinnying of the thirsty horses could be heard by anyone upwind of them. It was a chance Buck had to take. They led the horses into the dark interior and tethered them strongly. If they broke free they'd likely drift with the wind and no one would ever ride them from Lodestar.

There was only one place for water and it was only a matter of time before that lone water cache would be useless because of what it contained. There was no alternative for Buck but to return to the water. Somehow or another those horses had to be watered. Enough at any rate to keep them alive until he killed or captured Deeth and Stinger.

They all lacked water. Buck and Edith, the horses, and Deeth and Stinger. Deeth and Stinger would have to return to the water shaft. That place of sudden death was getting to be a horror to Buck Ruffin. He suddenly raised his head as the tolling of a bell came to him, then died away. The wind had shifted to ring the bell as it had done the night he had come to this place of death. Tolling for the new dead; tolling for those still alive in Lodestar, those who were doomed to die. Buck shivered despite himself.

He led the way from the warehouse. The plaintive whinnying of the horses died away behind them. He was afraid to take Edith with him but more afraid to leave her alone. The odds against them had lowered in a sense, but Hazen Deeth and Stinger were the most dangerous of the men Buck had faced and fought in Lodestar.

In a sense the wind had helped them that night, but it could be an enemy as well as an ally. Its whining and moaning would deafen a man to the sound of enemy footsteps. Buck led the way up the slope, knowing the girl would imitate his every movement, walking when he did, crawling when he did, lying quietly when he did, and the senses alert to the sudden death prowling Lodestar that blustery night.

He stopped at last underneath the rusted skeleton legs of a tall structure. From this vantage point he could see the dark mouth of the water shaft with the loose soil and rock scattered about the mouth. There was no sign of the two hard cases. Once again he'd have to go down into that dangerous drift for water. His own thirst was clawing at the back of his dry throat and he knew Edith must feel the same thing. The thought of being trapped down there was a sickening thought in his tired mind.

He handed the girl the rifle and took the Colt from her. He had to get water containers and he could hardly handle a rifle while loaded down with containers. He bellied along the slope until he found half a dozen rusty containers of various sizes and shapes, just enough to water the horses to keep a breath of life into them until he could supply more to them.

Buck peered down the slope. His eyes narrowed as he saw two men move quickly up the gully toward the supposed cache of treasure. For a moment or two he rested his head on the hard ground. Was there time enough to get the water? He had no choice. If they came back to the shaft they'd be sure to find him. There was no purpose in him lying there thinking about what he must do and the eventualities he might have to face. Water, as always, was the key of life in Lodestar.

He carried the containers to the hidden opening into the drift and let them roll down the sloped earth just below the hole. He bellied up to the lip of the larger hole and looked toward the place where Edith waited. He wanted her no closer. Then he slid down into the hole, dropped his long legs into the drift and landed with a rush of loose earth on the floor of the drift. He felt about for the containers, then lighted his candle stub, peering through the shifting darkness into the deeper part of the drift and he could feel the sickness rising within him. He forced himself to gather the containers, tie them together with a length of rope, then sling them over his shoulder. He walked into the dimness of the drift.

CHAPTER ELEVEN

B uck Ruffin carried the heavily laden water
containers down the slope to where Edith waited
for him. The two of them almost forgot caution
in their haste to get off the moonlighted slopes. Buck was
gambling on one thing. The greed of the two men would
probably transcend everything else, for the treasure fever
was upon them, and it was incurable. Buck placed the
water containers in the shelter of the warehouse wall.
"Stand guard," he said over his shoulder. Already the
horses had smelled the water.

The wind battered at the ruins of the warehouse,
sifting dust through cracks and crannies. The horses
drank steadily until Buck took the half empty containers
from them. Watering them had taken a great weight
from his mind. He concealed the remainder of the water
and walked outside to where Edith stood guard. "Did you
see them?" she asked.

"Yes." He eyed the mining ruins high above them.
"They're back in the gully, Edith."

"Let's leave at once," she said quickly. "We have
enough water to reach safety haven't we?"

"It's a calculated risk," he said. "I'm not sure of the
success of it at all, Edith."

She looked up at him. "Isn't it better than staying here with those two killers still on the loose?" Her eyes narrowed a little as she saw the look on his bruised face. "What are you thinking about, Buck?"

He looked down at her. "I came to Lodestar for a reason," he said quietly. "I haven't succeeded yet."

"You can always come back, Buck!"

He shook his head. "I came for four men. I got two of them. Two from four leaves two. It's as simple as that."

"It's madness!"

He shook his head. "It's my duty," he said.

She opened her mouth and then closed it. There was no arguing with this lobo of a man once he made up his mind.

He drew her close and kissed her. if anything happens to me," he said, "take all of the horses. Head south-west toward the California border. When you are far enough away from here, turn three of the horses loose. You'll just have enough water for yourself and one horse. It will be a tight squeeze, but as you told me the first time I met you, you're too tough to die."

The wind howled at that one as it swept across Lodestar, but there seemed to be a grudging tone of respect in it.

He checked his Colt.

"Take the rifle too," she said.

"You'll need it if you have to leave," he said. He kissed her once more, then strode off up the littered slope. Her eyes were bright with tears, but she knew in her own heart she would have done the same thing had she been a man like Buck Ruffin, a man who wore the star.

A good gambler knows the odds; so does a good lawman. The calculated risk plays a big part in tracking down and taking criminals. Deeth and Stinger had the map and likely the overlay. By now their greed for the treasure cache would have driven everything else from their minds. Or had it? That was the calculated risk.

He drifted like a shadow across the naked ground and past the many ruins trending slowly toward the mouth of the gully. He was within a hundred yards of it when he dropped to the ground and worked his way past the mouth and up behind the row of ruins on the north side of it. Building by building he worked his way closer to the stone structure where he and Edith had been trapped.

He stopped close behind it and pressed his ear against the stone. He listened for a long time, then he kept close to the side wall as he walked silently toward the front of the structure. He stopped to eye the moonlighted gully. The wind was dying but it was still, able to whirl dust and sand about with some of its old power.

There was no sign of life. Quin Scheel lay still on the humped earth across from the building. His hair ruffled in the wind. Buck drew and cocked his Colt. He pressed against the front wall until he reached the low arched doorway. He stopped and listened. The wind died away. Then Buck nodded in grim satisfaction.

He drew in a deep breath, then swiftly and silently rounded the side of the door and pressed himself flat against the inner front wall. Far at the rear of the low structure he saw a faint guttering of yellow light and the muffled sound of metal against metal. He padded forward.

"Damn!" said Hazen Deeth clearly. "It's got to be in here, Stinger!"

"I think you're loco," said Stinger. "Ain't nothing here but these damned metal bottles. You read the map and overlay wrong."

"I read it right, damn you! It's got to be in here."

Neither of them saw the lean figure closing in.

"Let's take another look outside," said Stinger.

"I tell you the swag is in here, Stinger!"

"Nobody can tell you anything," said Stinger. He picked up his rifle and pushed his body into the reopened gap between the timber boarding and the side wall of the building. His head and shoulders were clearly outlined. Buck pressed against the boarding. It was too dark for Stinger to get a clear look at anything in the darkened building. He pushed his way through and Buck Ruffin made his move. He darted forward and swung the heavy barrel of the Colt alongside Stinger's head, buffaloing him neatly. The man staggered forward and fell onto a pile of loose earth, dropping his rifle. He gasped once.

"What is it, Stinger?" said Deeth over his shoulder.

Buck pushed into the gap.

Deeth whirled. His left hand slapped down on the guttering candle while his right hand dropped for a draw. Two Colts blazed and boomed in the narrow area between flasks and timber boarding. Lead clanged against iron. Smoke swept past Buck's face. He dropped to one knee and fired twice into the darkness and in the quick spurting of gun-light he saw Deeth stagger backward and fall heavily.

Buck got to his feet and instinct—more than anything else made him jump through the gap. Dimly he saw Stinger rising with his rifle in his hands. The man fired. The slug cut a burning slash alongside Buck's skull creasing him neatly but even as he fell he emptied his hot Colt. The stabbing muzzle flames lighted the darkness for a fraction of time and then Buck Ruffin knew no more.

The water was cool but the hands were cooler and the lips that pressed against his seemed to bring him back to life. He opened his eyes to look up into the pale taut face of Edith Young. "Thank God," she whispered. She helped him to sit up with his back against the stone wall. He looked past the flickering, dancing light of the candle she had placed on top of a box. At the edge of the pool of light lay the crumpled figure of Stinger with his bloody hands twisted in his shirt front.

"Can we leave now, Buck?" she softly asked.

He drew her close. His head ached like the devil was

beating tanbark inside of it, but his release from having
to get those two killers made up for it.

"How did you know they'd be in here?" she asked.

"Help me up, Edith."

She helped him to his feet. He picked up the candle
and worked his way into the area behind the timber
boarding. Hazen Deeth lay still in death. Something
silvery bright was running lazily down the sloped earth to
one side of him, staining itself on his gun hand and Colt.
Buck picked up a tin can and held it close to the place in
one of the bullet punctured flasks where the silvery fluid
was leaking onto the earth. He turned and handed the
can to Edith. "Here," he said with a tired smile.

She looked curiously at it. "What is it, Buck?"

"Your father's treasure, Edith, only Deeth and Stinger
didn't know it. It's quicksilver. It's used on the amalgamating plates of the mills to separate the silver from the
ore. These iron flasks are filled with it. Each flask is
worth about fifty dollars a flask. There must be at least a
hundred of them stored in this vault. About five thousand dollars' worth of quicksilver on the present market,
Edith."

She stared uncomprehendingly at him. "Silver? Quicksilver?" She smiled. "Then *they* were looking for silver in
here with five thousand dollars' worth of treasure right
under their hands?"

He nodded.

Her eyes narrowed. "And you knew it was here all the
time? You knew they'd likely come here, for the overlay
would indicate this building. You took your calculated
risk."

"Yes, Edith." He pressed a hand against his aching
head. "We can board this up again. It isn't likely anyone
will come around and find it until we can get back here
with wagons to haul it out of here. It won't repay you for
the loss of your father, Edith, but he would have wanted
it this way."

"And you?" she said.

"I got my four boys," he said quietly. "The warrants said dead or alive. I would have preferred it the other way. Four thousand dollars, Edith. I can't complain about that." He studied her.

She-came close to him and cupped his dirty, battered face in her slim hands. "You said the quicksilver was used to amalgamate with the silver from the ore. Maybe we can do a little amalgamating ourselves, Buck. Five thousand dollars and four thousand dollars makes nine thousand dollars, and that, in my book, is a nice sum with which to start a long life as man and wife."

He kissed her and the two of them left that place of treasure and sudden death. They weren't out of the trap of the desert yet, but when two people are too tough to die, the desert really hasn't got much of a calculated risk to kill them.

THE VALIANT BUGLES

THE VALIANT BUGLES

To "Nick" Halseth

CHAPTER ONE

The rising skein of yellow dust whirled up beyond the serrated escarpment half a mile from the place where the detachment had halted and dismounted. The dust might be from a whirling wind-devil rising from the baked desert floor two hundred feet below the lip of the escarpment. But it might also come from the hoofs of Mr. McAllister's patrol horses—*if* the lost patrol was still alive in the very heart of Apache country.

Captain Holt Downey studied the dust through reddened eyes. It wavered against the shimmering heat veils which rose from the Spanish Desert of Arizona. The terrain seemed vague and unreal, almost as though seen in a dream, but this country was not a dream—rather, it was a nightmare, viewed and experienced while one was wide awake, the better to suffer from it.

Far across the vast depression of the Spanish Desert was a strange natural formation of jumbled rock, resembling the ruined walls and towers of some forgotten city of Asia Minor. In the center of the chaotic masses of yellow, salmon, and reddish rock rose the ugly excrescence that dominated the vast rock mass. It would have been the citadel in a man-made fortress. In fact, it *was* a natural citadel in the tortured and jumbled masses of decomposing rock and great tip-tilted slabs of granite which formed the half-sunken range to the south of the desert.

Holt Downey could hear his men talking in low, thirst-hoarse voices. Now and then one of the cavalry horses whinnied plaintively because of thirst. Holt did not look back at his understrength company. He didn't have to. He knew they were watching him, waiting for the command which would take them back the hellish miles to Fort Guthrie. He didn't have to see them watching him, for he seemed to feel their eyes boring into his back. Their dislike of him was a physical thing on that heat-soaked plain which stretched to the escarpment.

The furnace wind shifted and moved across the plain toward the detachment, and men opened their mouths to get their breath. It was then that Holt heard the faint popping sound carried to him on the wind. It came from the south, below the escarpment. "Yancey!" he called out.

The lean civilian scout shambled forward leading his raw-boned buckskin. "Yeah, Captain?" he said.

Holt did not look at the man. Yancey was little better than useless in that country. Holt himself knew the region better than the scout did, although that wasn't saying much either. No man seemed to know much about the Spanish Desert country. No white man did, that is, but the Apaches knew it well enough. *They knew it too damned well*, thought Holt.

Yancey shifted his feet. The man's body stench came to Holt on the wind and almost sickened him. They all stank from two weeks of patrol, but it was the mingled aura of sweat, dust and horse, clean in contrast to the powerful secretions of Yancey Tulvis. "Yeah, Captain?" he asked again.

"Listen."

Yancey cocked an ear. "Can't hear nothing."

Holt gripped the scout by the arm. "Sounds like shooting," he said.

The scout eyed the tall, hawk-faced officer. "You been out on patrol too long," he observed with a sly grin.

Holt held back an impulse to smash the lopsided and dirty face of the scout. "Is there a way down that escarpment?" he asked.

"Now you ain't thinking of taking thutty-five men and hosses down there, are you?"

Holt slanted his head sideways and looked at the scout, and the look from the hard gray-green eyes was like the blow of a club. "Is there a way down that escarpment?"

Yancey stepped back a little. "I don't rightly know," he said sullenly.

"You don't rightly know a goddamned thing, Yancey!" Holt turned. "Sergeant Caxton!"

The blocky noncom came forward leading his horse. He touched the brim of his campaign hat. "Sir?"

"Yancey and I are going ahead to the escarpment. Hold the company here. Look for arm signals. I may need you in a hurry."

Caxton nodded. "Yes, sir." He hesitated, touching his cracked lips with his tongue. "What about water, sir?"

Holt glanced back at the company. "We'll turn back to Socorro Tanks after I scout ahead."

The veteran noncom looked toward the raveled thread of dust. "Are you sure of that, sir?"

"Are you questioning my plans, Sergeant?"

There was a faintly malicious look in Caxton's blue eyes. "Why, no, sir!"

"How is Mr. Sturgis?"

"He'll be all right, Captain. Too much sun, not enough water. A hard patrol for a new shavetail fresh from the Academy, sir."

"He'll live," said Holt. He unwrapped the reins from about his left arm and led his bay forward, followed by

Yancey. He did not see the glances that passed between the two men behind him.

"Probably nothing but a wind-devil," said Yancey to Holt.

The dust didn't show any inclination to vanish as quickly as it had appeared. "More like the dust from hoofs," said Holt.

"Out here? Ain't nobody loco enough to come out here."

"Except the army, eh, Yancey?"

"Well—"

Holt looked at the scout. "Except Holt Downey, Yancey?"

Yancey flushed. He shifted his chew of tobacco and spat copiously. "You said it, I didn', Captain," he mumbled around his chew.

They left the tired horses in a hollow and went forward on foot, and the heat of the naked rock burned up through their boot soles. The wind shifted again, and the popping noise came again.

Holt walked to within twenty feet of the escarpment lip and then went down on his hands and knees. He moved forward until he was almost at the lip, then went down on his lean belly. The breath wheezed out of his lungs as the rock burned through his shirt and seemed to sear his skin. There was a place where a rock fall had allowed a little earth to form a pocket, which in turn afforded a precarious existence to scrub brush. Holt edged forward until he could look down to the Spanish Desert.

Yancey came up beside Holt. "Jesus God!" he said.

Far below them the escarpment was gashed by a narrow gully with almost vertical sides. To right and left of it the ground was an impassable mass of shattered rock interlaced with thorny brush, like chevaux-de-frise. At the junction of the gully and the harsh desert floor there was a dark, irregular circle. Holt dashed the sweat from his forehead and felt for his field glasses.

The popping noise was louder, like hot grease in a skillet. Cottony puffs of white smoke rose from the dark circle, and other puffs seemed to sprout among the rocks below the dark circle like strange desert growths. The wind raveled the smoke and carried it off. Beyond the mouth of the gully were tiny horsemen, and it was from beneath the hoofs of their mounts that the dust arose.

"It must be Mr. McAllister's patrol!" said Yancey. He spat juicily. "How in Christ's name did he get 'way out here?" He eyed Holt. "How did *you* know he'd be out here, Captain?"

Holt did not answer. He uncased his glasses, braced his elbows, then focused the glasses on the dark circle. Details swam into view. Dead horses, starting to swell in the intense heat. Troopers lying behind the horses with their carbines in their hands. Dead and wounded lying within the stinking ring of horses. The sun glinted for an instant, like a shard of molten gold, on the shoulder of one of the crouching men. The good German lens picked out the young officer and his shiny, gold-braid-bordered shoulder straps.

Yancey placed a dirty hand on Holt's arm. "Look! To the right! Mounted buck's!"

The scout was a pretty poor specimen of his calling, but his eyes were like a hawk's. Holt shifted the glasses. A score of bucks sat their horses in a deep natural bowl within the rocks to the right of the gully. One of them stood beside his mount and was talking and gesturing, swinging an arm toward the gully. Holt changed the focus of the glasses. The painted face of the speaker came into view. The face was one that might look from a smoky window of hell. A beaked nose, a thin slit of a lipless mouth. On the head was a sort of helmet made of matted fur from which protruded two yellow-stained horns. "Christ!" said Holt.

"What is it?"

Holt lowered the glasses. "That's the Butcher down there?"

"El Carnicero?" Yancey's lips drew back from his teeth in a quick grimace of fear and it seemed as though the stench from his body increased.

The guts in Holt's belly seemed to coil tightly and his breath came harshly in his throat. A reddish mist formed in front of his eyes. He lowered the glasses and rested his head on his forearms. He could feel the hot, itching tendrils of sour sweat working down inside his shirt, burning his skin. The heat soaked into him with enervating strength, and it took all the stamina he had to raise his head again. El Carnicero! The Mexicans had named him well, with the skill they had in such matters. The Butcher!

Yancey spat again. "They say there ain't no such 'Pache as the Butcher."

Holt did not answer. He was studying the terrain. If he could pin the Butcher against the foot of the escarpment or ambush him in the rock labyrinths he'd have him as cold as yesterday's rations.

"They say they's half a dozen 'Paches wear that damned horned helmet and that battle shirt, pretending like *they* was the Butcher."

Holt shifted a little. If the Apaches slipped out into the Spanish Desert they'd be gone like the morning mist burned by the rising sun. Holt's command was too beat, men and horses, to make a stern chase across that playground of Hell down there. Besides, no white man knew of any water out there, or in the brooding mountain range to the south of the desert. But the Apaches did....

Carbines popped futilely from the ring of dead horseflesh. Wasting ammunition. The Apaches could wait. The sun and thirst would do their preliminary work for them. The rest would be easy. A swift rush at dusk or at dawn. Bloody work with the knives. Another White-Eye patrol gone to the House of Spirits. *Aiyee!*

"Go back and get Sergeant Caxton!" Holt said, and then Holt focused the glasses on the mounted bucks. Some of them were dismounting to squat in the meager shade of their horses. They seemed to be in no hurry. The lenses picked out the demon face of the buck wearing the horned helmet. Holt's breath drew in sharply. It was the Butcher! Yancey was full of wind. There was such a man, if "man" was the proper name for the Butcher. If such a man did not actually exist, as many Mexicans and Americans thought, then the Apaches were using psychology indeed, for the name of El Carnicero was enough to make strong men wince. He had cut a swath of blood and loot across Chihuahua, Sonora, New Mexico, and Arizona in the decade since the Civil War, avoiding American and Mexican ambushes, appearing and disappearing like a wind-devil, killing for the sheer bloody pleasure of it, as though to sate some burning inner thirst.

Caxton and the scout crawled into the patch of scrub brush. Caxton wiped the sweat from his broad face. Holt handed him the field glasses, and the sergeant focused them on the terrain below the escarpment. His mouth worked a little as he studied the scene. He put down the glasses. "Mr. McAllister's patrol, sir?" he asked.

"I don't know who else it could be."

"That's true, sir."

Holt lay flat, studying the lay of the land. Minutes ticked past, and then Caxton spoke. "Yancey said you thought the Butcher was down there."

"Yes."

"You're sure?"

Holt looked sideways at the noncom. "If there is such a man is what you actually mean, isn't that it?"

Caxton flushed. "Well—yes, sir."

The agate eyes held Caxton's. "There is, Sergeant, before God Almighty, *there is...*"

The two men eyed the officer. Yancey leaned back a little, held a forefinger beside his head, and whirled it in a little circle. His lips silently formed the word *"loco."*

Caxton nodded.

Holt shoved back his sweat-soaked campaign hat. He looked to the right along the escarpment. There was a place five hundred yards away where mounted men might be able to get down to the desert floor. To his left a great talus had flowed down to the desert, forming a long curved ridge, like a gigantic fishhook. The gully, at the mouth of which the patrol was trapped, seemed to aim at the curve of the fishhook. If El Carnicero could be driven from the west into the curve of the fishhook, he could be hit and hit hard by a charge down the gully. There would be no way out. Horses couldn't carry men over that talus ridge. It was too loose. Men on foot could be picked off one by one as they tried to cross it.

The silence was broken only by the sighing of the furnace wind and the occasional report of a rifle or carbine far below.

"Poor devils," said Caxton quietly.

Holt looked at him. The noncom was looking down at the trapped troopers. The heat was hellish enough on top of the escarpment, but there was a little mottled shade from the scrub brush, and the wind, hot as it was, helped some. But down in that gully it would be like the interior of a blast furnace, with rock beneath them and on each side of them reflecting the heat while it blocked off the wind. With no water and no shade, and wounded men lying below the stinking rampart of dead horses, the patrol was doomed unless Holt Downey did something about it.

Yancey and Caxton eyed Holt. They eyed him with the expectancy of subordinates who knew they had nothing to do but obey his orders. The plan and the entire responsibility were up to him.

Holt wiped the salt sweat from his eyes. His orders had been clear enough. "Captain Downey," Colonel Fleming had said in his weighty voice, "you will take your B Company on a reconnaissance southwest of Fort Guthrie, to the vicinity of Socorro Tanks, then east to the Caballo Wash, thence north again to Fort Guthrie. Rations and ammunition for ten days. Your primary objective is to find Mr. McAllister and his patrol from F Company. If by any chance you strike the trail of El Carnicero, or any of his sub-chiefs, you will immediately dispatch couriers to this post and to Fort Parnell with information on his strength, direction of travel, and anything else you may learn. But your primary mission is to *find Mr. McAllister,* and it is hardly necessary for me to tell you why."

Holt shifted a little. He had thirty-five men. They were worn thin by heat and hard travel across harsh country, but they were soldiers.

"We wait much longer," said Yancey, "and Mr. McAllister will catch a bullet or die of thirst, and the *general* wouldn't like that at all. No sireee, General McAllister wouldn't like it one little bit."

Holt beckoned to Caxton. "Take the third and fourth squads to the right, well back from the edge of this escarpment. Have the men lead their horses down to the desert floor, and for God's sake don't let the Apaches spot you. You see that fishhook ridge? When you hear the trumpet sound the charge, sweep in like foragers, driving those mounted Apaches inside of that fishhook."

"Yes, sir." Caxton glanced at Holt.

Holt cased his glasses. "I'll take the first and second squads down the gully and catch them flat-footed within the fishhook."

"Yes, sir. One thing, sir, what about Mr. McAllister and his men?"

Holt crawled backward. "They'll be all right."

Caxton looked puzzled. He glanced down at the gully. There wasn't much room for a charge down it.

"Shake the dung!" snapped Holt. He got to his feet and strode toward his horse. He pumped an arm up and down, and the company slowly led their horses to where he stood. Ronald Sturgis, the new shavetail, fresh from the Academy, and the only other officer in B Company, came up to Holt. "I'm ready for duty, sir," he said crisply.

Holt eyed the handsome face, mottled red and white by the sun and heat exhaustion. "You'd better let Sergeant Caxton take over, mister," he said.

Sturgis flushed. "Are we attacking?"

"Yes."

"What about Mr. McAllister?"

"He's down there, mister."

Caxton led out the third and fourth squads. Ronald Sturgis turned to Holt. "I want to take command," he said.

"So?" Holt drew out his service Colt and checked it. Then he looked the younger man in the eye. "Then you go right along. First Sergeant Caxton will brief you."

"Thanks, sir."

Holt waved a hand. He reached out and held Sturgis by a fold of his damp shirt. "One other thing, mister: You're not fighting rebels when you fight out here. Give no quarter. Out here, in Apache country, it's kill or be killed. Forget any chivalry you may think is the way to fight wars. Fight dirty, dirtier than they do, and you may live to have a silver bar on that bare shoulder strap of yours."

Holt watched Caxton and Sturgis lead the two squads to the west. "Sergeant Lambert! Trumpeter Monahan!"

The two troopers came to him and saluted. Holt told them of his plan. "We'll approach the head of the gully and work down it as far as we can without being seen. We may get fairly close to Mr. McAllister's position without being seen."

"Yes, sir," said Lambert.

"And if we don't?" said Yancey Tulvis.

Holt ignored him. He led the way to the entrance to the gully. The men were quiet. The veteran yellowlegs had the quietness of professionals going about their business. The rookies had the silence of men who were damned well afraid, perhaps more of making fools of themselves than of facing the Apaches.

CHAPTER TWO

The heat was beating down on the two waiting squads. Holt took out his repeater watch and opened the cover. Sturgis had had half an hour to get into position. Holt had heard no firing from McAllister's men at the foot of the high-walled gully. Holt had led his command to within a hundred and fifty yards of the patrol's position, and he was sure they had not been seen.

"Mount," said Holt.

There was a smashing of saddle leather as the squads mounted. Holt looked at the quiet men. "We'll go in with the pistol," he said. "If we catch them within the fish-hook I want every one of them killed or captured. If they break into the open don't chase them. Open fire with the carbine. Above all, I want El Carnicero. You'll know him by his battle shirt and horned helmet. Pick a partner and stay together. No man will fight alone! If your partner goes down, stay with him to protect him—but keep shooting!"

The fourteen-dollar-a-month faces showed no expression. Holt looked at Trumpeter Monahan. "When I raise my hand, you blow the charge, and put some spit into it!"

Holt swung up on Brandy, then unsheathed his issue Colt.

"What the hell is that?" demanded Corporal Moore.

The sudden rattling of pistols came to them on the wind. Holt kneed Brandy forward and looked toward the sound of the firing. Ronald Sturgis had disobeyed orders. He was leading his men in a hell-for-leather charge along the base of the escarpment in true Yellow Tavern style, with sabers and pistols. The Apaches were milling about, close to the one place where they could still break for the open desert. *And once they got into the clear—*

"Now, Monahan!" yelled Holt. He was off down the gully even as the first notes ripped brazenly out from the C horn. Some of the men yelled hoarsely, and the echoes slammed back and forth between the high walls of the gully.

The Apaches who had kept McAllister pinned down were popping out of the rock crevices like deadly jack-in-the-boxes, racing to join their mates.

Holt tilted forward as the big bay plunged down the steep slope. It was far steeper than Holt had realized, but there was no going back now. The luck of the foolhardy would have to carry him through now.

The two squads pounded along behind him, a tight mass of horseflesh and men, like an avalanche gathering speed, and the noise of their wild passage was like the roaring of a winter storm along the New England coast

Holt shot a glance toward the Apache position. Beyond tumbled masses of rock, he saw the mounted bucks being driven toward the fishhook by Sturgis' men. The kid had disobeyed orders, but the attack might yet be a success. The Apaches were riding like furies, firing at the racing troopers, while red blossoms of fire sprouted from Colts' muzzles. Here and there a trooper had gone down, but there were more Apaches down than troopers.

El Carnicero was within the hook. Holt looked

beyond McAllister's position. He saw nothing but that damned horned head through a swirling red mist.

"For God's sake, Captain!" yelled Yancey Tulvis. "Look out!"

Brandy hurled himself over a rock ledge and plunged toward the mouth of the gully. It was narrow; it was too damned narrow!

The young shavetail stood up with his pistol in one hand and his saber in the other, with his mouth squared like a Greek mask, yelling in delight at the sight of his rescuers, then the forefeet of the big bay struck him and drove him to one side like a rag doll. Brandy was in and out of the circle of dead horseflesh like a steeplechase champion. All Holt saw out of the corner of his eye was screaming troopers being scattered like bloody chaff, then the bay was in the clear racing toward El Carnicero.

Holt did not look back when the avalanche of horses and men struck the circle within which McAllister's men were penned like trapped rats. He saw nothing but El Carnicero. His Colt seemed to rise automatically and crack twice to drive a screaming buck from his horse. Brandy slammed hard against another Apache mount and the warrior died with a neat blue hole between his eyes.

The big bay was wild with excitement as he took out after El Carnicero. Bullets hummed past Holt Downey. All over within the fishhook area rifles and pistols cracked and Apaches went down. El Carnicero screamed like an insane fury. His horse reared and pawed the air with his forehoofs, then the Apache swung him away from the howling troopers and crouched low on his back, riding hard toward Sturgis' men who had scattered to kill Apaches. There was no one in the chief's way but Sturgis.

For a moment it seemed like a poised tableau: the horned killer on his maddened horse; the young officer with saber in one hand and pistol in the other. There was no way past Sturgis for El Carnicero. The Apache swung his lance from its sling and poised it, aiming squarely for Sturgis.

"Shoot! Shoot! *For Christ's sake shoot!*" yelled Holt.

In the whirling mist of dust and gun smoke the figures seemed like wraiths from another world. Then Sturgis yanked savagely at his horse's reins, dropped his saber, and vanished in the thick whirling smoke and dust, letting El Carnicero pass.

Holt cursed savagely. He sank the steel into the tiring bay as he fired twice at the dim figure of the Apache. Then the bay was through the haze. El Carnicero was riding toward the open desert. The crackling of shots and the yelling of the fighting men rose from the base of the escarpment, but it meant nothing now to the two men who rode out into the yellow glare of the desert sun. The hoofs drummed like pebbles shaken in a gourd. Foam flecked from the bay's mouth. His stride faltered a little, but he kept on.

El Carnicero was out of effective pistol range, but Holt threw his last shot after him, then sheathed the pistol. He leaned forward and spoke to Brandy and felt the bay's pace increase.

El Carnicero looked back, and his face seemed etched in Holt's mind. The Apache was gaining a little. Holt drew his Spencer repeater from its sheath and began to beat the bay with it, but Brandy was losing ground.

Then the Apache's horse stumbled and went down. Holt yelled and began to close in. El Carnicero yanked a carbine from the fallen horse and raised it. He fired once. The bullet struck the bay with the sound of a stick being whipped into thick mud. Brandy was down and Holt struck the ground, his carbine flying from his hand to strike a rock and shatter the stock.

El Carnicero was up on his horse and off like a stone flung from a sling. He turned and looked back, and the look of triumph on his painted face struck Holt like a lance.

Holt stood there with the sweat cutting stinging channels through the dust on his face, and his face seemed like that of a graven image of hate incarnate.

Smaller and smaller became the figure of the Butcher and his racing horse until there was nothing to be seen but the thread of yellow dust rising to be raveled by the wind. He was heading for the fantastic range to the south of the Spanish Desert, and no white man could follow him there. His medicine was too good, and besides, no white man knew where the water *tinajas* were in that jumbled mass of rock and heat.

Brandy moved a little, and his great eyes looked at Holt. Holt knelt by the big bay. The leg bones showed through the hide. His right front leg was a shattered mess. Holt stood up and reached for his Colt. The holster was empty. He walked back toward the escarpment. The shooting had stopped. Here and there across the yellow sands tiny mounted men raced away from the scene of the fight. Apaches. It was their way. Scatter when the going got too tough. Meet at some prearranged place.

Holt could see his scattered company. One man was having an arm wound bandaged. Another lay on the ground while one of his mates staunched the flow of blood from a leg wound.

Sergeant Caxton stood with his arms folded looking up the dust-shrouded gully. There was a hideous mess of horses and bodies of men where Lieutenant McAllister's patrol had been overrun.

"Caxton!" said Holt.

The noncom turned. "Yes, sir?"

"Go back and shoot my horse. His leg is hopelessly broken."

Sergeant Caxton dropped his hand to his Colt and then drew out the heavy hand gun. For a moment he hesitated, then he reversed the Colt and held it out toward Holt. "Kill him yourself," he said. "You've done a damned good job of killing so far today, Captain Downey. Don't quit because you're ahead."

Holt took the proffered pistol. He walked back to the bay and fired without hesitation. The flat crack of the Colt echoed from the escarpment. The troopers watched him as he came back toward the big first sergeant.

Holt stopped in front of Caxton. He shifted the hot Colt to his left hand, then swiftly reached out to rip the big yellow chevrons and diamond from the sleeves of Caxton's shirt. Hard gray-green eyes met hard blue eyes and neither man looked away. Holt reversed the Colt and handed it to Caxton. Caxton took the weapon and his eyes never left those of Holt Downey. Then the ex-noncom sheathed the weapon. Holt walked past him. "Sergeant Lambert!" he called.

The noncom came forward and saluted. "Yes, sir?"

"Take over as temporary first sergeant."

Lambert's eyes flicked toward the man he had replaced. "Yes, sir."

"How many casualties?" asked Holt.

"Three men wounded, sir. None of them seriously." Lambert smiled thinly. "Seven dead Apaches and four wounded, sir."

"What about Mr. McAllister's detachment?"

Lambert paled a little beneath his tan. "All dead, sir."

"*All* of them?"

Lambert swallowed a little. "From the looks of them, there were only two men on their feet besides Mr. McAllister. The others were already dead—I think..."

Holt wiped the sweat from his face. He felt unutterably weary. "Bury them," he said.

Lambert looked up at the brazen sky. "Hot work with little water, sir."

Holt walked to a fallen Apache horse. A swollen intestine hung greasily over the dead horse's dusty flanks. "Plenty of water in these Apache canteens," he said.

"But, sir...!"

Holt turned and a faintly cynical smile flitted over his hawk's face. "Squeamish, Sergeant Lambert? You'll thank God for that water long before we reach Socorro Tanks. Now jump to it!"

Holt turned and looked toward the distant mountains, shrouded in shimmering haze. He thought he saw a thread of dust rising several miles to the south. The Butcher had made good his escape. But it had been close, so very close... One day his luck would run out. One day Holt Downey would reach him with his bare hands and laugh in that lipless face as the eyes bulged out.

———

DUSK WAS GATHERING across the Spanish Desert when the last man of Mr. McAllister's patrol was covered with the harsh earth. The dead Apaches had been dumped into a deep rock crevice. The four wounded bucks were bound and mounted on their horses. They might all reach Fort Guthrie if they didn't die of loss of blood long before that time.

B Company gathered silently in front of the mounded graves. Holt Downey took off his hat. "The Lord is my shepherd; I shall not want," he said quietly. "He maketh me to lie down in green pastures: he leadeth me beside the still waters...."

———

IT WAS dark atop the escarpment as the point led out for Socorro Tanks. To the east there was a faint suggestion of light from the rising moon. There was little sound atop the escarpment other than the thudding of the hoofs of the led horses and the creaking of leather.

Far out on the Spanish Desert a coyote howled. The wind shifted a little. Holt Downey rode from the rear of his little column toward the front. He could see Mr.

Sturgis leading the way for the main body of the company. Mr. Sturgis had had little to say since the attack. Holt held nothing against him for his failure to stop El Carnicero in his lance charge. Braver men than Ronald Sturgis had been frightened by the Apache chief. But Sturgis had jumped the gun in the attack. Perhaps, if he had waited a little, they might have gathered in El Carnicero or killed him. Perhaps... It was the unknown quantity.

Holt drew off to one side to watch the plodding troopers. Near the end of the column was ex-First Sergeant Caxton walking beside a footsore rookie, a kid fresh from a mill town in Massachusetts, in the army by way of Jefferson Barracks. Holt kneed his horse and turned toward the head of the column. There seemed to be a fraction of a moment when it was quiet. *"Murderer!"* the voice said clearly, and it came from the very rear of the column, but there was no way of knowing whose voice it actually was.

CHAPTER THREE

Fort Guthrie squatted like some ugly growth on the mesa overlooking the cut-up malpais country to the south. The scrub brush had been cleared for a hundred yards beyond the post buildings and the adobe and fieldstone buildings stood out starkly on the yellowish earth of the mesa top. Beyond the post were two elevations, hardly more than twenty feet higher than the level of the post itself, but on the flat land of the mesa they stood out almost like major elevations. One of the elevations had been dug into and walls of rock and adobe had been reared, pierced by gun embrasures, but the bastion had never been used in the memory of anyone at Fort Guthrie, so it had become a home for kangaroo rats, gophers, jack rabbits and snakes. The other elevation was stippled with white headboards, standing starkly from the barren earth; a wide path bordered with whitewashed stones led up to the grave-yard, while rusted wire surrounded it, serving little other purpose than to keep the tumbleweeds from rolling across the graves to plunge down the mesa side to the south.

Holt Downey rode silently ahead of his company. Mr. Sturgis seemed to prefer the company of Yancey Tulvis, the windy scout, who droned on and on about his adventures and experiences with Apaches, Navajos, Pimas, Papagos and Mohaves, with interesting sidelights on the sexual accomplishments of the women of each tribe. Holt was sure that no squaw would have looked with interest on Yancey Tulvis, and yet it was said that he had a daughter who was more than passing fair to look upon, although whether she was a breed or not no one had ever known for sure.

The post flag' snapped vigorously in the dry wind which scoured the mesa top. The pattern of stars and stripes stood out boldly and pleasingly against the stark blue sky. It was about the only spot of color at Fort Guthrie, for if the officer who had selected the site of Guthrie had planned specifically to choose the most isolated and barren spot in Arizona Territory for it, he had evidently succeeded.

"The rump av the universe," said Trumpeter Monahan, almost as though he had read Holt's thoughts.

"You can say that again," said Sergeant Lambert in a sour voice.

"Why, Sarge?" asked Monahan. "We all know it well enough."

Lambert stood up in his stirrups and eased his crotch. "Look, sir, there's a dougherty wagon coming up the road from the desert."

Holt looked at the vehicle. The green Maltese cross of the Medical Department stood out against the dusty side of the ambulance. A dozen troopers trotted alongside the vehicle.

"There's a woman in it," said Yancey Tulvis.

"Trust you to see that," said Lambert.

"What else is interestin' around Fort Guthrie?" asked the scout. He spat and leered.

Ronald Sturgis took out his field glasses and focused them on the vehicle. "There's a woman all right! Yancey, you've eyes like a hawk!"

"Sho," said the scout deprecatingly.

Sturgis suddenly lowered the glasses and glanced at Holt. "There's a general officer with her. I'd swear it was General McAllister. I saw him once at the Academy."

Holt saw that the company column would meet the dougherty at the gate of the fort unless he speeded up their march or slowed it down. But he would do neither. He'd have to face Talbot McAllister sooner or later. McAllister was Inspector General for the Department now. Some sanitary sink gossip said that he had been assigned to that duty because his power in Washington had become too much for President Grant, and a hint to "Cump" Sherman, commander of the army, had taken care of Talbot McAllister. It hadn't been too long before the hand of General McAllister had been felt throughout the department.

Holt turned in his saddle. "Straighten up there! Square those campaign hats fore and aft! Let's *look* like soldiers!"

Holt halted the company just short of the junction of the two roads which led to Fort Guthrie just as the dougherty reached the junction. The driver reined in the dusty mules, and the door of the ambulance swung open.

"Attention!" barked Holt as he saluted. Talbot McAllister returned the salute. "Back from patrol, Captain Downey?" he asked in his coal-voice.

"Yes, sir."

"Where did you patrol?"

"Southwest, sir, to the area south of Socorro Tanks, the Spanish Desert, thence back to Caballo Wash."

Talbot McAllister was still a handsome man and the resemblance of his son to his well-known father was rather startling, except that young DeWitt McAllister had had a warmth about him said to be inherited from his mother, a famous Southern beauty.

The gray eyes studied Holt. "Any news of my son, Downey?"

Holt could almost feel the tension along the dusty column of troopers just behind him.

"*Well,* Captain?"

Holt looked beyond the imperious face of the general. There was a woman on the seat next to him. A pretty woman, although it was hard to distinguish her features clearly. But she was young.

"Captain Downey!" snapped McAllister.

Holt looked down at the father of the man he had killed just as surely as though he had put a pistol to his neck and had drawn the trigger. "I am sorry to say, sir, that your son is dead," said Holt quietly.

There was a startled intake of breath from the woman beside the general. He turned quickly. "Katherine," he said.

"I'm all right, General."

The gray eyes struck Holt like a whiplash. "This young lady is...or was...DeWitt's fiancée. You might have been more considerate, Downey!"

Holt's face tightened. "The general insisted that I speak."

"True! How did he die, sir?"

In the moment's hesitation before Holt spoke again, he felt the tension from the quiet column of men like a living force at his back. "We had a fight with Apaches, general. It was the Butcher. He had Mr. McAllister's patrol trapped at the bottom of the Barrera Escarpment, north of the Spanish Desert."

"And my son died in action fighting the Butcher?"

"Not exactly, sir."

McAllister's lean jaws tightened as the muscles drew up like wires. "What do you mean—*not exactly,* sir?"

Salt sweat trickled down Holt's sides like rivulets from a hot spring. There was a feathery feeling in his diaphragm. Fifteen years of honorable military service hung in the balance. "We charged the Butcher, general. We had him trapped neatly... The trap snapped shut—

but the Butcher slipped through... In the charge, my detachment overran Mr. McAllister's position. Mr. McAllister was hit by a horse, thrown aside, and trampled to death under the rest of the horses."

In the silence that followed the noisy fluttering of the flag halyards, slapping against the warped flagpole of the fort, seemed inordinately loud.

"Who led that charge, mister?" asked the general quietly.

"I did, sir."

The gray eyes were like shards of floe ice. "There was no way to avoid running over my son's position?"

Now was the time to lie. Now was the time to wriggle into the clear a little to prepare a defense against that which would surely come, a court of inquiry. Holt shook his head a little. Those close to him were waiting. Mr. Sturgis had not seen Holt's charge, and he himself was hardly in a position to accuse anyone of improper conduct after his performance at the Barrera Escarpment. It would be the word of the company commander against the men of his company. Officer against enlisted men.

"Mr. Downey?" said the general harshly.

"I misjudged the width of the gully down which I led two squads in the charge—the width, and the steepness of it. There was no way of passing Mr. McAllister's position. We had to override it."

The young woman turned her head away and the general placed a hand on her shoulder before he looked at Holt again. "Whose horse first struck my son down?"

"Mine, sir."

Talbot McAllister nodded. He closed the dougherty's door and looked through the open window. "Present yourself in one hour at Colonel Fleming's office. I want to hear all about this mess, Captain."

"Yes, sir."

"And the Apache—the Butcher—he escaped?"

"He escaped, sir."

McAllister nodded. "Drive on," he said to the dougherty driver.

Holt saluted, but the general did not return the salute. The ambulance rolled to the gateway. The sentry presented arms. "Turn out the guard!" he called out.

Holt sat there watching the little ceremony. But he was not watching the general, but rather the young woman who had descended from the ambulance on his arm. The dry wind fluttered her honey-colored hair, and suddenly Holt Downey felt a green sickness deep within him, for he remembered what had been left of DeWitt McAllister after the charge down the gully.

Holt led the worn company into the post quadrangle. He swung down from' his horse and let Monahan take the reins. "Sergeant Lambert, take over," said Holt.

"What about the prisoners, sir?"

Holt was a little startled. He had quite forgotten the two sullen bucks who had survived the return trip to Fort Guthrie. Two of the original quartet had been dumped along the way for the buzzards and coyotes to clean up. "Guardhouse," he said. He eyed the noncom. "No rough stuff! I don't want those bucks kicked around."

Yancey Tulvis spat. "Considerate, of you, Cap'n, sir," he said.

Holt whirled quickly. "I don't give a tinker's damn for them, Tulvis! Dead or alive, it's all the same to me! But we might get them to talk! They might know the way into the Butcher's stronghold!" Holt stalked off to his quarters.

Yancey Tulvis spat juicily. "It's a cinch, if they do tell, *you* won't be the man to go in after the Butcher, Captain Downey!"

Ronald Sturgis slapped the dust from his trousers with the gauntlets he affected as part of a frontier cavalry officer's uniform. "What do you mean by that, Yancey?" he asked.

The scout looked about. Lambert had dismissed the beat company. "You think General McAllister is going to let High and Mighty Holt Downey keep his shoulder straps after what happened out there?"

Sturgis glanced toward headquarters. "You mean—?"

"Sure as shootin', mister!" Yancey thumbed his beak of a nose toward the back of Holt Downey. "They'll crucify that brass-bound sonofabitch or my name ain't Yancey Benedict Tulvis!"

Sturgis idly slapped his gauntlets against his thigh. The command, three companies of cavalry, one of infantry, with other post personnel, was terribly short of officers. That was why DeWitt McAllister had taken out a patrol into the Barrera Escarpment country when he hardly knew the terrain of the mesa upon which Fort Guthrie sat. That was why F Company had only two officers available for duty— Captain Holt Downey and Second Lieutenant Ronald Sturgis. Attrition of officers had been high in the department in the past year because of El Carnicero and his satellite chiefs.

Yancey leaned close to Sturgis. "You watch! They ask me what he done and I'll tell 'em."

"So? What will you tell them?"

Yancey grinned. "Sergeant Caxton figgered there wasn't enough room in that gully for a charge. He didn' say so, but he knew it. So did I. I yelled at him to pull up afore he ever reached McAllister's position, but he kept agoin' like the devil hisself was after him."

Sturgis nodded. "You'd testify to that at a court of inquiry?"

"Why not? I got no love for Holt Downey. Neither has Sergeant Caxton." Yancey grinned again. "I mean— ex-First Sergeant Caxton."

"Hey, Yancey!" called out a passing trooper. "They's a lady to see you over at your shebang!"

Yancey whirled in pleased expectation. "Lady? Who, Gillis?"

The trooper leered. "Your daughter, Yancey, and she ain't in no pleasant mood. Look ahere!" The trooper touched a finger to four parallel red marks on his right cheek. "She strikes like a damned wildcat. Drew blood, she did."

Yancey's face fell. "Jesus God," he said sorrowfully.

The young officer eyed him. "Is it that bad?"

"Sure is. You never met Annie. Bad as her old lady." Yancey shrugged. "See you later, Mr. Sturgis."

Yancey shuffled off toward the dismal row of sagging adobes and jacals at the far end of the post, not too distant from the edge of the mesa.

Ronald Sturgis passed a hand across his jaws. He needed a shave. The command was short of officers. He was second in command of F Company. Now, if Holt Downey was out of the way, a young officer might very well gain a silver bar for his shoulder straps without having to spend four or five years of hell as a junior officer at Fort Guthrie. Besides, Holt Downey had seen him run from the Butcher. The company commander might not say anything. He was of that breed. But he would *think* plenty, and none of it good for his junior officer. Sturgis walked toward Officers' Row. He saw the tall, spare figure of First Lieutenant Benjamin Loris entering the quarters he shared with Holt Downey. The adjutant must have heard something about the mess at the Barrera Escarpment. Loris disliked Ronald Sturgis almost as much as Holt Downey did.

"I'll screw them," said Sturgis. "I'll screw them all!"

The dry wind swept across the isolated post from the direction of the Barrera Escarpment and the Spanish Desert, slapping the flag halyards against the pole, rolling tumbleweeds across the hard-beaten surface of the parade-ground quadrangle, and it seemed as though the bitter laughter of El Carnicero rode on the wings of the wind, laughing at the garrison of Fort Guthrie.

CHAPTER FOUR

B en Loris scaled his forage cap at a hook and
nodded in satisfaction as it neatly struck the
target and hung there. The tall officer dropped
onto his cot and watched Holt as he swabbed his naked
upper body with a towel. "Pretty bad, eh, Holt?" he
asked.

"Damned bad, Benny."

Loris took a cigar from a case and lighted it. He
puffed out the smoke and watched it waver in rifts across
the room. "McAllister is raw-hiding the colonel."

"For what I did?"

Loris shook his head. "For letting DeWitt take out a
patrol."

Holt sat down and pulled off his boots. Feet and
socks seemed to be all one. He wrinkled his nose. *"Cavalry,"* he said in disgust. "We walked most of the way back
from Socorro Tanks." He looked at Loris. "The kid would
have been all right if he had stayed away from the Barrera
Escarpment. He had Sergeant Cassidy with him. Cassidy
was worth three second looies. McAllister must have
bullied Cassidy into letting him go into that goddamned
country. Cassidy knew better."

Loris nodded. "Cassidy dead too?"

"All of them, Ben." Holt stripped off trousers and under-drawers. "McAllister and two of them were still alive when we attacked. It was a hell of a mess. They had been out of water for some time, from the looks of them. Hardly enough cartridges left to hold off an Apache rush. All horses dead— and stinking to high heaven."

Loris blew a smoke ring. "The kid wanted to go to war, didn't he? To be a big man like his daddy. The hero of Chambliss Mills, Swift Run Creek and Missionary Ridge. Holder of the Medal of Honor. Contemporary of 'Cump' Sherman and 'Pap' Thomas."

"Shut up, Ben!"

The lean face turned toward Holt, and the strange green eyes studied him. "What do you aim to do, Holt?"

"Tell the truth."

"All of it?"

The look in Holt's eyes was enough to quiet the average man, but not Ben Loris. The adjutant sat up. "There isn't an officer or enlisted man in this department who doesn't know how much you hate the Butcher."

"So?"

"I have an idea you let that hatred lead you into accidentally killing DeWitt McAllister."

"You talk too goddamned much, Ben."

Stable call blew across the post.

"You admitted to the general that you had misjudged the width of the gully. You couldn't stop?"

Holt shook his head. How could he tell Ben Loris how tired he had been? How the heat and thirst had seemed to sap his thinking processes? How the sight of the horned head of El Carnicero had almost destroyed his reason?

"It would have to be McAllister's only son. Jesus God, Holt, you certainly did it up brown this time."

Holt took a towel and washing materials. He put on a faded robe. "I knew that was DeWitt McAllister down in that gully," he said quietly. "I also knew it was the only chance any of us have had in the past two or three years of getting the Butcher. I *had* to attack him, Ben. Don't you see that?"

Loris dropped his long legs over the side of the cot and gripped the cot edge with his lean hands. He tilted his head to one side as he looked at Holt. "Maybe you've forgotten that I'm the adjutant here in this sinkhole of Hell, Holt. I wrote out your orders. Your primary objective was to *find Mr. McAllister and his patrol.* You were not to attack El Carnicero or any of his men, but rather to report on his strength, direction of travel, and so forth."

Holt rested a hand against the wall. "He was right there, Ben! Like a rat at the bottom of a hole and I had him cold! What would you have done?"

The adjutant stood up. "I? I would have driven him off and saved DeWitt McAllister to bring him back in triumph to Fort Guthrie just about the same time General Talbot McAllister, accompanied by Miss Katherine Nolan of Boston, fiancée of Second Lieutenant DeWitt McAllister, arrived at Fort Guthrie. Think of the plaudits! The congratulations! The possible promotion! The possible *leave!*"

Holt opened the rear door and walked out of the room. The door slammed shut behind him.

Ben Loris took his cap from the hook and placed it on his dark curly hair. He tilted it a little to one side and smiled at himself in the cracked and faded mirror. He reached into one of his dress boots, drew out a bottle, opened it and took a stiff hooker. He wiped his mouth and replaced the bottle in the boot. "Yes," he said thoughtfully. "That's what *I* would have done, Holt, but then, I haven't got the reason to hate El Carnicero that you have." He tapped the top of his cap, opened the outer door and left the quarters.

IT WAS dusk when Captain Holt Downey, bathed and shaved, attired in his second-best uniform, left his quarters and walked across the empty parade ground toward headquarters. It lacked five minutes of the hour's time the general had allowed him and he had no idea of what to say to that officer beyond what he had already told him just outside the gates of the post.

A solid figure, dressed in dark clothing, leaned against one of the posts at the end of the ramada in front of headquarters building. "Good evening, Holt," the man said.

Holt stared at him. "For God's sake! Mark Lewis!"

The man held out a hand. "The same. How are you, Holt?"

Holt shrugged. "I could be better. You've heard the news?"

"I am sorry to say that I have. I wish that I had been scouting for you instead of Tulvis. Perhaps I could have dissuaded you from what you did."

Holt shoved back his forage cap. "It's true I could have used you out there. You know that country better than any man in this department. I'm not so sure you could have stopped me from attacking El Carnicero."

"Perhaps." The cultured voice of the chief of scouts always seemed to hold a note of sadness. Mark Lewis "had a story," according to those who knew him.

Holt eyed the scout. "How was it this time?"

The scout could not meet Holt's eyes. "Damned bad, Holt. I could have used you as much as you could have used me."

"I can't stop you from drinking, Mark."

"No, but I seem to gain a great deal of pleasure from your company."

"How? The last time I found you in Tucson you didn't even know me, or at least claimed you didn't recognize me."

Mark Lewis straightened his string tie and brushed

tobacco ashes from his broadcloth suit. "Perhaps I was ashamed to let people know that I had betrayed one of my best friends."

"You didn't *betray* me." Holt touched his left cheek. "I did have a neat bruise here for a week after you slugged me."

The scout cleared his throat. "I'm dried out now, Holt."

"For how long?"

"Permanently, Holt."

"I'm happy to hear that. Now I have to see McAllister. Can I see you after that?"

"I'll be in your quarters."

"Thanks." Holt turned to go, but the scout tapped him on the shoulder. Holt turned again to face him.

"Watch out for Yancey Tulvis," said Lewis. "He's talking."

"He usually is, Mark."

"He hates your guts, Holt. You know him for the charlatan he is. Yancey has been playing the part of the frontier scout for so long he actually believes in it himself. You have the faculty of showing him up. He's a small man inside, Holt, and men like that can be damned vindictive."

"Perhaps I won't have to worry about that after the general gets through with me," Holt said dryly.

"They can't cashier you, Holt! They need you here more than they do Talbot McAllister!"

"Thanks, Mark," I'll see you."

The scout watched the officer walk to the door of headquarters. He shook his head and walked across the parade ground to Holt's quarters. He opened the door, lighted the lamp, then sat down in a chair, eyeing himself in the mirror. His face was pale, as it always was after a prolonged debauch in the roaring fleshpots of Tucson or Prescott, and the dark areas beneath his eyes and where the quick stubble of his fast-growing beard showed gave him a deathly look. He felt for a cigar and lighted it. His eyes fell on Ben Loris' dress boots.

The scout examined his well-kept hands. His eyes wandered to the dress boots. He stood up, slipped a hand into the left-hand boot and withdrew it. He reached into the other boot and drew out the bottle. It was half full.

"Go ahead, Mark," the quiet voice said.

Lewis turned quickly. Holt Downey stood in the doorway. For a moment their eyes clashed, and then the scout replaced the bottle. "Thanks, Holt," he said.

"Think nothing of it. I might need you in a hurry, Mark. As it is, you've made me late now for my meeting with the general." Holt closed the door behind him.

GENERAL TALBOT MCALLISTER stood with his back toward Holt, studying the huge ordnance map that hung on the wall of the post commander's office. Colonel Milas Fleming sat at his desk, fiddling with a letter opener fashioned like a miniature cavalry saber. His heavy-lidded eyes flitted from the general to Holt and then back to the general again. A warm breeze crept from the partly opened door of the adjutant's office and dabbled at Holt's sweat-dampened hair.

It was quiet. Now and then a mule brayed discordantly from the corrals, or a trooper laughed in the barracks. The flag halyards slapped steadily against the tall pole. The wind never stopped sweeping across the mesa. A veteran trooper and an inveterate drinker had hanged himself in the stables just the winter before because of the wind. It said nauseating things to him, he had said. He had heard the voices of the men he had killed in twenty years of service, mumbling curses at him in the voice of the wind.

McAllister traced a line along the map. Holt could see what he was doing well enough. He was following the thin line of the trail southwest of Fort Guthrie, to Socorro Tanks, thence to the line of the Barrera Escarpment. The general turned to Colonel Fleming. "Milas," he said, "just what was my son doing in that area?"

Milas Fleming cleared his throat with deliberation. Everything Milas Fleming did was done with deliberation, as though the very existence of the universe depended upon what he would say or do. He had been a classmate of Talbot McAllister at West Point and, in fact, had ranked much higher in the class, but after graduation Talbot McAllister had followed his star through the Seminole War, the Mexican War, and the Civil War, with a record hardly second to that of any of the general officers in the service, while Milas Fleming had bumbled along, always reaching for a star and yet never finding it, not even the lone star of a brigadier, which thought obsessed him almost to the exclusion of all others.

"Milas?" asked the general patiently.

"Oh, yes, sir, yes indeed." Fleming straightened up. "The fact is that Mr. McAllister had strict orders not to go into the Barrera Escarpment country."

"So?"

Fleming fiddled with the letter opener. "He had Sergeant Cassidy with him. Cassidy was a veteran. One of my best men. Certainly of officer material, except for birth and education, General. I..."

"Get on with it, Milas."

"Perhaps Sergeant Cassidy—how shall we say it?" Fleming's voice droned to a halt.

"Yes, Milas?"

"Talked Mr. McAllister into it," said the colonel.

"Nonsense!"

Fleming looked desperately at Holt. "Captain, would you agree with me?"

"I would not, sir."

A slow flush crept over Fleming's broad face. "*Sir?*"

Holt stood up. "Cassidy knew better than to go into

that country with a ten-man patrol led by a green officer. In my opinion Mr. McAllister overrode Cassidy and went to the Barrera Escarpment."

"Why, Captain?" asked the general.

"I don't know."

"Can you guess?"

"I think so."

"Proceed, then."

Holt avoided the panic-stricken gaze of the colonel. "Mr. McAllister went into that country for one of two reasons, closely allied. He was either looking for Apaches, or they lured him in there."

McAllister studied the hawk face of the man who had killed his son—the hard gray-green eyes, the strong nose, the mat of thick reddish hair. "You really believe so, Downey?"

"I would swear to it, sir."

"Why?"

Fleming's face was mottled with controlled anger.

Holt saw a movement beyond the half-open door to the adjutant's office. Someone was listening in there. Perhaps a clerk, taking down what was said. He wouldn't put it past Milas Fleming. Holt looked at the general. "Mr. McAllister had bragged in the officers' mess that he would try for a brevet or a coffin on that patrol, General McAllister. I warned him about being careless or looking for trouble."

"So? What did he say?"

"He told me to mind my own damned business."

In the hush that followed Holt's last words he heard the rustling of cloth in the adjoining office.

"You did not prefer charges against him, sir?"

Holt raised his head, "No, General."

"Why not, if I may ask?"

"He had been drinking, sir. I was a shavetail myself in the first year of the war. I can recall a time when I might have done the same thing."

Fleming fiddled with the letter opener.

"For God's sake, Milas!" snapped McAllister.

Fleming dropped the opener.

The general paced back and forth. "None of these happenings can excuse you for what you did at the Barrera Escarpment, Captain Downey."

"No, sir."

"You had strict orders to find my son's patrol, *not* to attack El Carnicero or any other Apache chief's band. Is that correct?"

"The general knows it is."

The hard eyes clashed with Holt's. "Yes—I know. Let me ask you point-blank, then, Downey. Why *did* you attack El Carnicero, forfeiting my son's life in the process?"

Sweat worked down Holt's sides beneath his shirt, and his throat went dry. He looked past the general, and it seemed as though the lines and markings on the huge map became the open country to the southeast, on the eastern border of the Spanish Desert, and three years seemed to pass before his eyes. The hazy shimmering heat waves. The barren earth, reflecting the harsh, brassy glare of the summer sun with a thousand glittering points. The skein of smoke rising up in the windless air to lie like coarse hair against the blue cloth of the clear sky. "Has the general ever heard of Lost Springs, sir?"

The gray eyes half closed. "Yes...yes... A massacre, was it not?"

"In a way"

"Go on, man!"

Holt's voice took on a metallic ring. "There was a young woman from the east traveling in this department to meet her fiancée, an officer stationed here at Fort Guthrie. A young second lieutenant of cavalry was detailed to escort that young woman here, as well as a supply train. The young officer halted the train at Lost Springs for the night. He was careless. The Apaches under El Carnicero struck them at dawn. The escort was wiped out, and the stock run off. The young officer and the young woman were in the old adobe that stood by the springs in those days. El Carnicero found them in there."

It was quiet in the hot office. Both senior officers watched the face of Holt Downey as he fought for control.

"El Carnicero took them alive," said Holt at last. "He took them into the mountains south of the Spanish Desert. A week later the young officer was found near Lost Springs. He died there, but only after he had told of what had happened to him and the young woman."

"Go on," said McAllister.

The gray-green eyes looked directly at the general, but Talbot McAllister had an eerie feeling that Holt Downey did not actually see him. "El Carnicero amused himself and his warriors by having the young officer and the captured white woman make love before them, under threat of the knives and the fire. Again and again, until they were exhausted. Then El Carnicero and his bucks took over the woman. They left the officer for the squaws. What was left of him was dropped outside of the adobe at Lost Springs. The man who heard his story left him a pistol and then rode out into the desert until he heard that lone pistol shot. He buried the remains and brought the information to the nearest military post."

"And the woman?"

"Who knows? She is dead. I hope to God she is dead."

"What has this to do with you, Downey?"

The gray-green eyes looked like peepholes into Hell. "The young woman was my fiancée. The officer was my younger brother, Neville Downey."

"Good God!"

Holt saw a figure just beyond the half-open door. It was the young woman who had come to the post with the general. Her face was pale and she held a slender hand at her throat.

Holt looked at the general. "Now you know why I overrode your son's patrol, General. I would have overridden Jesus Christ himself to get at El Carnicero!"

McAllister turned away. "Get out," he said thinly.

Holt saluted and walked to the door. He opened it and walked out into the darkness of the desert night. The wind dried the sweat on his forehead. He walked toward his quarters with his forage cap in his hand. Somewhere, out in the darkness of the mesa top, a coyote howled mournfully.

CHAPTER FIVE

H olt Downey stood in the bastion with his arms resting on the wall, looking out across the low land to the south of the great mesa. The moon was just rising, and its light seemed to accentuate the deep shadows of arroyos and gullies on the wide desert plain. The wind caressed his face and seemed to whisper gently to him. Behind him he could hear the life of the fort. Yellow rectangles of light were etched against the adobe and stone walls of the post, but the lights seemed only to heighten the vast loneliness of Fort Guthrie. The nights always seemed to move in on the isolated post as though it were the only place of habitation on some distant planet.

There was almost a feeling of relief within him. He had brooded a great deal about what had happened at the Barrera Escarpment while on his way back to Fort Guthrie. But McAllister had been the catalyst for Holt's mingled and torturing emotions. There was nothing more that could be done to him. Reprimand, disgrace, dismissal, it was all the same.

The wind shifted a little. He turned slowly and dropped his hand to the butt of his issue Colt. No man went unarmed around Fort Guthrie unless he welcomed a gut-ripping knife slash from the shadows. Within the past two years Apaches had been shot down within the post confines. Something moved in the darkness beyond the entrance to the embrasure. Holt drew his pistol and cocked it as he sank down to get his head and shoulders off the sky line.

The darkness at the embrasure entrance suddenly grew darker. Then it seemed to flow across the ground toward him, and for a moment the green bile seemed to rise within him. He raised the pistol and tightened his finger on the trigger.

"Captain Downey?" the soft voice queried.

The faint fragrance of violets came to him. He stood up. "Miss Nolan?" he asked.

"Yes."

She came closer and dropped the hood of her traveling cloak, and he saw the smooth oval of her face and the soft border of her upswept hair against it. "Never walk up on a man like that," he said sharply.

"Why? Are you nervous?"

He let down the hammer of his pistol and sheathed the heavy weapon. Cold sweat trickled down his sides. It had been too close for comfort. "No, Miss Nolan, I'm not nervous. This is Apache country. Those people move like shadows, or ghosts, but I assure you, they strike like tigers when the time comes. Many a man has died in this country because he got careless. The time to look for Apaches is when you least expect to see them."

She leaned against the embrasure and looked back at the fort. "But this is a garrisoned post! Surely they wouldn't dare come around here to lurk and kill."

He laughed shortly. "Six months ago Major Mitzler left his quarters to go to the washroom not twenty feet behind Officers' Row. There were two sentries, veteran soldiers, not fifty feet away at the time. In the morning we found the major. We buried him with full military honors that same afternoon."

She shuddered a little and moved closer to him.

"Now no man moves around the post at night unless he is armed."

She tilted her head to one side. "But you came out here alone."

"I find it quiet out here. Often when my thoughts get too tangled I come out here." He looked down at her. "I'm sorry about DeWitt," he said softly.

"I know."

"You hate me for what I did?"

"No."

"But you loved him."

She looked out across the desert as the first silvery wash of the moon began to spread across it "I once thought I did," she replied.

He stared at her. "But you came all those hellish miles in that rattling dougherty in the heat of the summer to be with him. If that isn't love, I'm not sure I know what love is."

"Who does?"

He leaned against the wall of the bastion and looked at her curiously. "I must say you take DeWitt's death very coolly, Miss Nolan."

She opened her cloak and threw it back over her shoulders, and he could see the smooth whiteness of them in contrast to the dark material of the garment. "I heard everything that was said in there, Captain Downey."

"I know."

"It was the general's idea, not mine. I hated the thought of spying on you, but I didn't want to cross him. It isn't easy to cross General McAllister."

"I know."

She glanced at him. "This trip was his idea. In fact, it was his idea for DeWitt and me to be engaged."

"So?"

The wind rustled the scattered desert growths. A tumble-weed trundled along past the bastion toward the lip of the mesa.

"I was flattered. DeWitt *was* handsome and cultured, with a famous father and a great career ahead of him in the service. Quite a rise in social position for the only daughter of an Irishman who served thirty years in the army and died a sergeant."

"I thought I detected a trace of the Irish in your speech."

She smiled prettily. "My family was from County Fermanagh."

Holt felt the deep loneliness within him so acutely that it was almost a physical pain. "Why did you come out here?" he asked quietly.

The great eyes studied him. "Because I felt sorry for you."

He cut a big hand sideways. "Never do that!"

"Never? Is it that you *need* no one? That your great hatred for this red animal El Carnicero is a substitute for every other human emotion? Or is it that you are really an animal like him you hunt so avidly?"

"What have you to gain by coming to talk to me?" he asked harshly.

"Perhaps I need someone too, Captain Downey," she said simply.

He looked down at her, and the impulse to take her into his arms was a compelling force he could hardly resist, but the high wall of reserve he had built about his emotions since the death of his brother Neville and Emily Locke would not be breached.

She was beautifully shaped, with firm high breasts and narrow waist, and he knew her long legs must be a pattern of symmetry for the rest of her lush body. There was little wanting in her beauty and coloring either.

There was a vibrant force in the young woman that would take the eye and interest of any man—except, perhaps, the man she stood with at that moment.

"Do you know why General McAllister chose me for his son? The daughter of Irish immigrants without a penny to their names? The daughter of a drunken man who fell to pieces when he was retired from the army because of wounds suffered in the war?"

"Go on," he said quietly.

Her great eyes held his. "Because your General McAllister breeds blood horses on his place in Kentucky. Because he knows a breed when he sees one, my fine Captain Downey. A *brood* mare, if you will!"

Call to quarters sounded on the post, and the brass tones of it drifted out across the mesa and then died away.

Katherine Nolan turned her head to listen. "Aye," she said. "This would be the life for me if I had been born a man."

"God forbid!"

She turned quickly. "Then there *is* emotion for a woman beneath that mask you wear, Captain! I knew it!"

"You talk too much, Miss Nolan." He drew her cloak up over her lovely white shoulders and held the front of the cloak in his big brown hands, drawing her closer to him. "What will happen to you now, Miss Nolan?"

"Kathy!"

"Kathy, then."

She smiled a little. "I don't know. The general told me I would always have a home with him."

He laughed dryly. "What a blessing!"

"He thinks I am still part of DeWitt's life."

"That is foolish. You'd better tell him that, Kathy."

There was almost a frightened look in her lovely eyes. "You don't understand, Holt. He means it. He chose me to be DeWitt's wife. He paid my fare to St. Louis, all my expenses, and has taken care of me almost like a child. But all the time he spoke of me as though I would be a chattel to his beloved DeWitt. Don't you understand? He can't imagine my being anything more now than something his dead son left behind! No man can have me now!"

"That's madness!"

She looked away. "Yes, it is, in a way. But he's a strong man, Holt. Strong and vindictive. I'm afraid of what he will do to you."

He shrugged. "Have me dismissed. Broken. What else can he do?"

She looked at him strangely. "I don't know." She hesitated. "But I *do* know this: Somehow or other he will make you pay for what you did, no matter where you go or what you do."

He released her and straightened up. "I'm not worried about Talbot McAllister, Kathy."

She walked toward the entrance to the bastion, then turned. "You are a fool! Perhaps I am a fool too! But I *know* that man, Holt! Perhaps that is why I came here. He hates you for what you did, and he'll hate me for what I will do to him, *and* his dead son. Don't you ever forget that for one moment!" Then she was gone as quickly and silently as she had appeared.

———

HOLT RETURNED to his quarters to find that Ben Loris and Mark Lewis had turned in. There was a slight smell of liquor in the air.

"Holt," said Loris sleepily.

"Yes."

"You've heard of the man they call the Prophet?"

"No. Who is he?"

"*Quién sabe?* He's allied with the Butcher, they say. The Prophet is supposed to interpret omens and give advice to the Butcher. They say the Butcher never does anything without the advice of the Prophet."

"You've been drinking."

"Certainly I have! But stories are cropping up all over the Territory and in Mexico too about this Prophet hombre. I heard McAllister mention it to Fleming. The man is dangerous."

"No more than El Carnicero."

"Don't delude yourself! El Carnicero may be physically dangerous and possessed of a native shrewdness and guile, but this Prophet is supposed to be a man of great intelligence and foresight. Apaches from all over the Southwest know about him now. It's said he may be able to muster all of them under the leadership of the Butcher."

"Crap," said Holt. "Mark, you ever hear of this Prophet?"

"Yes."

"Who is he?"

"No one really knows. Some say he's Yaqui, others Apache; some think he is a Mexican or an American. One story has it that he's a breed of some other tribe."

"So? What do you think?"

There was a moment's silence. "He exists, Holt. You can bet your life on it. He'll be heard of more and more in the days to come. His Apache name is Dobe-gusndi-he."

"What does it mean?"

"Invulnerable."

Ben Loris laughed.

"Don't laugh, Ben," said the scout quietly. "There is more truth to this thing than you or anyone else knows. He'll make himself well known before too long, as I said before, and God help the white people in this country when he does."

Holt Downey closed his eyes. Slowly the thoughts of El Carnicero and the Prophet drained from his tired

mind to be replaced by thoughts of Kathy Nolan, with
her soft Irish beauty and quick Irish tongue. He fell
asleep thinking about her. It was the first time in over
three years he had not fallen asleep thinking of Emily
Locke.

CHAPTER SIX

F Company was answering roll call in the pale cold light of early morning on the parade ground of Fort Guthrie. The sour voices of first sergeants could be heard rattling off the names of the men in the three cavalry companies and the lone company of dough-boys, as well as the men who formed the small detachments of medics, quartermasters, ordnance, signal corps, and other ancillary units.

Captain Holt Downey was standing roll call, for Mr. Ronald Sturgis had been temporarily assigned as aide to General Talbot McAllister.

"Caxton!" called out Acting First Sergeant Lambert.

There was no answer.

"Caxton!"

No one answered. Lambert looked at Corporal McCormick. "Where is Caxton, McCormick?"

"I don't know, Sergeant."

"He's in your squad now!"

"Aye, Sergeant, that I well know, but he has not been seen this morning, and his cot was not slept in."

Lambert turned to look at Holt.

"Mark him A.W.O.L., Lambert. Have Corporal

McCormick round him up after roll call. If he has left the post let me know."

"Yes, sir."

Lambert finished the roll and turned to Holt to report. Holt dismissed him. Lambert took his post. "At ease, F Company," said Holt.

The line moved and then settled down. Holt walked closer to them. "You men will spend this morning getting your equipment, uniforms, and horses cleaned up. It was a tough patrol, and I'm proud of all of you."

There was no expression on any of the brown faces beneath the brims of the campaign hats.

"Sergeant Lambert is to be promoted to first Sergeant vice Caxton, demoted. Corporal Cassidy will get his third stripe vice Lambert, promoted. Both of these noncommissioned officers earned their stripes the hard way. I am not promoting any of you privates to replace Cassidy until I see some improvement in this company. We are at war out here just as surely as though we were facing rebels or Mexicans as the army did in the past two wars of this nation. We are fighting a deadly and treacherous enemy. We can't let up for a moment. Some of you men have requested leaves. I'm sorry to say that I will not recommend any such applications until things settle down."

"Sergeant Lambert!"

Lambert came forward and saluted.

"Dismiss the company, Sergeant!"

Holt heard the shuffling of feet and the movement of the men as the company broke ranks. "The brass-bound bastard," a high-pitched voice said. "I'll bet he'll let *himself* in for a leave before too long."

"The hell he will," said another anonymous voice. "He's got his eye on that new filly the general brought along with him. He'd be a damned fool to let a tasty bit like that get away from him."

Holt did not turn. It was no use in trying to find the

owners of those caustic voices. Probably everyone on the post knew by now that he had been with Kathy Nolan the evening before. Nothing was secret on a small post like Fort Guthrie. Innocent or not, the two of them would be linked together in the minds of the curious and the filthy-thinking, and it wouldn't be long before the general himself found out about it

———

HOLT CAME OUT OF THE OFFICERS' mess to see Corporal McCormick waiting for him. The big Irishman saluted. "Sorr," he said. "I have located Sergeant Caxton, that is to say, 'Private' Caxton, sorr."

"So? Where is he?"

McCormick flushed. "Well, 'tis a bit av a problem, ye might say."

"Where is he? Speak up, man!"

McCormick lowered his voice. "He's in a lady's quarters, sorr."

"Get him, then."

"It's not as aisy as that, sorr. He's drunk, and armed, and I did not want to start a Donnybrook, without I spoke to the captain first, sorr."

Holt nodded. "You did well, McCormick."

The Irishman looked down at his huge freckled fists. "I cud break his jaw with these."

"He's a big man, Mac, and hard as nails."

The blue eyes danced a little. "It is so, but it wud be a broth av a foight."

"Where is he?"

"In Yancey Tulvis' shebang, sorr."

"Is Yancey there?"

"No, sorr."

"I'll get him then."

McCormick hesitated. "Yancey's daughter Annie is thayer too."

Holt walked along the front of the quarters. "Get back to duty, McCormick," he said.

"Aye," breathed the big noncom. "Aye, but I'd give a month's pay to see ye and that man Caxton tangle. That I wud!"

Holt stopped at the end building of Soapsuds Row, the quarters for married enlisted men and civilian government employees. A baby was squalling from Sergeant Torrio's quarters. The heat in that country had killed two of the quartermaster-sergeant's brood in the past year.

Yancey Tulvis lived in a shebang all right. It had once been a storage building until the post had outgrown it. Then it had been the post bakery, and after that a catch-all for odds and ends until Yancey had taken it over. For a time his "wife," a breed of undetermined blood origin, had lived there, but instead of making it more livable the slattern had made it worse, until now nothing could free it of the stench of unwashed clothing, food slops and sour liquor fumes.

Holt tapped on the door.

"What is it you want?" a woman called out.

"Private Caxton."

"Who are you?"

"Captain Downey."

Feet grated on the floor. "You can take him and be welcome to him, Captain." The door swung open. A young woman stood there pushing back her thick mane of jet-black hair while she surveyed Holt with bold black eyes. Her dress was clean and neat, but rather thin from too many washings, and the full breasts of the woman were unhampered by anything but the thin cotton material and a shift beneath it. The deep cleft of her breasts stood free of the material.

"Well, Captain Downey?"

She was damned good-looking. Her slightly olive skin was in vivid contrast to her full red lips.

Holt touched his cap. "You must be Annie Tulvis."

She leaned against the door side and her eyes swept up and down him as though she liked what she saw. "Yes," she said.

"I'm sorry to trouble you, Miss Tulvis."

"*Annie,* Captain."

"Annie, then."

She stepped back and jerked a thumb over her shoulder. "He's in there."

Holt walked into the small living room. Surprisingly enough, it was neat and clean. The mingled odors of strong issue soap, lye, and carbolic hung in the air. A door at the rear of the room was closed. Holt looked at the girl.

"The bedroom there," she said.

He hesitated. "You could get yourself in trouble because of this."

"What do you mean?"

"Who's making that damned racket out there!" roared Caxton drunkenly from behind the closed door.

"It's Captain Downey, Caxton," said Holt.

There was a moment's silence. Holt reached forward, turning the handle of the door and shoved the door back, stepping prudently to one side as he did so. A whisky bottle shot through the open doorway and smashed on the packed earth floor of the living room.

"Damn him!" said Annie Tulvis.

Holt looked at her. "Blame yourself," he said.

"Damn you too, Captain Downey!"

"*Gracias,*" he said dryly. "Caxton?"

"What do you want?"

"You."

"That figures."

"I'm coming in there, Caxton."

"Do," said Caxton with drunken politeness.

Holt walked into the darkened room, and as he did so he heard the crisp metallic double clicking of a gun hammer being cocked. A shard of morning light came through a split in the drab window shade. Dust motes danced in it, and beyond the path of the yellow light was a hunched figure sitting on a sway-backed bed. The room was a foul aura of sweat, sour liquor, and unwashed bedding.

"Get up," said Holt.

"I'm no longer a soldier."

"You may be right at that, but you have a contract with the government for two more years of service, and until that time comes, Private Caxton, you *will* soldier. At least as long as you are in B Company."

"You know what the men call B Company? I'll tell you!" Caxton hiccupped. *"Bastard* Company! Maybe because of the letter. Maybe because of the men in it. But probably because of the man who commands it."

"I'll forget that."

Caxton stood up and the gun, at waist level, was in the pathway of the light from the window.

"Put up that gun, Caxton," said Holt quietly.

"Why? I could kill you."

"You'd never get away with it."

"There are six rounds in it. One for you and then one for me."

Annie Tulvis laughed. "You'd do it too, wouldn't you, Joe? The easy way out for a yellowbelly like you!"

"Shut up, you!"

"Put up the gun, Caxton," said Holt.

"Go to hell."

"It's the liquor talking. You never could drink."

"I can drink you or any other brass-bounder shoulder straps under the table."

"A great accomplishment," sneered Annie.

"You may be right, Caxton," said Holt. "Pick up the uniform you've disgraced and put it on. At least look like a soldier."

"I can outdrink you, outfight you, and outscrew you, you yellow bastard!"

"Hear him," said Annie in disgust.

The pistol barrel wavered in the path of light. Holt stepped quickly to one side, cut his left hand down hard on Caxton's gun wrist, then hooked a smashing blow against the man's unshaven jaw. The gun crashed and the slug thudded into the floor. Caxton went down heavily through a cloud of stinking gun smoke.

Holt picked up the pistol and emptied it. He threw it on the bed. "Get up, Caxton," he said quietly.

The big noncom got up and touched his jaw.

"Get dressed."

Boots thudded on the hard earth' outside of the shebang. Annie glanced at Holt. "He did it this time," she said. "I'll get run out of here by the colonel. He warned me when I come back that he'd stand for no nonsense."

Holt walked to the door just as a fist struck it. "Wait," he said loudly. He spoke out of the side of his mouth. "Close that door back there. Tell Caxton to keep his mouth shut."

Holt opened the door. Corporal Ganning of A Company stared at him, then saluted. "Corporal of the guard, sir. We heard a shot." There were three other troopers from A behind him, and other members of the garrison and women from Soapsuds Row watching Holt.

"It's nothing, Ganning," said Holt easily. "I dropped my pistol and it went off."

"In there, sir?" blurted Ganning. He looked past Holt at Annie Tulvis.

"Yes," said Holt.

Ganning nodded. He turned to his men. "Get back to the guardhouse." He looked at Holt. "We've been told to look for Private Caxton, sir. Is he in there?"

"No."

"Thank you, sir." Ganning saluted and strode off.

A broad-beamed corporal's wife sniffed. "That Annie Tulvis! Had every enlisted man except my Hennery looking at her with sheep's eyes and bad thoughts. Now she's got shoulder straps coming down here in Soapsuds Row." She nudged the skinny wife of Farrier Corporal MacGinnis. "Eh, Ruby?"

Ruby drew herself up so that her bones showed through her thin and dirty dress. "I can't see what men see in her anyways, Sylvia."

"I got some coffee on. I seen enough this mornin', Ruby." The two of them marched virtuously along Soapsuds Row. Thin bottom and broad-beamed stern in righteous motion.

Holt closed the door. Annie Tulvis was cleaning up the mess made by the broken bottle. "You see how it is?" she asked.

"In a way."

She stood up and dumped the glass into a can. "What do you mean, Captain?" she asked over her shoulder.

"Fort Guthrie isn't a hog ranch."

She turned slowly. "Just what do you mean?"

"It didn't take you long to get into business. Liquor and soldiers. You didn't really think you'd get away with it, did you now?"

Her right hand swung up in a full arc and caught him flush and hard on the left side of his face so that he staggered a little with the blow. Her breasts rose and fell spasmodically. "You think I invited Joe Caxton in here? The drunken fool had no other place to go! He was going to look for you with that gun in his hand. I couldn't sleep last night and went for a little walk. I found him prowling around your quarters early this morning. Your lights were on. I could hear you talking in there. I got him to come back here and luckily he passed out from the rotgut he had filled his belly with! Now, for doing him a service, I'll be run outa here!"

Joe Caxton opened the door. He was dressed and didn't look too bad, but he had the look on his face of a man who has just lost the contents of his gut the hard way. The sour stench of vomit hovered around him. The white worms were moiling in his belly, and a farrier's hammer was doing yeoman service against the inside of his skull. The dark bruise mark where Holt's fist had struck him stood out lividly from his pale face. His eyes held Holt's. "Well, sir?" he asked sarcastically.

"Report to Corporal McCormick for extra fatigue duty."

"You'll have a fine time when you turn me in."

"I'm not turning you in, Caxton."

"Gracious of you, sir."

Holt pointed to the door. "Get out! You've made a damned mess of things, all right. You've got Annie Tulvis in trouble."

Caxton's face worked for a minute. He shot a frightened glance at her.

"Not *that* kind of trouble," said Annie. "I wouldn't let a drunken fool like you touch me."

Caxton walked to the door and then he turned. "If the captain isn't going to prefer charges against me, I'd like to put in for a transfer to another post, or at least another company."

"No."

The bloodshot blue eyes studied Holt. "You'll have to get the last turn of the screw out of me, eh, Captain? Make my life a hell. Drive me to drink, desertion, or suicide."

"Get out."

The big ex-sergeant drew himself up. "Ah, if you were only an enlisted man like myself for half an hour! I'd break your damned brass jaw for you."

Holt's anger seemed to froth up inside of him so fast that he could hardly control it "You think I'm hiding behind these bars?"

"It looks like it."

"I can take them off."

"Ah, but would you?"

Holt moved closer to Caxton. "The old bastion is the

usual place isn't it? After taps is usually the time. It's a post rule that the guard doesn't go near there when a debt is to be settled with fists and boots."

Caxton smiled thinly. "You'd actually *be* there?"

"Come and see."

"That I will!"

"Tonight then."

"Tonight."

Caxton left and closed the door behind himself.

"You're loco," said Annie.

Holt turned. "Maybe. I may not be here much longer in any case."

"He'll lick you, Captain, drunk or sober he can lick you."

"Maybe."

"The damned fool! Drunk and out of his mind he was. Calls himself a soldier!"

Holt rubbed the place where she had struck him. "He *is* a soldier. One of the best."

She stared at him curiously. "But why are you letting him get the chance to maim you?"

Holt walked to the door and opened it. "The army can't afford to lose a man like Caxton."

"If he beats you and the news gets around it will be the end of you, Captain."

"And if I beat him he'll be as good a soldier as he ever was."

"I can't figure you out. I've heard about that mess at Barrera Escarpment. You may not have those bars long."

"Yes. But if I keep them, I'll need Caxton for what I plan to do—get El Carnicero."

"And if you don't keep them?"

Holt smiled. "Maybe I can use him anyway. Good day, Miss Tulvis."

"Annie!"

"Good day, Annie." He closed the door behind him. A shambling figure was staggering from one side of Soapsuds Row to the other, with a mass of dusty blankets hanging on his back. It was Yancey Tulvis, onion-eyed drunk.

The scout stopped and tried to focus his eyes. "Hangin' around Annie, Cap'n?" He blinked owlishly. "My, my— she's come up in the world!"

"Shut up, you damned fool!"

Yancey hiccupped. He placed a dirty finger alongside his beak of a nose. "Sure, sure, I'll shut up. Scared of you, Cap'n Downey. Scared like everyone else when you get that loco look in them green eyes. Well, anyways, Annie ain't bad. They say she's good in bed if for nothing else."

Holt raised a hand.

"Hit me!" Yancey staggered closer. "Go on! Hit me! Kill me like you done Mr. McAllister!"

Holt felt an urge to smash the lean face of the drunken scout, but then Yancey staggered back, fell heavily and lay still.

Holt walked toward the quadrangle, hearing the doors open up along Soapsuds Row. In five minutes Yancey's words would be all over Fort Guthrie. It didn't really matter. Holt's career had tumbled like a house of cards, and for some indefinite reason it didn't really matter.

CHAPTER SEVEN

A frontier army post is a little world all of its own. The only connection with the soft outside world is a pair of rutted wagon tracks stretching off into infinity on the sun-ravaged desert and a thin thread of telegraph wire that is dead more often than it is alive. Nothing escapes the tongue of the gossip, and there is always at least one pair of eyes or ears to see or hear that which is going on and which might feed the fires of perpetual gossip.

The word went around Fort Guthrie. Captain Holt Downey had been bold enough, or careless enough, to visit Annie Tulvis in her father's shebang in the broad clear light of morning. Some said that the captain had struck down poor Yancey Tulvis right in the middle of Soapsuds Row. Some said Sergeant Joe Caxton had been broken by Captain Downey, not because of anything that had happened on the Barrera Escarpment patrol, but rather because Joe Caxton had become enamored of Annie Tulvis and had wanted to marry her.

The gossip went the rounds. Through Soapsuds Row and the sanitary sinks; through the low barracks and the stables; the corrals, wagon-yard and quartermaster warehouse; through the hospital, the bakeshop, the farrier's shop, and the enlisted men's mess. In time it reached the officers' mess and then headquarters. It had taken exactly one hour and forty-five minutes to cover the post and to let two hundred and twenty-five people, soldiers, civilian employees, and the women of Soapsuds Row know of the very latest scandal in the little isolated sphere of Fort Guthrie. The tale had grown longer and longer and had been garnished and embellished with delicate touches here and there.

Holt Downey stood with Ordnance Sergeant Orrin Elwood in the old powder magazine, which was just off the row of service shops at the southeast corner of the post proper. In early days, during the Civil War, the post had been established by California Volunteers to keep the Apaches in check. At that time, in pursuance of regulations concerning camps, posts, and stations, the powder magazine had been built of heavy fieldstone and mortar beyond the post buildings, with a ridge of earth turned up between it and the post, for purposes of safety. But after the war, the post had been abandoned for a time, then hastily regarrisoned in the Apache scare of '67. The buildings had been either moved or replaced on higher ground, but for some reason the magazine had not been moved, pursuant to regulations, a safe distance from the new buildings.

Sergeant Elwood tapped the low arched roof of the magazine. "It's very weak, sir. While you were gone I had to shore it up in several places near the rear. I spoke to Sergeant Major Stokes about getting a detail to build a new magazine at the place you picked out, but, what with patrols, fatigue details, and a heavy sick list, he just couldn't get the men."

Holt rubbed his jaw. "General McAllister is here on a tour of inspection. The last time an inspection was made Colonel Fleming was ordered to have this magazine replaced by a new one, in the proper place."

"Yes, sir."

Holt eyed the rear of the structure. "There's a hell of a lot of explosives in here, Elwood."

The ordnance man nodded gloomily. "There is, sir. We have several hundred cases of .58 caliber paper cartridges in here."

Holt shook his head. "For muzzle-loaders we don't have."

"Not to mention powder charges for six-pounder Napoleons. The only cannon we have now is the little mountain howitzer we use for salutes and as a sundown gun."

Holt leaned back against cases of cartridge ammunition for the .45/70 caliber carbines with which the cavalry was equipped. "I'd like to get permission from the department to either have this obsolete ammunition taken to Fort Lowell for disposition or to take it out on the mesa and blow it up."

Elwood sniffed. "*Waste* it, sir? By God, Quartermaster Sergeant Torrio has been trying to get rid of some cases of hardtack left at the old post back in '65 by the California Volunteers. The damned stuff is so hard that some of the prisoners in the guardhouse carved chessmen out of it rather than break their teeth on it. The Army doesn't throw *anything* away except good men, Captain."

A shadow darkened the low doorway of the magazine. An orderly saluted smartly. "Captain Downey, sir, Colonel Fleming sends his compliments and requests that the captain report to him at the old bastion immediately."

Holt looked at him curiously. He returned the salute. "Sergeant Elwood," he said. "I'll speak to the colonel about rebuilding the magazine, although God alone knows how we'll get a detail to do it—and He won't tell."

Elwood nodded. "That's the truth, sir."

Holt walked across the quadrangle toward the western side of the post. Odd that the colonel should want him at the bastion. Surely it could have no connection with his being there with Kathy Nolan the night before. He passed between his quarters and the end of the officers' mess. Out on the mesa, to his right, he could see two riders. One of them was a woman and the other a man. The sun glinted on polished brass. The man was a soldier.

Colonel Fleming and Adjutant Ben Loring were in the bastion studying something to the south through field glasses. Captain Wiley Foster stood beside them, setting up a telescope on a tripod.

Holt entered the bastion, and as he did so he saw a flash of light far out on the desert near Caballo Wash and a thin thread of smoke rising toward the clear skies. Holt saluted as Fleming turned. "The colonel sent for me," he said.

"Ah, yes, Downey." He handed his glasses to Holt. "See what you think of that smoke out there."

"I'll have this glass set up in a minute," said Captain Foster. The infantryman wiped the sweat from his face. "It's far more powerful than those field glasses."

Holt rested his elbows atop the bastion wall and held the glasses to his eyes. The flat desert floor swam into view. There was a faint movement on the desert not far from the source of the smoke, like worms wriggling. The light flashed again. Quickly Holt shifted the glasses.

"You're looking the wrong way!" snapped Fleming pettishly.

A naked shaft of rock towered up from the flat desert floor, to the west of Caballo Wash, and a good twenty miles from the source of the smoke. Even as Holt put the glasses on it he saw a shard of brilliant light lance out from the top of the shaft, to wink again and again.

"Well?" asked Fleming.

Hoofs rattled on the harsh earth. The officers turned to see General McAllister helping Kathy Nolan down from her horse. She wore a semi-military riding dress and blouse, with a tiny blue kepi perched on her honey-colored hair. Wiley Foster whistled softly as he saw a little expanse of shapely leg above the low-cut riding boots she wore. Colonel Fleming fixed the infantryman with a basilisk stare, and Foster turned to work on his telescope.

"What is it, gentlemen?" asked General McAllister as he returned their salutes.

"There is smoke out on the desert, sir," said the colonel.

"So?"

"Probably a forgotten fire, sir."

"No," said Holt.

McAllister and Fleming stared at him.

"That's the Caballo Wash swing station of the stage-coach line," said Holt. "It's burning. Apache raid."

"Poppycock!" snapped Fleming. "They wouldn't dare come this close to Fort Guthrie."

"Agreed," said McAllister. "Fleming, you told me last night that no Apaches had been within fifty miles of Fort Guthrie for over a year."

"Well, sir, I—"

Foster whistled softly. Fleming turned quickly on him, then saw that he wasn't eyeing Kathy Nolan, but was peering through the telescope.

"Those flashes are Apaches signaling," said Holt.

"Now, Downey!" said Fleming.

"Look at Piloncillo Rock, sir," suggested Holt, pointing at the naked shaft of rock. Even as he did so the shards of reflected light seemed to dance atop the tall pinnacle.

McAllister took over the telescope. For a few minutes, he was quiet. Worms of sweat worked down Fleming's plump cheeks and neck. Holt looked away. Old Milas would be in a hell of a fix in a little while. The magazine unmoved, one of his officers in trouble for accidentally killing the general's son, and now Apaches raiding veritably in the back yard of Fort Guthrie.

Holt looked at Kathy. She stood to one side, looking through an embrasure toward the south. For a moment she stood there, then she slowly turned her head and looked at him. A silent message of understanding seemed to flash between them even as the mirror signals flashed between Piloncillo Rock and Caballo Wash swing station. She had felt his gaze on her, and now he seemed to see deep within her eyes into her very soul—and he knew he must have her.

The general turned toward Holt, saw the look passing between Kathy and Holt, and his face seemed to grow taut beneath the freshly shaven skin. "Mr. Downey!" he said sharply.

"Yes, sir!"

"I want you to take a detachment out there to Caballo Wash swing station at once."

Holt eyed the general. "May I ask why, sir?"

"Dammit, man, there are Apaches out there. You said so yourself!"

"We'd never catch them there, sir. As soon as we hit the desert below the mesa they'd see our dust from Piloncillo Rock. The lookouts up there would signal to their mates at Caballo Wash, and they'd be gone hours before we got there."

"Very true," said Foster.

"Be quiet!" snapped Fleming.

McAllister looked out over the desert again. After a while he turned to look at Holt again. "May I ask what you *would* do, Captain Downey?" he said sarcastically.

Holt walked to the bastion wall and thrust an arm to the west. "There's an old road that cuts down the side of the mesa ten miles from here, shielded by an outcropping of the mesa itself. No one out on the desert can see troops coming down that road. At the base of the mesa there a ridge, which you can't see from here, slants transversely across the desert toward Piloncillo Rock. Good troops could make that passage in four or five hours without raising enough dust for the lookouts on Piloncillo to spot."

"With what purpose, may I ask?"

"There's no sense in going to Caballo Wash. The Apaches wouldn't have attacked it if they hadn't been sure they could get away with it. They're guerrilla fighters, and they hate to lose warriors. Caballo Wash was a soft touch for them. Plenty of horses and mules, stores, guns, and ammunition. Those lookouts are watching the whole desert for troop movements, and when they see any they'll signal to the bucks at Caballo Wash, as I said before. But if we can nail those lookouts, we might, by a long chance, manage to trap the raiders."

McAllister rubbed his jaw. He nodded. "Meanwhile we can wire the garrisons at Forts Parnell, Liscomb, and Roscoe to converge on the trails leading south from Caballo Wash."

Holt eyed the general. He was a soldier after all.

"You'll have to move fast, Downey," said McAllister.

Holt saluted. "I'll leave at once."

Ben Loris followed Holt from the bastion and strode alongside him toward the fort. "Give me your orders," he said. "I'll have everything ready."

"Two squads. One hundred rounds carbine ammunition and fifty rounds pistol ammunition. No sabers. One pack mule for extra ammunition. One for extra water. Three days' rations for the men. I'll take Sergeant Lambert, Corporals McCormick and Donigan, Trumpeter Monahan."

"Right!"

"Snap to it, then!"

Holt ducked into his quarters and stripped off his uniform to change into field uniform. He swung his gun belt about his lean waist and buckled it, then reached for his battered campaign hat. "Good God," he said. "I forgot about Mark Lewis! I'll need him!"

Holt reached into Ben Loris' dress boot and pulled

out the bottle. It was empty. Old Ben was sure playing the bottle. Holt unlocked his foot locker and took out a bottle of rye. He took a good dollop and replaced the bottle in the locker. He snatched up his Spencer repeating carbine and walked outside into the full glare of the summer sun. The rays seemed to cut across his eyes like a hot saber blade. It would be hell again out on that desert.

Loris had managed to get things moving. Men tumbled out of the barracks to the accompaniment of noncoms' whip-crack voices. Others trotted up saddled horses. A detail was loading the mules at the corral. Trumpeter Monahan saluted Holt. "Reportin' for duty, sorr!"

"Find Mark Lewis. We'll need a scout."

Monahan shook his head. "Mark Lewis left the post this mornin', sorr."

Holt stared at him. "You're sure?"

"Yis, sorr!"

Ben Loris trotted up. "All set, Holt."

"Thanks, Ben. What's this about Mark taking off?"

"By God, I wondered if *you* had been swilling the last of that bottle."

They looked at each other. "Not *again*," said Holt.

"I can't believe it. He was good for at least a month to dry out, Holt."

"Aye," agreed Monahan solemnly.

"There's always Yancey Tulvis," said Ben.

"I'd rather take his daughter," said Holt savagely. "He's no damned good, to us or himself."

In less than half an hour the command was ready to move. Far out on the shimmering desert the smoke still rose thinly like a pencil mark against the sky.

Talbot McAllister stood beneath the ramada watching the command. "Downey," he said.

Holt turned and saluted.

"I'm sending Lieutenant Eaton and two squads of A

Company down the east road toward the head of Caballo Wash. Captain DeVoto of F will go down the old road just south of the fort to debouch out onto the desert."

"They'll raise a lot of dust, General."

"Right, Downey. If the Apaches at Caballo Wash swing station see that dust they'll tend to drift west. The messages are being sent to Forts Parnell, Liscomb, and Roscoe. We may yet weave a net around the Butcher's neck, if that is him out there."

"It isn't like him to fool around with a small-time raid."

"Perhaps. Move out then, Captain."

Holt rapped out his commands. In minutes the detachment was moving out from the post. As Holt looked back he saw a woman standing at the entrance to the bastion. She waved a handkerchief at him. It was Kathy Nolan.

The dust had hardly settled on the road to the west when the telegraph orderly came into the colonel's office, where Talbot McAllister stood before the great ordnance map. "Sir," he said, "the messages—" He hesitated. "The messages—"

"Go on, man!"

"The wire must be down. I couldn't get any of them through."

McAllister turned slowly and looked at him. "*None* of them?"

"None, sir."

The general nodded. He could hear the commands rattling out on the parade ground as Eaton and DeVoto readied their detachments.

The telegrapher shifted his feet.

"Well?" demanded the general.

"If the troops at Forts Parnell, Liscomb, and Roscoe don't move out, that means the troops from this post will be the only ones out there."

"So?"

"Captain Downey hasn't got enough men to stop the Apaches, sir."

The man shuffled his feet. The ticking of the wall clock seemed to get louder. "Maybe the general should send a courier after the captain to turn him back. If he goes down on that desert, sir, he may never come back."

The general turned, and his eyes were as hard as brightly polished steel. "Get back into your office! Keep your mouth shut! You understand? You are not to tell anyone that those messages did not get through! Is that clear?"

"Yes, sir."

The door closed behind the telegrapher. Talbot McAllister sat down at the colonel's desk and began to fiddle with the colonel's letter opener, which was shaped like a miniature saber. Suddenly he raised it and drove it down hard on the desk. It snapped, and one of the pieces drove into his flesh. He plucked out the bloody piece of metal and watched the bright blood drip onto the blotting pad. "He said he'd ride over Jesus Christ to get at El Carnicero," he said. *"Well, maybe now he'll have his chance!"*

CHAPTER EIGHT

Mr. George Eaton, commander of A Company, led his men down the east mesa road at a smart trot. Dust rose and settled on the uniforms and on the dark bays of A, turning men and horses into a neutral color. Halfway down the mesa they could still see the distant smoke to the south.

Sergeant Carnahan grinned at Eaton through the dust. "Does the lieutenant think we might get a crack at them?"

"Hardly. We're what is known as a diversionary force, Sergeant. The troops from the other posts will have all the fighting."

"Captain Downey should have a bit of a fight too."

"The lucky cuss usually does."

The hoofs clattered on the hard earth. Eaton looked down the road. Another hundred yards and they'd be on the hard desert and could head for the wash. Maybe he'd have a good fight at that, get a promotion and leave. Evelyn was getting impatient. After all, they had been engaged for three years, and she had kept on insisting that she come out to Arizona Territory so that they could get married. So romantic, a military wedding, under crossed sabers, and so on and so on. She had no idea of "what Fort Guthrie was like. The hellish summers and the bitter winters. Nothing like Savannah, Georgia.

Sergeant Carnahan suddenly stood up in his McClellan. He opened his mouth to yell, and as he did so a creosote bush at the side of the rutted road seemed to blossom red flame. The heavy slug struck at an angle, entering the sergeant's mouth and smashing up into his brain. Blood and gray matter struck George Eaton across the face, blinding him. His bay pitched hard, and George Eaton went over his head to strike his skull on the hot naked rock.

Gun flashes rippled from the brush and the jumbled rocks to right and left of the road. Men screamed and horses pawed the air frantically. A rookie lost control of his horse and it broke for the desert. A slug broke the bay's neck, and as the kid went down an Apache bounded from his hiding place and raised a club, a hideous thing formed of a round stone encased in tightly drawn rawhide. The club came down and splattered the kids brains all over the road.

One after the other the little detachment fell and died until only George Eaton lay in the road, trying to get up while he pawed at the mess on his face. The shooting died away. The young officer at last cleared his face and got up on his hands and knees. Then he saw something dimly in front of him, like two slim tree trunks colored light brown. But they weren't tree trunks. They were strong legs clad in the *n'deh b'keh,* the thigh-length, thick-soled, button-toed moccasins of the Apaches.

Eaton looked up into a face that chilled his guts. White bands of paint across a beak of a nose between two flat black eyes like chips of ebony. Eaton tried to get up, but his senses wavered. The Apache spoke quick in slurring speech. Strong hands gripped the officer and threw him on his back. In seconds they had stripped him of weapons, boots, and clothing. The sun began to scorch his white flesh. It was quiet now. No wounded moaned or screamed, for the wounded had died with crushed skulls. The cavalry horses had been led off.

Twenty warriors watched the naked officer, and there was no expression on their flat faces.

Eaton struggled a little as the tall Apache reached down into the top of one of his moccasins and drew out a thin-bladed knife. He tested the edge with his thumb and looked down at Eaton.

"I demand the honors of war!" said Eaton thickly. The words were silly, the whole thing was silly. It couldn't happen within three miles of Fort Guthrie. It was impossible He was still babbling about the "honors of war" when the knife cut home between his thighs. He screamed like an animal and kept on screaming until they stuffed his mouth full and left him thrashing and rolling in the road until his life left him because of loss of blood.

———————

Captain Sebastian DeVoto led his detachment down the old road just below the site of Fort Guthrie. The smoke was still rising out on the desert. Sergeant Schmidt turned his head. "Sounded like shooting over to the east, sir," he said.

DeVoto looked to his left. He was an old soldier. He had fought with Garibaldi's Red Shirts in Sicily and in Italy, and had served in the Papal Guard before he had heard of the Civil War in the United States. Veterans were needed to lead the green Union troops, so the adventurous Italian had been welcomed and soon commissioned. Heroism at Cold Harbor had been awarded by a lieutenant-colonelcy of volunteers, and his wartime record had brought him a regular army commission as first lieutenant of cavalry.

"Maybe we'd better investigate, sir," said Schmidt.

"No time, *sergente*. Maybe it is a hunting party, yes?"

"I doubt it, sir."

DeVoto thrust up an arm and halted the little column. He slid from his horse and got his field glasses. He walked to a tall boulder just at the edge of the desert and scrambled up on it, uncasing his glasses. He raised them to his eyes.

The handful of troopers sat their horses on the flats, just off the place where the road debouched onto the desert. The area was stippled with creosote bushes and gaunt ocotillo rising from the rock-hard surface of the ground. There was a place where a shallow wash had softened the ground to a certain point, and here the area showed low humps dotted haphazardly about among the brush.

The captain lowered his glasses and focused them, then raised them again. He looked the very picture of the frontier cavalry officer with his rakish campaign hat, worn but neat trail uniform, and bright yellow scarf about his brown neck. Suddenly DeVoto stiffened as he studied the terrain to the east. He lowered the glasses and turned to call out to Sergeant Schmidt.

There was the sound of a sharply cracked stick. DeVoto jerked as the bullet struck him just over the heart. He pitched backward from the boulder and was dead before his body struck the ground.

The troopers fought their restless horses. At that moment there was a curious movement along the winding wash. The low humps moved, shook, and then seemed to sprout men— Apaches, covered with the dust which had settled on the gray blankets over their hiding holes. Rifles crackled from the crescent of warriors, and before Schmidt got his new command under control three troopers were dead in their blood and a shrieking rookie had his hands clasped over the horrible gouge where his eyes had been before a chewed slug had ripped across them to plunge him into everlasting darkness.

Schmidt's Colt barked. "Retreat!" he yelled. "Up the

road! We can't fight them here!" A bullet tore into his right shoulder and he thrust his reins into his mouth, did the border shift with his Colt and closed in behind the yelling troopers as they forced their panicked horses up the road. Two more troopers went down. One was dead. The other was a veteran and his partner charged at him, kicked his left foot free from the stirrup and leaned forward. The dismounted trooper tried to swing up behind his partner, but a fifty-caliber slug broke his spine just as his feet left the ground.

The dust rose behind the retreating troopers. Flashes of gunfire still dotted the chaparral. But Schmidt, in ignominious retreat, had at least saved half of the detachment. There was no hope for any of the wounded left behind. War clubs and rifle butts crushed the skulls of the helpless, and strong hands ripped uniforms and equipment from the still-warm bodies.

The gun smoke drifted out across the desert. A painted buck began to sing a victory song. In a few minutes some of the Apaches were riding hard across the desert on captured army horses while others of the band trotted alongside them. It would be a long time before the White-Eyes could organize a pursuit, and by the time they did the Apaches would have vanished like wind-driven smoke.

———

HOLT DOWNEY LAY flat on his lean belly with his field glasses to his eyes, studying the heat-shimmering terrain. He could see the long length of the low ridge which rose from the desert floor like the overturned hull of a long-forgotten shipwreck three-quarters buried by the sand. Far across the desert was the lean needle shape of Piloncillo Rock, and it seemed to waver and dance grotesquely in the hot air rising from the yellow earth.

Holt lowered his glasses. To his left was the great

naked rock shoulder which thrust out from the south side of the mesa like a ship's prow, with a gentle talus burying its foot like the crested wave at a ship's cutwater. He could see nothing past that rock shoulder. They were cut off from sight or sound of the fort ten miles to the east and high above them.

The thread of smoke from Caballo Wash swing station had died away in the time it had taken Holt to lead his detachment northwest from Fort Guthrie, then angling back to meet the old road. It had been slow going down that bitch of a road, but at least it was rock for the most part, and no dust had arisen to mark their passage.

The detachment squatted in the meager shade of their sweating mounts. One of the troopers was watching Holt Downey. It was Joe Caxton, and he was a sick man. The hammer still thudded in his skull, and the harsh heat and reflected sunlight did his head no good either. But his eyes hardly left Holt Downey.

None of the other men spoke to him. He had been a good noncom, but damned tough. Too tough to haze, now that he was a buck private again, and the look in his bloodshot eyes boded no good for anyone, least of all his company commander.

Sergeant Lambert crawled up beside Holt. "How does it look, sir?"

"*Quién sabe?* You never can see those red bastards unless by accident."

"Yeah—or when they're confident of themselves."

Holt closed his eyes. "Why did you bring Caxton along?"

"He's in McCormick's squad now, sir. You asked for Donigan and McCormick as corporals."

"Dammit! The man should have been left behind."

"He wasn't confined or under arrest, sir."

Holt grunted.

"Besides, he said he wanted to keep an eye on you, Captain."

"So? Why?"

Lambert shrugged. "All he told McCormick was that he had an important appointment with you and he meant to keep it."

Holt opened his eyes. "Out here?"

"He didn't say, sir."

Holt looked back over his shoulder. Lambert looked back also. Caxton squatted beside his horse, and his campaign hat brim was pulled low over his eyes.

Lambert grinned. "God, he must have the father and mother of all hangovers. And on top of that a night with Annie Tulvis!"

Holt looked at the noncom. "He had nothing to do with Annie Tulvis. She took him in because he was blind drunk."

Holt got up and left the noncom. He walked behind a rock ledge until he could see to the east side of the ridge.

Lambert looked at Monahan, the trumpeter. "You hear that, Mike?"

"Aye."

"What the hell riled him so much about Annie Tulvis?"

"I wud not know, Sergeant."

Lambert spat and grinned lecherously. "I'll bet Downey has his eye on that buxom filly. Jees, what a woman! What do you think, Mike?"

Monahan wiped the sweat from his red face. "I think ye have a damned filthy mind, Sergeant. The girl is all right."

"Be damned to you, Monahan!"

"And, beggin' yere pardon, be damned to ye, Sergeant dear!"

There was an uneasy feeling in Holt Downey. There was no chance that the Apaches knew his detachment was in that area, but still a subtle warning came to his honed sixth sense. It was still a long way out to Piloncillo Rock, and they couldn't travel fast because of raising dust while the keenest eyes in the world were watching every movement out on the desert. But then too, if McAllister's quickly devised plan worked, the troops from the other posts might get a fair crack at the raiders. It was like grabbing a handful of shelled corn. Most of it would slip out between your fingers, but some of it would still be retained. It was all you could hope for in Apache fighting, to get a small part of them. It was their country. They knew every water hole and trail and could live comfortably in a land where a white man would soon starve to death.

Holt moved back to his command. "Let's move out, Lambert," he said.

They led the horses down onto the desert, behind the ridge. Holt went ahead on foot while Monahan led his horse and Holt's mount. Holt picked the best way to go, and they had made a good mile along the way before he stopped again and crawled up the slope of the ridge to scout the terrain with his field glasses.

There was dust out on the desert, but whether it was caused by Apaches, troops, or wind-devils he had no way of knowing. The tall pinnacle of rock seemed deserted. There had been no flashes from it for some time.

They went on. Now and then Holt looked back at the rim of the mesa. He could have used Mark Lewis. But the quiet scout had slipped again. Damn the luck in having two scouts at Fort Guthrie, one of them inefficient and practically useless, and the other one of the best men in his field, if and when he was sober.

The pinnacle of rock didn't seem to get any closer, but gradually its coloring changed as the sun traveled west. And then, before one realized it, the tall shaft of rock was looming overhead, not a mile from the tired troopers.

"Looks deserted," said Lambert. He shifted his chew of sweet Wedding Cake and spat at a lizard.

"What did ye expect to see?" asked Monahan sarcastically, "a gaslight parade up thayer?"

"Scratch my rump, Monahan."

"Ye'll have to wash it first, Sergeant love."

"Shut up!" snapped Holt. Something had caught his eye.

Just a quick flash of movement on the brush-stippled lower slopes of the pinnacle.

"By Jesus!" said Lambert. "That's a buck!"

Monahan nodded. "Aye, but how many more av thim are up thayer?"

Holt studied the pinnacle with his glasses. He had scouted Piloncillo Rock many times before. There was only one way to get to the top and down again, on the northwestern face of the pinnacle, and with the exceptions of scant brush and few low ledges of rock, the passage was open to sight from anyone on the western side of the pinnacle. The small area atop the pinnacle was also exposed to view. There were no warriors up there, and he couldn't see any others on the slope.

Holt cased his glasses. "Hold the men here, Lambert," he said. "Monahan and McCormick come with me. Leave your carbines here and take off your spurs."

The three of them threaded their way cautiously through a jungle of cactus and ocotillo which covered the western slope of the ridge until they were within fifty feet of the trail from the top of the pinnacle.

It was quiet. A lone hawk floated high overhead. The dry wind rustled the brush a little. Sweat ran down Holt's face as he lay there beside the two big Irishmen.

"Hist!" said Monahan.

Holt saw the movement before he heard anything. Then the buck appeared. A small man trotting toward them carrying a repeating rifle. Holt jerked his head at the two troopers. They left Holt and circled about, one on each side of Holt.

The warrior was ten feet from Holt when he saw the

blue uniform against the glaucous green of the grease-wood. He jumped back and raised his rifle. Monahan rose from the brush like a jack-in-the-box and dived at the buck. He heard the thudding of Monahan's boots on the ground and turned. Holt was on him, and as he whirled again, Holt gripped the rifle forced it up and to one side, and smashed a hard knee into the buck's groin. As the warrior bent forward in agony, Holt ripped the rifle away from his nerveless hands and struck him down with the butt.

Monahan kicked him down as he tried to rise, then swiftly plucked the sheath knife from the buck's waist. He cast it into the brush. McCormick closed in. "Fast work," he said. "I was afraid ye'd let that rifle go off, sorr. If any more of these divils are about they'd sure hear it."

Monahan wiped the sweat from his face. Holt emptied the rifle. The brass cartridges struck the hard earth. "Look at this," said Holt. "Brand new Winchester Model 1873, caliber .44/40. A helluva lot better weapon than the ones we troopers are issued."

McCormick nodded. "Now where do ye suppose he got it?"

"In a raid maybe."

"Let's hope so, sorr. If the Butcher gets a lot of these he'd be in a good position to drive us out of this country."

Holt looked down at the unconscious warrior. He looked like an Apache and wore the usual clothing. Buck-skin breechclout, thigh-length mocs, dingy headband. But there was something different about him.

"Looks like a greaser," said Monahan suddenly.

"Aye," breathed McCormick.

Holt studied the lean brown face. Apaches usually killed adult males. But they usually kept small captive children for adoption into their band or for ransom. More than one Mexican kid had been raised amongst them, as fierce and as predatory as they were.

The buck opened his eyes and glared at Holt.

"Habla español, hombre?" asked Holt.

There was a faint nicker in the dark eyes.

Monahan nudged him with a boot. "Speak when the captain speaks to ye," he said.

McCormick spat on his hands. "Let me work him over a bit, sorr." He bent to reach for the buck. The Apache suddenly seemed to coil and spring like a released trap. A hideout knife, short and crooked, a real *saca tripos,* flashed in his hand and the keen blade sliced through McCormick's right sleeve and deep into his arm. The blood spurted freely. "Holy Mother!" said McCormick. "He's cut me to the bone!"

Monahan kicked out hard against the buck's head. The knife flew from the warrior's hand and Holt kicked it to one side. "Don't kill him, Mike!" snapped Holt

Mr. McCormick groaned thickly as he gripped his slashed arm. The blood ran between his big fingers, and he stamped his feet on the ground in his agony. He started for the warrior, but Holt stopped him. He ripped off the trooper's bandanna scarf and formed a tourniquet about the arm. "Tie that sonofabitch up, Mike," he said over his shoulder.

The trumpeter cut a stick, thrust it in front of the elbows of the Apache and behind his back. He lashed the stick tightly, then shoved him toward the waiting troopers.

"All right, McCormick?" asked Holt.

The pale-faced noncom wiped the cold sweat from his face. "I'll be all right, sorr. He was like a striking rattler, so he was."

"You can't take chances like that, Mac."

The troopers looked curiously at them as they returned with the prisoner. Lambert grinned. "That the best you could do, Monahan? One undersized buck?"

"I didn't see ye out thayer, Sergeant mine."

Holt eyed the prisoner. He was sure he was Mexican, or at least part Mexican. He had tried to get pure-blooded Apaches to talk before, but no threat or violence could force a word out of them. A pure Mex or a breed, though, might be more imaginative, particularly with the application of a little force in the right place. Holt figured he could make this hombre talk.

Holt led out. The troopers were quiet. They hadn't even had the dubious pleasure of a fight to alleviate the hell of the trip.

The sun was slanting down. The edge of the mesa was already getting barred with dark shadows where gullies ran down to the desert. A purplish hue tinted the mesa. Something glinted for an instant near where Fort Guthrie was, although the fort itself could not be seen.

Holt turned and rested a hand on his cantle. Piloncillo stood naked and lonely. No smoke was to be seen near Caballo Wash. No dust marred the dusk air. Nothing. The desert seemed wrapped in the eternal peace which was its normal lot, until man entered it.

The sun was almost gone when they neared the foot of the mesa road. A cool breeze swept down from the mesa. "Ah," said Lambert. "At least we'll have a quiet, cool ride back to the fort."

"I'd rather have a quiet, cool beer," said Monahan.

Holt wiped his face and raised his head, then he stiffened in his saddle. Something had moved among the shadows at the foot of the road. Apaches, and a mess of them! There was no time to maneuver, and he knew he'd have his command cut to pieces before he could retreat "Blow the charge, Trumpeter!" he yelled as he ripped his Colt free.

The stirring brazen notes were lipped out by the Irishman. The troopers were startled, but most of them were veterans. Colts were drawn and cocked, and spurs sank deep into the dusty flanks of the light bays.

Holt's horse struck a running buck and a pistol shot, fired at five feet, blew off the back of his head. A second shot struck a warrior in the chest, and as he went down the hoofs of the big bay smashed him into pulp.

Rifles flashed from the ambushers, to be answered by the sharper cracking of the cavalry pistols. Smoke and dust swirled up and shrouded the racing, yelling troopers. Most of them broke through, then turned in their saddles to shoot. Holt's bay staggered, then went down, and he cleared the stirrups, ripping his Spencer repeater from its sheath as he did so. He struck the ground running, levered a cartridge into the chamber, and rapped out a shot. He moved forward as fast as he could, levering and firing at hip level, cutting a path through the shrieking bucks.

He was all alone in the middle of the damned melee, with dust and smoke swirling around him and blood-hungry bucks yelling to eat his guts with a spoon. The ghastly feeling came over him that this was the end.

A horseman crashed through a knot of Apaches, turned his big bay in a hoof-pawing rear and kicked out an empty stirrup for Holt. Holt gripped it, and as the bay set off up the road he ran beside it, striking out at the warriors with his empty carbine. He gripped the trooper's cartridge belt and swung up behind him.

The frustrated warriors poured fire up the darkening slope from their Winchester repeaters; but the detachment had a charmed life, and they disappeared around the great rock shoulder which thrust itself out from the mesa.

Holt looked back as the bay topped the edge of the mesa. The rest of the detachment was already there. "Ye have the luck av the Irish, sorr!" yelled Monahan.

Holt slid from the horse. "Thanks, soldier," he said. He looked up into the face of Joe Caxton.

"It was nothing," said the ex-sergeant. "For this we are soldiers." He smiled thinly. "Besides, we have an appointment, if the captain remembers."

CHAPTER NINE

Fort Guthrie had a pall of tragedy over it. Two officers and twenty-four enlisted men had died that day. Only the grace of God and the quick thinking of Holt Downey had saved B Company from the bitter tragedies that had overcome A and F Companies at the foot of the mesa. All the garrison of Fort Guthrie had to show for that bloody day's work was one undersized and sullen Apache buck kept in solitary confinement.

Women wept along Soapsuds Row. One officer in each of the two stricken companies gathered together the personal effects of First Lieutenant George Eaton of Savannah, Georgia, and Captain Sebastian DeVoto of New York and Turin. Twenty-four enlisted men's foot-lockers were taken from the barracks and placed in the quartermaster warehouse.

Surgeon Angus Logie and his medical detachment were still busy as the faint light of the moon showed atop the dark mountain range far to the east. Now and then the surgeon's eyes flicked toward the cot in the far corner where a nineteen-year-old boy lay with a thick white bandage across the place where the merriest blue eyes in F Company had once been.

Logie finished swabbing out the great gouge in Corporal McCormick's muscular right arm. It was as neat an incision as the good surgeon could have made himself.

"Will I lose it, sorr?" asked McCormick.

"No. You'll be up and about in a few weeks. You'll have a beauty of a scar to show off to the girls in the whorehouses, Mac."

"Away wid ye, sorr!" laughed the big Mick.

Talbot McAllister sat at the colonel's desk listening to Holt Downey's report. He looked up as Holt finished. "I don't think much of you, sir," he said coldly. "One captive for this whole afternoon's work and twenty-six dead, seven wounded for our side of the ledger."

Holt's face darkened. "Surely the general doesn't accuse me of being responsible for those ambushes?"

McAllister made an impatient gesture with a bandaged hand.

Holt leaned forward. "That captive is Mexican, or at least part Mexican. If I can get him to talk, we may get some information about El Carnicero."

"Perhaps."

Holt smashed a fist into his other palm. "I just don't understand it! It was almost as though they *knew* what we planned to do! They've never been bold enough to come this close to the post."

"Carelessness, Captain, sheer carelessness."

Colonel Fleming cleared his throat. "Captain DeVoto and Lieutenant Eaton were both experienced Indian fighters, sir. As fine as any man in this department, with the exception of Captain Downey perhaps."

The cold eyes flicked up at Holt. "Yes, so I understand. Nothing, *but nothing*, stops him from attacking the enemy."

Holt wet his lips. He could feel the unreasoning, implacable hatred of the general officer sitting in front of him. "There's a chance that the other troops from

Parnell, Liscomb and Roscoe may have cut off some of the raiders, sir."

"No. That would be impossible, sir."

Holt eyed him. "Then the general received a wire to that effect?"

"I did not, Captain."

Fleming wiped the sweat from his thick jowls. "The wire has been down most of the day, Downey."

Holt turned quickly. "When did you know *that*, Colonel?"

Fleming swallowed, shifted his feet, then looked at the general. "I—" he said, and then he closed his mouth.

"Was the wire down *before* we left, sir?"

"Well, Downey, that is to say, I—"

"Hell's fire, Fleming!" snapped McAllister. "Get this officer out of here! It's time for mess."

"Dismissed, Downey," said Fleming. It was the first definite thing he had said since Holt had been in the office. Holt turned to salute the general and their eyes clashed like tempered steel. Holt knew right then and there that no messages had been sent to alert the troops at the other three forts.

———

BEN LORIS SAT at the edge of his bunk in his underdrawers, sucking a long nine cigar. Holt stood at the front window looking out across the moon-washed parade ground.

Boots grated on the harsh earth outside the rear door. Both officers reached for their Colts. A dark-clad figure filled the rear doorway and the rich odor of whisky drifted in on them. Mark Lewis stood there in the full solemnity of a person as drunk as he can get without falling down. "Good evening, gentlemen," he said.

"Good Christ," breathed Loris. "Look at him."

"You look," said Holt in disgust. "I'm sick enough as it is."

Lewis walked in and sat down on Holt's bunk. "I fear I am not too welcome here," he said gravely. A hiccup spoiled the effect.

"You're putting it mildly," said Holt.

Lewis tried to fix Holt with a stern look but he had difficulty in focusing his eyes.

"Where did you go, Mark?" asked Ben.

He waved a hand. "I need a drink," he said.

"Sure. That's all you need."

"Give him one," said Holt. "I'm curious to see how far he'll go. His bilges are awash right now with rotgut."

Ben passed the bottle to the scout. Lewis measured the contents with his eyes, then tipped up the bottle. The liquor gurgled down, and then he took the bottle from his mouth. "Mother's milk," he said solemnly.

"Some mother," said Loris.

Holt picked up a chair, twirled it, then sat down, resting his forearms on the back. He studied the drunken scout. "I could have used you today," he said.

"Sorry."

"Sorry hell! I could have used you. Seb DeVoto and George Eaton died because they didn't have a decent scout with them. I damned near didn't get back either. You're through, Mark. By God, you're through!"

"I'll be all right in the morning."

"Yes? You'd better be. I have a job for you."

"No scouting in this heat with a hangover, Holt."

"I'd like to see you sweat out that rotgut. No, it's a job of questioning."

"So?"

"I brought in a prisoner. He's not a pure-blooded Apache. Maybe a full-blooded Mex. Maybe a breed. But he's not a real rimrock Apache."

"What do you want me to do?"

"You speak fluent Spanish and damned good Apache.

I want you to go with me in the morning and start talking to this prisoner."

"What is it you want to know?"

Holt hitched his chair a little closer and lowered his voice. "No rimrock Apache would betray his mates, or their leader. I'm sure these raiders today were part of the Butcher's *corrida*. If we can force this prisoner to talk, we may find out a way to get into the Butcher's stronghold, or maybe even make him guide us in there."

The dark eyes studied Holt, and it seemed to Holt for an odd moment that the man wasn't really drunk at all.

"It's against regulations to use force to make a prisoner talk, Mark, but be damned to the regulations!"

"From what you've been doing lately the regulations can't mean much."

"They used to. But this is a bloody war, Mark! If I had my way with you, for example, I'd have you in a sweatbox or standing on a barrel top in the sun for a day until you pleaded for mercy and swore off liquor for life."

Tattoo blew sweetly out on the night air and echoed from the hills.

"Half an hour until taps," observed Ben dryly.

Holt shot a glance at him. Any soldier knew it was half an hour from tattoo to taps. The adjutant's face was devoid of expression. *How much did he know?*

Mark hiccupped and reached for the bottle. "So you think you can make this prisoner squeal, Holt?"

"I'll bet on it."

"And if he does squeal and tells you how to find the Butcher, or agrees to show the way to the stronghold, what happens then?"

"I'm going in after the Butcher."

"You're loco!"

"Listen, Mark," said Holt thinly, "and keep this inside your drunken skull. Paste it on the bottom of that bottle. Whether I'm cashiered or not, whether I get orders or not, I'm going in after the Butcher."

The bottle hid the scout's face. "He'll flay you alive, Holt."

"I mean to get him first."

He lowered the bottle and wiped his mouth. Then he slowly sagged down to lie on his side. Holt took the bottle from the weak hand.

"He's gone, Holt," said Ben.

Holt eyed the drunken scout. "I'll sober him up in the morning."

Holt walked over to his wardrobe and changed his uniform. Ben Loris watched him through half-closed eyes. "Going for a walk?"

"Maybe."

"Miss Nolan?"

"No."

"*Miss* Tulvis?"

Holt turned and the look in his eyes was enough to silence Ben. Holt picked up the bottle and allowed himself one drink. He was tired, but Joe Caxton would be tired too. Joe had just lived through a bitch of a drunk. But he was a bigger man than Holt and a stronger man. The odds would be about even, or so Holt hoped. He couldn't afford to be badly beaten by Joe Caxton this night. He put on his forage cap, buckled on his pistol belt, saluted Ben gravely, then left the room.

Loris reached for the bottle and took a slug. "Ah hell," he said softly. "Next to a good woman there's nothing like a good fight. This promises to be the best one I might have seen in my whole life, and custom forbids me go."

Mark Lewis began to snore.

In a little while taps sounded soft and clear on the dry wind sweeping across the post.

CHAPTER TEN

The area between the post and the bastion was silvered by moonlight and as level as a billiard table. Holt looked back toward the post as he walked. No one had seen him leave. He had waited until the guard had gone its rounds. The post was quiet, and one light showed at the end of Soapsuds Row. Yancey Tulvis' shebang.

Holt stopped at the entrance to the bastion. It was so quiet he wondered if he had arrived before Caxton or whether Caxton was coming at all. He placed his hand on his pistol butt and stepped into the moonlit bastion. A solid figure squatted in the shadows at the southeast corner. "You won't need that gun, Captain," said the big man. "Or did you intend to kill me with it?"

Holt walked into the middle of the bastion. No one could see them from the post, for the central part of the little fortification was lower than the fire step which was next to the walls.

"It would be easy," said the ex-sergeant. "Deserting, resisting arrest, attacking a superior officer—which would it be, *sir?*"

Holt unbuckled his gun belt and placed it and the Colt on the fire step. He rolled up his shirt sleeves and scaled his hat to lie beside the gun belt. "Did you come here to fight or to talk? You called me a yellow bastard and other things. You said you wished I could be an enlisted man for half an hour so you could break my damned brass jaw, as you called it."

Caxton stood up and peeled off his shirt. He wore no undershirt, and his thick upper body was solid and padded with heavy muscles. There was no fat on the man. He weighed a good hundred and ninety pounds, twenty pounds heavier than Holt. "I'll not hit shoulder straps," he said. "I'm still that much of the Regular, Captain Downey."

Holt wordlessly took off his shirt. His muscles were flat and lean but small in contrast to the cords which covered the big, enlisted man's torso and arms. "You really want to go through with this, then?" he asked.

Caxton smiled and ran thick fingers through his yellow hair. "Why not?"

"Why not, indeed?" said Holt quietly.

Caxton walked forward into the middle of the bastion and dragged a toe across the hard earth, marking a hardly distinguishable line. Holt smiled. Caxton was acting like a kid challenging the new kid on the block to mortal combat, preliminary to starting a long friendship.

Holt moved quickly. He stepped across the line, measured Caxton with a left, tapping him hard twice alongside the jaw, then threw a short right cross which shook the big man. Caxton staggered back a little and covered up while Holt moved in closer and closer, hitting Caxton like a butcher chopping meat, driving him back almost to the fire step. Caxton stopped and swayed his body from side to side. The punch came out of thin air, smacking hard and solidly against Holt's jaw and dumping him on the ground so hard his rump stung from the contact.

Caxton moved back, feinted once or twice, drew in a deep lungful of the dry night air, and waited with a faint smile on his face. It was then that Holt knew he was in for a hell of a beating, for the man had a professional style about him.

Holt got up and brushed the dirt from his hands. This time he raised them and waited. Caxton circled, his hard jaw tucked in behind his big right fist, while his left fist was no more than a foot and a half in front of him. Holt circled with the big man, threw a left, then a right, then a left, all of which stirred up nothing but air. Caxton laughed. He threw a wild left which Holt went under, and as Holt came up for a counter punch he caught a right in the pit of his lean gut which bent him over to meet a whistling left uppercut. It drove him back so that his heels struck the fire step, and he sat down, striking his head back against the bastion wall. Blood trickled into his mouth, warm and salt.

Caxton stepped back. "Time," he said. He sat down on the opposite fire step, looking at Holt like a solid and methodical bulldog who knew his business.

They studied each other. Holt knew Caxton had won his stripes in the field, but he had also won them in the old B Company, the hard way. B had been known as the "Battling Bastards of B" long before Holt had joined the company as commander a few years before. But Captain Jim Jarvis, who had led B through the Civil War, and later against the Comanches and Kiowas, had always insisted that his non-coms be able to use their brains as well as their fists. Holt had walked into the boots of a good man, respected and beloved by the men of B. Jarvis had been killed by a flint arrowhead, driven into his sternum by an Apache at ten-foot range.

"Time—sir," said Caxton.

The next round was fast and furious. Holt got in a few good blows which might have hurt a lesser man. He was still on his feet when Caxton said, "Time." Holt sat down and his breath was harsh in his throat.

Caxton rubbed his abraded knuckles. "Not bad," he

said. "There's no need for you to fight on until I say "Time," sir. When you feel like it you can say it too."

"Thanks," said Holt dryly. "I figured you needed the rest more than I did."

Caxton thrust forward his head and stared belligerently at Holt, then he laughed. "You're game enough, Downey," he said.

"Just call me 'Sport', Caxton."

They stood up for the next round. Caxton was sure and methodical now, for he knew he had his man. "I won't—mark—you up," he said, driving home body blows to time his words. "No need—for that—I don't—want—the boys—to know—I licked you—That—is for—my own—personal—satisfaction—"

Holt backpedaled, blocking the vicious punches with fists and forearms, but his rib cage ached from the thudding mallet blows. Caxton was breathing hard, though, harder than Holt. The big man plunged in, eager to get it over with, only to walk into a straight left. His head snapped up in surprise, and Holt threw a right from the heels, catching Caxton flush on the button. It was so well timed that the big man's feet flew up as he was dumped into a corner of the bastion.

Blood dripped from Holt's mouth. He spat, and the patch of blood looked black on the moonlit earth. "Time," he said thickly.

Caxton waved a hand. He sat up and felt his jaw. "I didn't know you had it in you, sir," he said.

"Neither did I."

They grinned at each other like two Cheshire cats.

But Holt knew there was to be no quarter. They were both fighting men, and they both wanted to win. If he won, nothing would be said about it at the post, and B Company would still be his. If he lost, Caxton would keep his mouth shut, but the company would know, and Holt could never control it again.

Holt stood up. The moon was full above them now,

slanting its light down into the bastion, and Holt could almost see each separate curling hair on the big enlisted man's chest. He could see the drying blood on the stony knuckles and the hard set of the strong jaw. They feinted slowly at each other, trying the defenses, watching for an opening. Caxton moved first, driving a right to the pit of Holt's stomach for his old one-two, belly and jaw. Holt turned sideways and took the bruising blow on the hip. The startled man drove in his uppercut, expecting to meet Holt's down-coming jaw, but Holt blocked the uppercut with his right forearm and smashed a neat short jab to Caxton's jaw, staggering him.

Holt drove in, throwing everything he had, belting gut and jaw, heart and chest, until Caxton retreated quickly, covering up until he got a chance to stand. Then it was toe to toe, two big hard-hitting men. Sweat and blood sprayed their faces and glistened on their upper bodies. Holt felt a tooth crack, but he had the satisfaction of seeing a mouse start under Caxton's left eye.

Caxton slammed Holt to the ground with a right cross. He danced back, but his footwork was getting clumsy. "Time?" he said.

"Time, hell!"

Holt got up, wiped his mouth, and rushed the big man. He was driven back three times with sickening blows. Again Caxton tried his right to the belly. Again Holt had the wit to turn away, block the left uppercut, and crack Caxton a smashing jab that dumped the big man flat on his back with Holt falling on top of him. Caxton shook his head and shoved Holt from him. Blood leaked from his slack mouth.

It was two weary and almost beaten men who stood up once more to the mark. Holt felt that his sand was running out. How much more could he take and deal out? He had whipped bigger men than Caxton and had taken a few beatings himself, but this was the first time he had ever experienced such an even match.

Caxton moved in, slowly and ponderously, shooting out his stubborn left, keeping his massive right fist cocked for the lethal explosion against Holt's jaw. Holt rocked him with a left to the gut and a cracking right hook to the jaw. Caxton swung wildly, and as Holt moved back he stumbled. The blow was glancing, but enough to send Holt down.

Caxton mistook Holt's fall for the preliminaries of victory. He laughed. "Get up! I'm not through until I knock you cold, *Mr.* Downey."

Holt opened his mouth to retort. Something moved in the gun embrasure on the south wall of the bastion. Holt rolled over, ripped his Colt free from the holster, and cocked it

Caxton jumped back toward the embrasure. "I knew it," he said. "You couldn't take a beating like a real man!"

The shadow in the embrasure moved quickly, and a figure jumped for the broad, sweaty back of the ex-sergeant. "Down, Joe!" yelled Holt. The veteran obeyed the command automatically. Holt fired from the ground, and the big .44 slug hit the Apache in the throat. He fell sideways, dropping his knife, and clutching at his throat as blood spewed from his mouth and glistened on Caxton's white skin. The echo of the gunshot sounded from the nearby hills. Smoke drifted in the bastion.

A thick-maned head showed at the outer side of the bastion, and Holt rolled up to his knees and fired. The head went down. Caxton snatched up the Apache knife, sank it into the back of the first writhing Apache, and looked at Holt. "We'd better pull foot!"

They could hear men yelling at the fort. Holt snatched up shirt and gun belt but dropped them again to fire at a buck who showed in an embrasure with raised rifle. He fell backward with a hoarse scream.

Then a knot of warriors came over the wall. Caxton met the first one with a left to the jaw, and as the head went back the knife went deep into the belly and was ripped sideways. Caxton's hard right shoulder drove against another Apache. A knee came up into the Apache's groin and the knife almost decapitated him as his head went down.

Holt fired from the hip, knocking a buck back against the wall. A warrior clubbed a rifle and swung it at Caxton. The Colt rapped. The buck fell against the white man and staggered him. A squat warrior raised a rifle at point-blank range ten feet from Caxton. Holt fired his last round and the warrior fell to one side. Caxton snatched up the rifle, reversed it, and laid about him like a farmer threshing wheat.

Then the Apaches were gone as quickly and as silently as they had arrived. Smoke was thick in the windless air. Half a dozen of them still lay in the bastion. Two of them writhed in silent agony. Caxton spat. He raised the rifle and drove the steel-shod butt down between the eyes of one of the wounded warriors, crushing the life out of him. The other warrior rolled away and ripped a hideout knife from his breechclout. It fanged up brightly toward the crotch of the big white man, but Holt stepped in close and smashed the butt of the smoking Colt down on his head. Caxton finished the job with the rifle butt.

They stood there staring at each other, while their glittering chests rose and fell. Boots thudded on the hard earth. "Who's in there?" yelled a voice.

"Captain Downey and Private Caxton," said Holt.

A corporal came into the bastion with a squad of infantrymen. He looked about at the carnage. "Jesus God," he said in awe.

Caxton spat leisurely. "You doughboys got here just in time to clean up the cavalry's leavings." He bowed a little to Holt. "Now, if the captain is quite ready, I think we ought to go and get patched up a little—from the fighting." He winked at Holt.

They pulled on their shirts and walked from the

bastion together. The quadrangle was full of men lining
up in company formation. Lights had gone on in most of
the buildings. Noncoms barked orders. A tall figure stood
beneath the ramada in front of headquarters, buckling on
a dress sword.

"Good God!" said Caxton.

Holt cupped his hands about his mouth. "For Christ's
sake! Don't line up there like clay pigeons! Get those
lights out! Get under cover! Pronto!"

The men scattered, running with rifles and carbines
at the trail, to take up the positions long ago designated
to them by Holt Downey when he had formed a defense
plan in case Fort Guthrie should be attacked. Lights
winked out. Holt crammed cartridges into his Colt.
Caxton ran to the little howitzer near the flagpole, of
little use other than for the morning and sunset gun
salutes. He took a charge from the ready box and
rammed it into the muzzle, placed a friction tube in the
firehole, and attached a lanyard to it. He grinned over his
shoulder at Holt. "Can't hit 'em, but it sure as hell can
scare 'em, and they don't like artillery fire one little bit!"

It suddenly grew quiet on the post. Now and then a
man coughed or a breech block was opened as a nervous
rookie checked to see if he had loaded his piece. It was
quiet out on the mesa too. The moon drifted behind a
bank of clouds, and Holt walked to the edge of the gate
area and looked toward the bastion.

"Ain't seen a damned thing out there, sir," a sergeant
said softly.

It was likely they were gone. They didn't like stand-up
fights, but rather the swift dusk or early-morning attack,
or the deadly ambush. They knew now that the post was
alerted, and they knew too that they had left eight good
fighting men to stiffen in the moonlight staring upward
with eyes that did not see. Those dead warriors would
wander forever in limbo, denied entrance to Chidin-bi-
Kungua, the House of Spirits over the Shadow Waters.

A coyote howled to the west, and a moment later one of his mates answered from the south, close to the lip of the mesa.

"Listen to them," said the sergeant. "The shooting must have roused them up."

Holt raised his head. There was a subtle difference in the calls. The imitation was close but not quite close enough. They were still out there, watching the post.

Holt walked back toward the center of the quadrangle. Caxton was prowling back and forth carrying a Long Tom .45/70 infantryman's rifle. "What about a sortie, sir?" he asked eagerly.

Holt leaned against the flagpole. "Haven't you had enough fighting for this night?" he asked.

Caxton's big hands gripped the rifle. "No," he said. He looked quickly at Holt. "You saved my life."

"Even up, Caxton. You saved mine earlier this day."

They eyed each other. Caxton laughed shortly. "And I thought you were going to kill me because I thought I had you licked."

Holt smiled. "Fact is, you did have me licked."

Caxton shook his head. "I was about done myself. That right low in the guts and the left uppercut never let me down before."

Holt gingerly felt his belly. "You nearly got me with it the first time."

Caxton shook his head sadly. "Like I said: it never let me down before."

They eyed each other again. Caxton shifted the rifle to his left hand and thrust out his right hand. "Before God," he said, "I don't always agree with you, sir. You turned me sour when you rode down poor Mr. McAllister and his boys. But maybe I understand a little better now."

Holt took the man's hand. "Thanks, Joe," he said quietly.

Ben Loris sauntered up through the moonlight.

"Holt," he said quietly. "The colonel wants to see you at once in headquarters."

Holt looked quickly at him. "So? Why?"

Ben shrugged. "Look out for a blow," he said.

Holt strode toward the building. Ben Loris eyed Joe Caxton. "You sure got hit a lot in that fracas in the bastion, Caxton. I didn't know Apaches were experts in the gentle art of pugilism."

Caxton rubbed his battered face. His left eye was beginning to close.

Ben leaned against the flagpole. "For example, I'd say that mouse under your left eye was caused by a hand, doubled so," he said, demonstrating with his right hand, "with the knuckles in this position, then driven by a man, say about six feet tall and weighing in at about one hundred and seventy pounds. How about that, Caxton?"

Caxton looked at the top of the flagpole, then down at the ground, then directly at Ben Loris. "Sir, if it's all the same to you, I fell up that damned flagpole there."

Loris grinned. He walked away. He had been right. It probably had been the best fight he *might* have seen under other circumstances. "I wonder how those Apaches felt when they came over that wall figuring they had two dead pigeons in there. It must have been like walking into two buzz saws."

CHAPTER ELEVEN

Once again he entered the drab and familiar office of the post commander. Colonel Fleming, as usual, was standing near the door to the next office, with a petulant look on his heavy face. The general was standing in front of the map, with his hands clasped behind him. The lamplight glittered on the hilt of the dress sword the Ladies' Patriotic Society of his home state had conferred on him after his heroic fight at Chambliss Mills, when though half of his brigade had been shot to doll rags in the leaden Confederate sleet, Talbot McAllister had won his star after carrying the Union flag to the ramparts and pistoling three rebels who had tried to take it from him.

Holt saluted, but the general did not return the salute. Holt held his hand at his cap brim until McAllister snapped out a salute. "Captain Downey," he said coldly. "Since when have you deluded yourself into the idea that you can contradict the orders of superior officers?"

Holt stared at him. "I wasn't aware that I had, sir."

Then an awfully chilling thought came to Holt. Colonel Fleming had long ago made Holt responsible for the defense plan for Fort Guthrie. Holt had triggered it into action as soon as he had entered the post proper. Then he remembered something. The tall man standing beneath headquarters ramada buckling on an ornate dress sword. *God help me,* he thought.

McAllister held Holt with cold eyes. "I had taken command, *Mister* Downey. I too am a soldier, in case you have forgotten. Colonel Fleming was not in sight. You, the appointed officer in charge of defense, were missing. Yet you barge in out of nowhere, yell out commands, make me look like a fool, then come in here and act as though you knew nothing of what you had done."

"I'm sorry, sir. I—" Then the old Army rule came swiftly into Holt's mind. *"Never complain and never explain."* He closed his mouth.

Fleming looked at the general. "I'm sure Captain Downey was doing what he thought was right, General."

"I didn't ask you for an opinion, Milas."

Milas Fleming flushed. He glanced at Holt. "No," he said slowly. "But Captain Holt had been appointed by me to handle the defense of the post. He saw those troops lining up in full moonlight and the lights of the post like targets at a carnival."

The glacial eyes swiveled from Holt to Colonel Fleming. *"You mean you agree that he was right,* Milas?"

It was a hard thing for Milas Fleming to do. He had only a few years left to serve before he could retire and go to live with his two widowed sisters in Cincinnati in the big white house he had bought for them to make ready for him when he returned, full of years, but not too much glory. The man standing before him could break him like a match-stick by a few words or suggestions.

"*Well,* Milas?"

Fleming raised a hand. "I am afraid I do agree with him, sir," he said steadily.

Talbot McAllister stared at Fleming as though the man had suddenly gone insane. "Colonel," he said, "I—" His sentence was snapped off short by the flat crack of a gun somewhere near the guardhouse. The report echoed between the buildings.

"To your post, Downey!" said Colonel Fleming. He doused the light and drew his pistol to follow Holt out of the office, leaving a set-faced general standing in the oil-reeking darkness.

Holt cut recklessly across the moon-washed parade ground. Somewhere to his right a gun roared, an infantryman's .45/70 from the sound of it. "Dammit, Mahoney!" roared a voice, louder than the rifle, "Don't shoot that thing unless you got something to shoot at!"

Ben Loris ran up beside Holt. "Guardhouse?" he asked.

"Sounded like it was there, or near there."

The guardhouse door swung open and shut in the rising wind. Holt pushed the door back and looked into the guardroom. It was empty. He could smell gun smoke. Then he saw feet sticking out from under a desk. He rounded the desk. An enlisted man of the infantry company lay face downward on the floor. Holt turned him over and looked into sightless eyes. There was a spreading stain on his flannel shirt.

Holt stood up and drew his pistol. Ben Loris snatched a rifle from the rack near the door and checked it. Holt opened the heavy door which led into the corridor where the prisoner cells were. It was quiet and dim in there, as there was no light, but pale moonlight streamed through the small barred windows. The cell which had held the two Apaches he had captured at the Barrera Escarpment was empty. He turned to look into the cell where the other prisoner had been kept. The one who was of Mexican blood, full or part. The man lay face downward on the floor, and the haft of a knife protruded from between his shoulder blades. The door swung open easily at Holt's touch.

"What do you make of it?" asked Ben.

Holt looked at him. "We wouldn't have been able to

get those two rimrock bucks to talk, no matter what we did. This one was our only chance."

Sergeant Lambert came into the guardhouse with a file of men. He whistled as he saw the dead guard and whistled again as he saw the dead buck.

Holt turned to the noncom. "Did any of you see who did this?"

Lambert shook his head. "I had charge of the area along Headquarters Row, sir, and that includes the guardhouse, as the captain knows. We were looking for Apaches when we heard the shot."

"One shot," said Holt. "That accounted for the guard. Someone killed him, then released the two rimrock bucks. You all know how fast and silently they can move."

"They don't waste any time," agreed Lambert.

Holt looked down at the dead man in the cell. "But why didn't they let this one go free?"

Ben Loris rubbed his jaw. "He probably could have made it as well as the others."

"Whoever killed that guard wanted to make sure this man didn't talk. He didn't want to take a chance of letting him make a break and getting captured again. *He wanted to make absolutely sure.*"

Holt walked outside and stood in the shadow of the guardhouse. Ben Loris leaned against the wall. "You don't suppose an Apache, or Apaches did the job, Holt? It was like their work, except for shooting the guard. They would have used the knife."

Holt looked across the moon-washed parade ground. An ant couldn't have crossed it without being seen. "No," he said quietly. "I'll swear it was someone on the post, Ben."

The tall adjutant shivered a little. "But who? And why?"

Holt looked at him. *"Quién sabe?* Who knows?"

Holt walked to the gate and looked out across the

mesa. There wasn't a sign of life out there. "Sergeant Vickers," he called to an infantryman.

"Yes, sir!"

"Take a squad out to the bastion. Scout about it, but don't let your men. wander off."

"Yes, sir!"

The squad moved out, rifles at the ready. Their feet crunched on the hard earth, and their heads swung from side to side as they advanced. Vickers reached the bastion and moved into it slowly. Then he waved his men in. Holt could see their campaign hats bobbing about in there, and then Vickers could be seen looking to the south and west over the wall. He led his squad out of the bastion and beyond it, circled wide, then led them back again.

Vickers saluted Holt. "Nothing, sir. Not a trace of them." He hesitated. "Even the bodies are gone out of the bastion, sir, although how they did it is beyond me, for we've hardly taken our eyes off it since the alert."

"They must be gone, then," said Loris.

Holt nodded. He was about to give orders to call off the alert, but the memory of the interview he had had with Talbot McAllister was too fresh and raw. He turned to Ben. "You'd better tell the colonel what we've learned. Suggest we call off the alert, but keep the guards doubled until reveille."

Loris nodded and hurried off. Holt walked slowly toward his quarters. His strength seemed to have drained from him. The loss of the breed Apache had hit him hard. The Butcher was playing with them as a cat plays with a mouse. He had trapped young McAllister at the Barrera Escarpment and then slipped out of Holt's net. Somehow his warriors had managed to be at the right place and at the right time to wipe out Eaton's command, cut DeVoto's command to pieces, and almost trap Holt's detachment. His men had crept up to the bastion, within spitting distance of the fort, and had almost trapped Holt and Caxton. Then the last slap in the face had been the mysterious occurrences at the guardhouse.

The wind shifted. Far out on the desert a coyote howled. Holt shivered a little. It was almost as though the Butcher had eyes and ears everywhere. What was it Ben Loris and Mark Lewis had been talking about just the night before? About the mysterious man known as the Prophet? *"Apaches from all over the Southwest know about him now. It's said he may be able to muster all of them under the leadership of the Butcher."*

He stopped outside his quarters and took a badly bent cigar from his shirt pocket. He struck a lucifer on the adobe wall and lighted the cigar.

"No one really knows who he is. Some say he's Yaqui, others Apache; some think he's a Mexican or an American. One story has it that he's a breed of some other tribe."

Holt sucked in on the cigar and blew out a cloud of smoke. The tobacco tasted good. He was damned tired and he needed a drink.

"He exists, Holt. You can bet your life on it. He'll be heard of more and more in the days to come."

Holt opened the door and walked into the quarters. He peeled off his shirt and trousers, wincing as he began to feel the places where Caxton's fists had pounded him. He'd be black and blue before too long.

"Don't laugh. There is more truth to this thing than you or anyone else knows. He'll make himself well known before too long, as I said before, and God help the white people in this country when he does."

Mark Lewis still lay on Holt's cot, snoring drunkenly. Holt accidentally upset a washstand. The scout moved. "That you, Ben?" he mumbled.

"It's Holt."

"Oh? You been out carousing?"

Holt shook his head. It was incredible that the scout could have slept through all the racket that had been going on. "No," he said.

"Oh."

Holt lay back on the scout's cot. "Mark," he said, "what was the name of that man you called the Prophet? His Apache name I mean?"

"Who?"

"The Prophet."

"Dobe-gusndi-he—the Invulnerable."

"Some title. Can he live up to it?"

Mark passed a hand across his eyes. "They say he can pull his intestines out of his mouth, yard by yard, and swallow them again. He's a *diyi*, a big medicine man. He can draw fire from the sun. He is supposed to have a medicine, or battle shirt which is impervious to bullets, knives, and arrows."

"Crap!"

The scout raised himself on one elbow. His voice was steady, not that of a drunken man. "Don't kid yourself, Holt. You're too intelligent for that. Maybe the stories are false, but the fact of the matter is that he has the ear of the Butcher! The Apaches believe in him because he has proved himself to them. You can't laugh off a man like him, and don't attempt it!"

The scout lay down again. Holt reached for a bottle and took a stiff drink. In a little while he heard Mark Lewis stirring again. "Something happened here tonight, Mark," said Holt. He told the scout of the attack at the bastion and what had happened at the guardhouse.

"Good God," said Lewis. "You might have gotten some information from that Mexican."

"Too late now."

Mark sat up. "Well, dammit, give me a drink! It's a cinch I won't have to help you question him tomorrow anyway."

Holt passed the bottle to him. The scout drank and gave the bottle back to Holt. Holt sat up. "For God's sake, Mark, I'm in a mess on this post. The Butcher seems to be getting a damned good hold on our short hairs. I need your help. Lay off of the bottle until we get him accounted for and I'll finance you to the biggest drunk in the history of Arizona Territory!"

Lewis laughed shortly. "All right, Holt. I'm sorry I let you down. You can depend on me."

Later, when the scout was asleep, Holt lay awake looking at the dim ceiling. *Dobe-gusndi-he*—the Invulnerable. The Butcher was menace enough and deadly dangerous like a crazed dog. But the Prophet was unknown to Holt, and yet his menace seemed even greater for its unknown quality. Together the two of them, Butcher and Prophet, might sweep the White-Eyes from the Territory of Arizona in a flood of blood such as had never been seen before in that bloody arena of warfare between white man and Apache.

CHAPTER TWELVE

H undreds of square miles were darkened by the twin shadows of the Butcher and the Prophet. The Apaches moved more boldly now. The hit-and-run raids increased, and the troops always seemed to be chasing a will-o'-the-wisp, for wherever they moved, the Apaches struck somewhere else. They struck harder each time, let more blood, and garnered more loot.

Veteran commanders began to sweat blood. They had always been at a disadvantage in fighting in the Apache country.

They didn't know it as well as the enemy did; the enemy could live in it without carrying heavy loads of supplies and water; the enemy gathered together, struck hard, then vanished into the hills or deserts, singly or in small groups, to assemble again by their efficient means of communication, far from the scene of their last raid, ready for yet another, and another...

Fort Guthrie was a smoldering mass of fear, anger, helplessness, and hatred. There were twenty-eight freshly mounded graves in the post cemetery, with their white headboards, neatly stenciled with name, rank, and organi-zation. Twenty-six of them marked the last resting places of the men of A and F Companies who had died in the ambushes planned, without doubt, by the Butcher. One was that of the guard who had been shot to death in the guardhouse the night of the alert. One was that of Captain Frank Carberry, who, after twenty years of service, none of which had placed him in action against an enemy, white or red, had been ordered by General Talbot McAllister to take out a patrol of F Company in the general direction of Piloncillo Rock. Carberry was an expert on administration, supply, and courts-martial, but he had not led a detachment of men since Jube Early had raided the very suburbs of Washington in 1864 with his ragged foot cavalry. Captain Carberry had led a scratch detachment of War Office clerks, convalescent soldiers, militiamen, and government employees into one of the forts that ringed Washington. After one night of sleeping in the open, they had heard the distant muttering of cannon when the wind shifted, until the fighting was over, and Captain Carberry led his unshaven command back into the city and returned to his desk in the War Office.

Carberry had been the innocent victim of the hatred of one man for another—that of Talbot McAllister against Holt Downey. McAllister had called for the patrol. Downey had remonstrated against weakening the post. McAllister had insisted. Colonel Fleming had said he had no line officers to spare, and, in fact, F Company had no officers at all because of the deaths of Mr. McAllister and Captain DeVoto. McAllister had therefore combed the post, found bumbling Frank Carberry happily and drowsily seated among his papers, and had ordered Fleming to send Carberry out into the field. Carberry had had a simple solution, however. So simple. He shot himself through the mouth while the patrol waited for him on the parade ground. The blood did not drip on Carberry's beloved papers, for he had wisely removed them from his desk top, filed them, and covered the issue desk with old newspapers. Captain Carberry was a very efficient and neat officer.

Holt Downey was back in the old powder magazine. The site of the sagging structure was a festering sore in the flesh of Fort Guthrie. There was no doubt that the magazine should be moved to a bigger and better structure, farther away from the post proper. But the post was short of men. The time of the year had come when it wasn't too long before the full fury of the summer heat would be upon them, and men would suffer hell digging in such weather unless they were lucky enough to suffer heat exhaustion or sunstroke instead.

Feet grated on the path just outside the magazine. Holt turned to see Mark Lewis. The scout was chewing an un-lighted cigar. "Cool in here anyway, Holt," he said. "Comparatively cool, that is."

Holt nodded. He sat down on a box of paper cartridges ball, musket, caliber .58, for which there wasn't a weapon on the post. "I'm surprised McAllister hasn't been yelling for the new magazine to be built."

"What's wrong with this one?"

"It's too old. Look at the props. It isn't regulation to have it this close to the post anyhow."

"So?"

"It should be moved farther out on the mesa. In fact, most of these ammunition and powder stores are obsolete."

The scout's dark eyes peered into the gloom. "You mean none of this stuff would go up if it had a spark?"

"Sure it would! It's got plenty of life for that. I don't like it, Mark."

The scout squatted near the door and moved his ragged cigar from one corner of his mouth to the other. "Sure would make a blow," he said.

Holt walked to the door and looked toward the post.

Just in line with the magazine was the quartermaster warehouse, with the stables and corrals beyond it, while on the other side was Headquarters Row. If the magazine blew it might take the warehouse with it and kill many of the horses and mules, and Headquarters Row would take a shellacking too.

He saw the fluttering of a dress on the little side porch of Colonel Fleming's quarters. It was Kathy Nolan. General McAllister had taken over Fleming's quarters and the colonel had moved in with Captain Carberry, senior officer on the post next to himself, and now Carberry was dead.

"There's a real woman for you, Holt," said Lewis quietly.

Holt glanced sideways. "Is that a figure of speech, or do you mean it specifically, Mark?"

The scout leaned against the crumbling side of the magazine entrance. "She was too fine a catch for young McAllister," he said quietly. "Every time I thought of him pawing over that body it made me a little sick."

"Talk about something else, Mark. This isn't like you."

The dark eyes were thinly veiled. "You mean you haven't thought of her yourself?"

"Have you?"

Lewis chewed on his cigar butt, then spat it out. "Frankly, Yes."

"You're at least twenty years older than she is, Mark."

The scout eyed Holt. "Older than that, Holt. But that's not important, is it? She's a real woman. The kind of woman a man would fight for. The kind of a woman who would stand beside a man through thick and thin, for better or for worse, as they say."

A hawk's shadow flitted over the bare yellow ground in front of the magazine. Holt looked at the bird, floating motionless on the wind. "You were married once, weren't you, Mark?"

"I never said that."

Holt glanced at him. "Yes, you did. That time in Tucson."

There was no answer from the scout. There was no expression on his face. Mark's drunken speech that night had bared his soul, probably to the only man he still trusted and liked, Holt Downey. His wife had been beautiful, talented, shapely, and an outright bitch. It was what had started him drinking, or so he had insisted. But she had been out of his life for years, at least out of sight and knowledge, but her ghost still lived with him. A vicious, vindictive ghost.

"You think a woman like Kathy Nolan could make you forget your wife?"

Mark slapped a hand against the crumbling wall of the magazine and watched the mortar drop to the ground. "Perhaps," he said, "although, if I ever got another woman, it would be more like an Annie Tulvis."

"Is she that bad, Mark?"

"I never said she was bad, Holt. I've always had a theory about women. Nothing new really. It's older than recorded history. The ancients practiced polygamy and found it good. The Indians still do. Why couldn't a man like you, or me, for that matter, have several women? One for each mood, each desire we have buried in our subconscious. One for the fireside, leisurely talk about home and family, deep love, and children. Another, a wanton, wild and passionate, but still a lover. Perhaps another to run the household, steady, patient, wise, always there when you needed her for comfort. I could go on."

Holt smiled. "I'll bet you could. If you had to have one woman for each mood of yours, Mark, you'd have more wives than Solomon, or, on a lesser scale, Brigham Young."

There was a slight fire of anger in the dark eyes. "And why not? Man should be supreme! No woman should ever be allowed to torture him as my wife..." His voice trailed off. Then he stood up straight and brushed the mortar dust from his dark suit. "Solomon was a mighty king! A strong and wise man. So was Brigham Young. There was no weakness, physically or mentally, in those men. And they begot a great many children."

Holt eyed the scout. There was something different about him, something Holt had never seen before—and he had seen this quiet, well-educated man in many moods. "Have you chosen your harem yet, Mark?" he asked, trying to say it jokingly, but knowing he had failed.

Mark Lewis glanced at Kathy Nolan. "She'd make the Number One wife," he said. "A strong, proud woman, who'd love you with everything she had."

"Go on."

"Annie Tulvis too."

"The wanton?"

The dark eyes flicked toward Holt. "In a sense. That woman could love a strong man with a master hand on her. She's never had a break, Holt. Her father is a spineless jellyfish, a stinking bag of flesh and bones trying to act like a man when he should be crawling in the slime."

"You mentioned others."

The scout walked up the little ramp toward the path, then turned. "All in good time, Holt," he said quietly. "All in good time."

Holt watched him walk between headquarters and the warehouse, tipping his hat to Kathy Nolan.

The scout was out of sight when she came down from the porch and walked toward the magazine. She made a pretty picture. The dry wind whipped her skirts about her long shapely legs and pressed the material tightly against the cups of her breasts. Holt, for an instant, wanted to beat it out of there, then he turned and walked into the semidarkness of the magazine. If she wanted to come to him, there was no way of stopping her. The whole post would know about it soon enough.

He heard her light feet on the path and turned as he felt her presence. God, but her eyes had a spell over him! Almost as though his benighted soul could drown in them. Then he knew why he had been in hell in the days since he had first talked to her in the moon-washed bastion. He was in love with her.

"Holt," she said quickly, "I won't take up much of your time."

"You shouldn't have come here. You know how quickly word spreads around a place like this."

"I know," she said.

There was something about her tone, her expression, that was different from that night in the bastion. "What's wrong, Kathy?" he asked quietly.

She cut him short with a quick wave of her right hand. "I didn't come here to talk about us, Holt."

"So? Why *did* you come here?"

"The general is going to leave here before long. I will go with him. In fact, he has ordered every woman at Fort Guthrie to get ready for a quick move. They are to be evacuated to Fort Lowell."

"That's not a bad idea, Kathy."

Her great eyes studied him. "That includes Annie Tulvis, Holt."

"I would expect so!"

Then a chill seemed to creep into the magazine, and he realized what was bothering her. Since that morning when he had gone to Annie Tulvis' quarters to get Joe Caxton, he had known gossip had linked his name with that of the scout's daughter, although he had only seen her a few times since that morning, and then at a distance. He had not spoken to her.

She looked away from him. "I have asked the general to send me back East, Holt."

"What did he say about that?"

She shrugged. "He didn't commit himself. He said he

would take me back there himself when he was ready, but that might not be for some time."

"How so?"

"He has wired to General Sherman, requesting a field command here in this department for the purpose of running El Carnicero to earth."

Holt shook his head. "He knows nothing of Apache fighting, Kathy."

"He is a good soldier, Holt."

"I'll agree. Against white men. But he doesn't know what he's up against."

"Last night he spent two hours telling Colonel Fleming what fools the officers in this department are. The defeats this garrison has suffered. He went on and on."

"I can imagine," said Holt dryly.

"I think he is sure that he can get the field command. He has also asked for additional troops from departments not affected by Indian troubles."

Holt smiled wryly. "That should be an interesting effort."

She leaned against one of the thick balks that supported the sagging roof. "Mr. Ronald Sturgis has requested that he lead the escort which will convey the women, and the general, to Fort Lowell."

"Him! Good God!" I beg your pardon, Kathy!"

She smiled a little. "Mr. Sturgis has attached his dougherty wagon to a star, Holt. The star of General McAllister. Perhaps he thinks he can replace DeWitt in the general's affections."

"Mr. Sturgis is ambitious. He can't wait for the slow grinding of the army mill. What did the general say about Sturgis leading the escort?"

"He was noncommittal. I do know this: He means to strip this post of every man he can take with him as escort."

"For the women, of course?"

She shook her head. "For himself, Holt. He left Washington because he was ordered out here to duty. He was politicking and had many friends. President Grant takes care of his friends, and Talbot McAllister isn't one of them. I think General McAllister wants to take this field command he has requested so that he can reap some glory out here, as well as to avenge his murdered son."

"Murdered?"

Her great eyes lifted to hold his. "That is what he calls you, Holt—murderer."

"Is his revenge to be on El Carnicero or on me? If I had not arrived at the Barrera Escarpment, DeWitt McAllister would have surely been killed outright—or worse, captured and tortured."

She studied him. "But you did kill him, Holt."

He looked away. "This is a hard and bloody game, Kathy. You've seen enough in the short time you've been here to know what we are up against. We get to be savages too. I've seen things done by El Carnicero's warriors, *and* squaws, that..." His voice trailed off.

He turned, and she was close behind him. He placed his hands at the small of her back and drew her close. She bent back her head and closed her eyes, and he kissed her. Instantly he knew he had started a fire that nothing but having her entirely would ever quench.

They clung together and his hands passed over her firm, yet soft upper body. Her breathing became harsh and erratic. She turned her head away from him. "I'll hate myself for this," she said.

"You know what it means?"

"I am not a child, Holt. But we must wait! You know the general. To him I'm still a chattel, a possession, which was to have been his son's and now is his. My desires are nothing to him. He couldn't fathom my belonging to any other man but his son, and certainly not you."

He placed a hand beneath her chin and turned her face to his. "He doesn't mean anything to me, Kathy."

"No? He can ruin your career."

"There are other things."

She shook her head. "Not for you, Holt. *Never for you.*"

A shadow darkened the doorway. Holt looked over her head into the taut face of Mr. Ronald Sturgis. "Well?" he asked. He could never disguise the dislike on face or in voice for Ronald Sturgis.

"The general sent me to find two people, Captain Downey. I'm in luck. I never expected to find the two of them *together.*"

She turned slowly. "What does he want of us?"

He smiled. "I'm not sure that he wants to speak to both of you together, or about the same matter."

She brushed the mortar dust from her clothing and walked past him. He gallantly touched the brim of his forage cap and bent himself a little from the waist. His eyes followed her shapely hips as she walked up the ramp and out of sight. "God," he said throatily. "What a filly! Lithe in the flanks and slender in the pasterns! What a partner for a bedroom canter, trot and gallop!"

The big hands clamped on his shoulders, whirled him around, gripped the front of his neat and expensive shirt, and slammed his head back against the wall so hard that loose mortar pattered down on his forage cap and shoulders. "Captain!" he husked.

Once again his head slammed back against the wall and he felt the blood beginning to trickle down the back of his neck. The hard gray-green eyes were inches from his and he could have sworn to God he saw racing red flecks in them. His breath would not come. He opened his mouth and could not speak, and he knew he was facing death or a merciless beating. "The general!" he managed to gasp.

The mad light went out of Holt's eyes. He brushed his hands against the front of his shirt as though to rid them of some unclean mess. "Mister," he said softly, "you ever say anything like that again in my presence, and I'll break your goddamned neck like a match stick!"

Holt walked from the magazine.

Sturgis shivered a little. He walked unsteadily to one of the balks that supported the roof and leaned against it. Then fear made him vomit and he felt the weak urine trickling down his shaking legs.

CHAPTER THIRTEEN

The general was in his favorite stance in front of the great map on the wall of the colonel's quarters. Colonel Milas Fleming had aged since Talbot McAllister had moved in on his little command. Fort Guthrie was isolated and a hellhole for most of the year, blazing hot in the summer, windy cold in the winter, but it was a good place for a man to wait out the last few years of his service. Certainly the Apaches were dangerous. They always were, even near places like Tombstone and Tucson. But he had been lucky in getting good junior officers who made good patrols, grappled with the Apaches, and, although they did not defeat them, at least kept them in check to embellish Milas Fleming's long and precise reports rendered to Department Headquarters.

But now Talbot McAllister had moved in, as he usually did. According to regulations he had no authority to take over Fleming's command—but he had. He had no right to order Fleming around like an aide or an orderly—but he had. He had absolutely no authority to take the major part of Fort Guthrie's already inadequate garrison along with him as escort to Fort Lowell—*but he would*.

Talbot McAllister could move into any post, camp, or station and take it over. More than once during the war he had flagrantly disobeyed orders from his superior officers and by the grace of God had won small but brilliant victories, and always at a time when the Union needed such stars to add to its dulling crown. That was why he had steadily climbed the ladder of promotion when more reliable, more brilliant, but less lucky men were bypassed. Even Grant had favored Talbot McAllister for a time, mentioning him in dispatches, giving him excellent commands, helping him along the way, until the war had ended, and Grant had eventually become President. Then it was that Talbot McAllister had overplayed his hand. He was a shrewd politician, but he had always had a bad habit of talking too 'much about what he intended to do, and then doing it. This time he had talked, but before he could move he had been swiftly shunted out of Washington, given a post commensurate with his rank, and had received a eulogy in the Washington and New York papers. Such a eulogy that he did not dare fight back against the men who had neatly backwatered him and left him to rot out of the main current of American history.

McAllister turned. "Milas," he said quietly, "I don't like to do this to you, but I must get to Fort Lowell. I can't take the risk of being captured by Apaches. And then, we must consider the fairer sex here at Fort Guthrie." He smiled.

Milas thought of some of the beefy laundresses along Soapsuds Row. "Yes, the fairer sex, General."

McAllister paced back and forth. "You will have enough men left to hold this position, I assure you."

Milas Fleming stood up. "The general doesn't seem to realize that Fort Guthrie was never intended to be a 'defensive' position. Our role has always been to be on the offensive. We cannot—and I must repeat that—*we cannot,* fulfill our role in the general plans of this department by remaining on the defensive. Our strength is in our patrols, small though they are."

"Yes, the patrols—my son ..." McAllister's voice trailed off.

"Mr. McAllister either disobeyed his orders or was lured into an ambush, sir."

The icy eyes lanced at Fleming. "You talk like Mr. Downey, sir!"

"Mr. Downey happened to be right, General!"

The general waved a brusque hand. "That is neither here nor there, sir!"

The colonel flushed. He had been a man once. At the Academy he had been undefeated in some of the rough-and-tumble scraps forced on plebes by bigger upperclassmen. His war record, although never distinguished, had at least been honorable. In actual fact, Milas Fleming was a far better officer than most people thought he was, but because of his droning voice and his rather unimposing appearance, he had always been underrated, even by his superiors. In time Milas Fleming had begun to accept their opinions of him at face value, allowing less capable officers to forge ahead of him. Milas Fleming lacked spark and daring. Perhaps that was why he had stayed back in the mire watching men like Talbot McAllister rise in the profession.

McAllister paced back and forth. "I'll need a full company of cavalry. Four wagons for supplies and impedimenta. One wagon for infantry, a squad at least, two wagons for the women of the post, and a dougherty for Miss Nolan and myself."

Fleming opened his mouth and then shut it. McAllister was taking exactly half of the wagons allotted to the garrison, wagons for which Milas Fleming himself would be held accountable.

McAllister turned away and said, "I am afraid that I

must take Captain Downey with me to command my escort, Milas."

Fleming stared at him. "But, sir! I've lost four of my officers in the past few days! If you take Mr. Sturgis as your aide, which you mentioned earlier today, and Captain Downey as your escort commander, I will be stripped of officers as well as of men. Really, you can hardly do a thing like this, sir!"

McAllister stood up. "Just what do you propose to do about it, Milas?"

Fleming drew himself up. "I will have to send in a report of this matter to headquarters."

"I can counteract that, Milas."

"I am sure you can, but I insist on doing so."

McAllister walked to one of the windows and looked toward the sagging powder magazine. "Not to change the subject, Milas, but wasn't that powder magazine to be moved farther out onto the mesa?"

"I am afraid that will have to be included in my report. That is, in addition to the report on the loss of my son and the loss of two other officers and twenty-four enlisted men virtually within the limits of post boundaries. The report, of course will include subject matter relative to the conduct of Captain Holt Downey. The entrance of Apaches right onto the post. The murder of an enlisted man in the guardhouse, the escape of two Apache prisoners, and so on and so on and so on ..."

The sweltering office was very quiet. The wind rustled and whispered about the eaves of the building and slapped the flagpole halyards in a steady rhythm.

Talbot McAllister yawned a little, covered his mouth, and then spoke over his shoulder. "How many years do you have left before retirement, Milas?"

"Three, general."

His timing was perfect. Talbot McAllister, as well as being a child of fortune, had the rare gift of perfect timing.

"The Benzine Board has been washing out quite a few junior officers, who, for one reason or another, mostly inefficiency, do not come up to the standards of the service. Just before I left Washington I heard that the eyes of the Board have lifted up a little. Raising their sights, so to speak. Colonels and generals are beginning to feel the strain, Milas."

A fly buzzed into the office and circled about Milas Fleming, but he made no move to brush it away.

"Do you understand, Milas?"

"Yes, sir."

Talbot McAllister turned with a quick smile lighting his usually austere face. "I knew you would! Now, about the manuscript?"

"It stays here, General."

Their eyes clashed, and Talbot McAllister knew he had gone too far. "All right, Milas!" He looked at the clock. "I sent for Captain Downey. Where is he?"

"Mr. Sturgis is looking for him, sir."

McAllister looked toward the magazine. He stiffened a little as he saw Kathy Nolan walk from it, to be followed a moment or two later by the lean, striding figure of Holt Downey.

"General McAllister, Sir," said Milas Fleming softly.

He did not turn. "Yes."

"I have often wondered if the general ever had any pastimes or hobbies?"

"Why do you ask?"

"I have never heard of you having any."

"The service is my whole life, Milas." He waved a hand. "There was a time, years ago, as a boy in fact, when I collected insects. You know, mounting them on cotton and displaying them on the walls of my room at home. Very interesting."

"I'm sure it was. May I ask a question about that hobby, sir?"

"Certainly, Milas!"

There was a moment's pause. "Were those insects *dead* before you thrust pins through them, Talbot?"

The general whirled in time to see Milas Fleming walk out of the door of the office just as Holt Downey's boot heels popped steadily on the worn boards of the ramada porch.

CHAPTER FOURTEEN

The sour voices of the noncoms crackled through the cold air of pre-dawn, like a heavy-booted man walking through thin sheets of scum ice. Now and then a mule brayed loudly in protest at being harnessed or being loaded with the clumsy issue pack saddle. Lights showed in yellow rectangles through the windows of the quarters and the mess hall. Babies cried from Soapsuds Row and the cold wind keened across the top of the mesa, swirling up sheets of gritty dust, rolling tumbleweeds in frantic flight through the dimness and banging the doors and shutters of Fort Guthrie in a wild discordance.

The wagons were lined up and last items were being pitched over the tailgates to be stowed by cursing troopers. Other troopers led their saddled mounts out onto the parade ground. The strong odor of issue coffee mingled with the acrid smell of mule and horse stallings. Frantic mothers screamed at the kids they had in sight and screamed still louder for those they couldn't find.

Holt Downey lighted a cigar as he leaned against the wall next to the door of his quarters. He looked up as Ben Loris appeared through the darkness. "If the general had any idea of secretiveness in this departure, he sure has lost it now," he said dryly.

Ben nodded. "A deaf man could hear this uproar. But *Talbot* thinks you will be well away and off the mesa before the sun comes up. He's over at Headquarters now getting a map talk from Mark Lewis."

"I hope to God he listens. I had a hell of a time with him yesterday when he told me I was to command his escort. I don't get it, Ben. Why me? He hates my guts."

Loris shrugged. "He wants to get through, Holt." He grinned. "Mr. Ronald Sturgis is as sour as a bag of lemon balls. He figured *he* was going to lead the escort, then go on as McAllister's aide on this forthcoming campaign of the general's. Don't turn your back on him, Holt."

"I wish you were going along, Ben. Isn't it about time you were relieved from the adjutancy and returned to a line company? Mine, for example?"

The tall adjutant shrugged again. He looked about the post. "I'd like to go, but at the same time, Colonel Fleming needs experienced officers here, Holt. I couldn't very well walk out of here and let him face this mess alone."

"You don't think the Apaches would attack, do you?"

Ben Loris reached into Holt's pocket and took out the silver cigar case. He scraped a match down the adobe wall of the quarters and lighted the short six he had selected from the case. "Mark Lewis and Yancey Tulvis went out yesterday afternoon. They came in half an hour ago. Not a sign of Apaches. Mark reported it to the general. Said it was as quiet as a graveyard in New England."

"Nice simile," said Holt dryly.

"Yancey Tulvis scouted out toward Caballo Wash and said he had seen nothing."

"He usually does."

Loris leaned back against the wall. "Fleming is as sour

as Sturgis. He told me a little while ago that he wanted loopholes cut into any of the newer buildings that didn't have them. He said that no patrols would go out until he either got his men back from McAllister's escort, or troops to replace them."

"That's strictly against orders, Ben."

"I know that! But what can he do? If he sends out patrols he weakens the post. You know well enough what would happen if El Carnicero struck here while you were gone. We wouldn't have a chance if we let patrols go out. I agree with Old Milas."

"He's not a bad sort."

"No. That's why I'd almost rather stay here than go with you. The Old Man needs help. He isn't as keen as he used to be—not that he was ever a brilliant soldier— but I know he can hold this post until hell freezes."

Holt relighted his cigar. "I'm sure of that. But it won't help him much even if he does. He's supposed to carry out offensive patrols to keep the Apaches in check. The last few days have been damned rough on him. He can't send out patrols and weaken his garrison; yet his orders are to carry out patrols."

"He's damned if he does, and damned if he doesn't."

Holt straightened up and spat. "McAllister's rising star has burned him in cold light," he said quietly.

It was almost time to go. They had a good two hours before the sun would tip the eastern ranges. In that time they would be off the mesa top, through the winding canyon which led to the road to the southeast, and under cover where they would remain until dusk. Holt had insisted on night traveling. He had also insisted that they leave the post at such a time that the Apaches would not realize that they had left. Mark Lewis had said there were no Apaches in the vicinity and that was enough for Holt. No man knew them better than Mark Lewis. He could feel them, he had often quietly told Holt on patrols. He had never been wrong.

Ben slapped Holt on the shoulder. "I'll scout about and pick up the loose ends, Holt. Give you time to get your gear together and do a little quiet thinking before all hell breaks loose."

"Thanks, Ben." He watched the tall adjutant stride through the darkness like a great ungainly stork. A good man, almost like a brother. He had, in fact, replaced Holt's kid brother Neville in Holt's affections. Holt walked inside and sat down on his bare cot. "Neville," he said quietly. He smashed a big fist down on the edge of the cot.

It was dark in the room. He leaned back against the wall and closed his eyes. There was a feeling of foreboding in him. Talbot McAllister had no use for him other than as a leader of his escort. The man let nothing stand in his way when he saw what he wanted in his next stride on to greater successes.

Someone tapped on the rear door. In a reflex action Holt was up off the cot and had his hand on his pistol butt "Who is it?"

"Annie Tulvis, Captain. Can I talk to you?"

"This isn't the place, Annie."

She laughed dryly. "Where is the place? This is like a beehive out here."

He opened the door. She came in, and her feminine aura was strong in his nostrils. She threw back the shawl she had over her head. "I've been trying to talk to you but you always seem to be busy."

He smiled a little. "It seems as though we have a movement on, Miss Tulvis, and I'm the escort commander."

"I know. That's why I came to talk with you."

"I'm listening."

"I've been ordered to leave the post."

"All of the women have."

She looked up at him, and although it was dark he could almost see the deep tragedy in her eyes. "For safety, Captain. That wasn't what I was told, about me, that is."

"So?"

She looked away, "They said I was undesirable."

He couldn't help but laugh. She stared up at him with fists clenched below her full breasts. "You too?" she demanded fiercely.

He placed his hands on her shoulders and they met bare warm flesh rather than cloth material. "I didn't mean it that way, Annie," he said gently. "I mean that you *are* desirable. Tell me more about this thing."

"It was all the talk. First about Joe Caxton staying in my place, then you coming over there. You know how it is in a place like this."

"Yes—I certainly do."

"Then it was my father. He got to be one of the worst. The things he says about me."

His hands tightened on her shoulder. He had wondered how a polecat like Yancey Tulvis had ever begotten a child like Annie.

"I didn't want to travel with the general's party, Captain. They'd look at me like I was a hurdy-gurdy girl from Tombstone or Tucson. I couldn't stand that!"

"I'll be there, Annie."

"Yes—I know—but it's the women I fear worse than the men. The things they can do to another woman! They're not like men. Men have it out, one way or another, and settle it. But women never let up. Particularly when they themselves are little better than the trash they think I am?"

"What is it you want to do, then?"

"Stay here!"

He shook his head. "You know the orders. This garrison will be greatly weakened. If the Apaches attack here, and take the place, you'll wish ten thousand times over that you had suffered the jibes and looks of the other women for the few days' trip to Fort Lowell."

"I'm not afraid."

"I know. But you'll have to go. Either way, for your safety, or because they say you are undesirable, you'll have to go with us."

Her shoulders slumped a little. She was a proud, fearless soul, perhaps a little tarnished, but she had a lot of—"

"Someone had to make a specific accusation."

"Who specifically said you were undesirable? The other women?"

"They agree, but I don't think any of them went to the colonel to make the accusation." She laughed. "A good many of them wouldn't want their own pasts looked into, I can assure you, Captain."

"Someone had to make a specific accusation."

She looked up at him again. "I'm not sure. I heard it was Lieutenant Loris."

"I can assure you it wasn't him, Annie."

"My father said it was him, Captain."

"Ben? I can't believe it!"

"That's what my father said, Captain. He was drunk when he said it, and he always blurts out the truth when he's drunk."

"It's a cinch he doesn't do that when he's sober."

She looked away again and her body shook a little. "I came back here to be with him. I have no one else. It's been a long time since I've seen him, or wanted to see him. But I got tired of the life I was leading. I thought maybe I could make a home for him here where no one knew me. I should have known better."

"Then it is best for you to leave. Stick it out on the trip. You'll be all right."

"I hate to admit how I feel about those women, Captain. But I'm afraid of them."

He lifted her head by cupping a hand beneath her chin. "Miss Nolan will be with us. I'll ask her to take you as her maid, Annie. Then no one can bother you."

"But she's a lady!"

He smiled a little. "Certainly she's a lady! That's why I know she'd take you as her maid."

"But the general wouldn't like that."

"The general has no claim on her now that his son is dead. Miss Nolan is a lot like you, Annie."

"How you talk! She's a real lady! Not like me!"

He grinned. "Your spirits are alike. Don't worry. She'll take you. If by any chance she doesn't, I'll take you as *my* personal maid."

She smiled quickly in the darkness, and he could see her oval, olive-skinned face, with the deep soft lips. The girl *was* beautiful. No wonder men chased after her. "I'd like that," she said fiercely.

Now the mood had changed, from fright, and later humor, to one of fierce passion, and the words of Mark Lewis came quickly to Holt Downey. *"That woman could love a strong man with a master hand on her."*

She pressed close to him and slid her arms about his corded neck, drawing herself up on her toes to reach for his lips. Her lips were warm and soft, sweet and promising. She looked up at him. "You can have anything you want," she said huskily.

"I wasn't bargaining, Annie."

She stepped back and stared at him. "No?" she said in a low voice. "Men always bargain. Even a man like you, Holt Downey. What do *you* want?"

A minute fled past. Then she reached up and began to unbutton her dress swiftly while her eyes held his. In a moment her dress was open to the waist and she was throwing it back over her smooth brown shoulders. Her unhampered breasts swung a little as she worked at the dress to get it free from her body. "No, Annie," he said. It had been a long time since he had had a woman, nor had the desire really been in him after he had heard of the death of Emily Locke at the greasy hands of El

Carnicero. Annie Tulvis was a real woman. Mark Lewis hadn't been wrong when he had named her for one of the wives in his mythical harem, next to Kathy Nolan. *"A wanton. Wild and passionate, but still a lover,"* he said.

"This is not the time and place, Annie," he said, and he felt like a double-damned fool when he said it.

She came close to him and raised her face to his. "You mean that?"

"Certainly!"

She slid her arms about his neck again and he could feel her naked upper body warmly through his thin shirt. *"Gracias,"* she said. "You won't think poorly of me for offering myself to you in payment?" She hesitated, and her body shook uncontrollably. "After all, Holt, it's all I have to offer."

He lifted her face to his and kissed her and felt her press against him like a child that has been lost and then found.

The front door of the quarters banged open and yellow light from a lantern flooded the room. Holt looked over the head of Annie Tulvis into the yellow eyes of Yancey Tulvis. Beyond the scout he could see Ben Loris and Mark Lewis. "For Cris' sakes!" said Yancey Tulvis. "We been lookin' all over for Annie! She been here alla time too!" The girl stepped back and swiftly pulled up her dress and a flood of blood darkened her face. She stepped behind Holt. Yancey spat into the fireplace and hurriedly wiped his slack mouth with the back of a hand. "They been lookin' for you too, Cap'n." His evil eyes flicked at Holt and then at the naked brown shoulder of his daughter which showed behind Holt. "Didn't know you was whorin' with Annie there. But pleasure before business, eh, Cap'n?"

The fist hit him so hard that the lantern flew out of the room and smashed at Mark Lewis' feet. Tulvis struck the wall with the back of his head and slid down to the floor. Holt heard the door which led to the wash row open and close behind him. Annie was gone.

Holt picked up his campaign hat and placed it on his head. He walked past the unconscious scout and out into the darkness of the parade ground. The parade was crowded with people, civilians and soldiers alike. Those who were going and those who would see them off. There wasn't any doubt that most of them had heard the loud-mouth of Yancey Tulvis condemning his own daughter.

He walked toward the headquarters building. A woman stood beside the dougherty wagon watching him. It was Kathy Nolan. He stopped and looked at her. "Well?" he asked.

"It was only yesterday that I was sure about you, Holt," she said quietly. "You didn't waste much time. But you might have timed this latest conquest of yours a little better. It's somewhat below your usual skill in such matters, isn't it?"

There was no one really close to them. The wind lifted her traveling skirt and whipped it about her long, graceful legs. "You talk like a little fool," he said quietly.

"You would say that."

It was no use. They would soon move out. Perhaps to meet El Carnicero in bloody combat—and in that combat he might die. He wanted to tell her the truth, but there wasn't enough time. Still, Annie Tulvis depended on him. "She needs your help, Kathy," he said. "They're driving her from the post. She asked me to have you take her as your maid. Only to Fort Lowell."

For a moment she stared at him and then she laughed. "This is priceless," she said.

"Perhaps."

"You're a strange man, Holt."

"You don't have to tell me. Will you take her? She needs your help."

She brushed back a stray wisp of her honey-colored

hair. "Let him who is without sin amongst ye cast the first stone," she said quietly. "Yes, Holt, I'll take her."

"Thanks," he said. He touched his hand to the brim of his hat and walked toward headquarters. Her eyes followed him, and somehow the bright light which had always showed in them was gone now.

CHAPTER FIFTEEN

The eastern sky was touched with the pale pearl light of dawn. A sentry at Post Number Five, near the quartermaster warehouse of Forth Guthrie, shifted his heavy Springfield from his right to his left shoulder. The post was quiet except for the cold wind which swept across the mesa. It was always blowing at Guthrie.

The sentry glanced at the eastern sky. Christ, but it was cold! He figured he had about fifteen minutes more of sentry duty, then he could doss down in the guardhouse until it was time for breakfast.

He eyed the low, sagging hump of the post magazine where it stood above the dun earth like a half-buried turtle. Somehow it looked different from the way it usually did. He walked a little closer to it. The ramp that led down into the doorway seemed a little hazy. Then he knew what it was. "Corporal of the Guard! Post Number Five!" he yelled at the top of his voice. "Fire in the magazine!" He turned to run.

There was a dull rumbling noise and then the roof of the magazine seemed to lift slowly upward like the lid on a Dutch oven raised by a gigantic, unseen hand. There was a coughing roar, and the roof and sides of the magazine flew upward and outward. A mass of gas and flame shot toward the warehouse, engulfing the racing sentry. It struck the warehouse wall and collapsed it, then shattered the stable walls, burying screaming horses and mules inside. The colonel's quarters leaned over lazily, then dropped flat like a house of cards. A ton of stone and earth alighted squarely on F Company's barracks, collapsing the thick earthen roof, burying what was left of F Company in a gigantic mound.

A huge stone came through the roof of the bakehouse, killing the baker, and smashed the big cast-iron stove. Blazing coals scattered across the floor, danced into the coal box, set fire to the wooden table, and lighted the apron of the dead baker. The corporal of the guard and three men got as far as the middle of the parade ground when the sky seemed to darken just above them and a thick blanket of earth and stone smashed them to the ground.

The post area was lighted in a hellish orange-red glow which made the remaining buildings stand out in stark reality like an etching. The flagpole swayed in the blast, then cracked near the base and fell swiftly to brain Sergeant Johanson as he came out of his quarters.

The thunder of the explosion raced across the mesa, struck the serrated hills, then slammed back and forth in the canyons to die muttering away in the dark distance.

A vast undulating ring of smoke rose slowly from what had been Fort Guthrie, and as if it had been a signal, men appeared from the draws and gullies of the mesa edge and from the broken ground to the west, moving swiftly toward the ravaged post. Men with thick manes of hair bound by dingy cloths; wearing flapping buckskin kilts and buckskin moccasins folded down about their knotty calves. They closed in like buzzards on an animal that was still alive but with no strength left to protect itself.

Adjutant Ben Loris saw them first. He had been badly

shaken by the explosions and the left side of his face was smashed and bloody. "Apaches!" he screamed at the top of his voice. His first shot dropped the closest warrior. His second broke the leg of another warrior. He fell back toward headquarters, looking wildly from right to left and then back again for support, but there was no support. Here and there a few moaning men lay scattered on the ground, and other bundles of bloody clothing that had once been men lay about among the shattered debris of the explosion.

His Colt was empty when he reached the steps of *the* ramada, but he had killed three warriors and wounded three others. The bucks closed in on him swiftly, their hard-soled moccasins husking on the dry earth and their kilts flapping steadily.

Beyond the closing ring he saw a lone Apache standing in the center of the parade ground holding a brass-bellied Winchester in his hands. His mane of hair was topped by a matted fur helmet from which protruded two yellow-stained horns. There had been times when Ben Loris had doubted that such a man as El Carnicero existed. He knew now that he did exist.

The lean adjutant went down under a rush of hard-muscled bodies, but they made no effort to gut him, smash his head in, or cut his throat. They lashed him firmly to one of the posts of the ramada. El Carnicero strode forward and spat full into Loris' face, and Ben knew there would be no pity for him when his time came to die slowly under their knives and fires.

After the first flurry of action the post was quiet except for the crackling of the flames in the blazing bake-house and the occasional thudding of a stone war club against the skulls of the wounded and the dying.

Colonel Milas Fleming had been in his office all morning since the general and his escort had left. The explosion had smashed his quarters to the ground and cracked the thick wall between them and the office. A piece of the wall had struck Milas Fleming on the head and he had fallen forward, striking his head on the desk before him. He was still in that position, but conscious, when he noticed how quiet it was. He raised his head and looked full into the face of a man standing just inside the doorway watching him. Milas Fleming knew who it was. Holt Downey had described the man, if he could be called such, a number of times to him. It was the Butcher —El Carnicero.

The colonel's hands tightened on the mass of paper just in front of him. The big clock on the wall ticked steadily, undisturbed by the blast.

There was an issue Colt in the desk drawer just under Milas Fleming's right hand, but somehow he could not move. The basilisk eyes of the Apache had him almost hypnotized. The colonel opened his mouth. "I—" It was as far as he got. He had broken the spell. The big Winchester cracked flatly, driving a puff of smoke toward the officer. The heavy slug smashed into Fleming's mouth and drove his head back. His hands scrabbled on the table, while blood spewed from his mouth to cover his hands and papers; then he fell heavily to the side and struck the floor.

The Apache padded forward and looked down at the officer. He raised his rifle and drove the metal-shod butt down hard on the skull to crush it. He fired a shot into the metal guts of the clock, then methodically searched the office for weapons. The Butcher strode from the office.

The wind began to rise suddenly, rifting the thick smoke over the post. It swirled through the open door of the headquarters office, picked up the sheets of his paperwork, blowing them through the inner office and out through the swinging back door, scurrying them and hurrying them across the mesa top intermingled with tumbleweeds.

The warriors carried the captured weapons from the

post, along with anything else that caught their fancy. A gingham dress, red flannel underdrawers, a brass pot, a child's rag doll, a civilian's bowler hat, anything and everything they wanted. There was no one to stop them. Certainly there was one White-Eye still alive, but he was hardly in a position to bother them, as' they rode west from the burning post, to vanish down the mesa side, leaving a vast caul of smoke as a marker against the brightening sky.

THE general's party was safely situated out of sight in the wide cleft between two flat-topped hills. No one could see the wagons and the animals unless they climbed to the top of those hills, and if they did they'd run into taut-faced troopers and infantrymen who lay hidden amongst the rocks and thorny brush.

There was no noise from the camp, in direct contrast to the din which had existed before the party had left Fort Guthrie. Even the smallest children seemed to know they must keep quiet, for the strange men with the bronze faces and the odd clothing were said to be about.

There were no fires. Movement was to be kept to a minimum so as to prevent the raising of dust.

Holt Downey squatted on a flat rock looking down at the camp. "What do you think, Mark?" he said to the scout.

"We'll be all right. The Apaches would lose too many warriors tryin' to get at us. They wouldn't like that."

Holt nodded. "I'm not worried about this position. It's getting caught out in the open that bothers me."

Mark shifted his unlighted cigar from one side of his mouth to the other. "I know a way we can have maximum cover," he said reflectively. "The way is rough, but it will be safer than the open desert."

"You didn't tell me this before."

The scout smiled. "Seems as though you were a little busy—with Miss Tulvis."

"Shut up about that, Mark!"

The scout placed a hand on Holt's shoulders. "Forgive me," he said.

Holt turned and looked along the mesa wall toward distant Fort Guthrie. "I hope to God the post is safe. It's weak, Mark, too damned weak. If the Butcher knew—"

"He doesn't. There wasn't a sign of Apaches anywhere near the post."

"Lookit that, sir!" called out Sergeant Lambert from the brush.

There was a bright flash of reddish light followed by what looked like an outburst of summer lightning near where the post was situated. It etched the serrated hills blackly against the sky. Then a dull rumbling roar came across the desert.

Holt jumped to his feet and reached for his glasses, then dropped his hand. They would be useless in that light.

"It's near Fort Guthrie," said a trooper.

Mark Lewis studied the smoke rising from the site of the flash. "It *is* Fort Guthrie," he said quietly.

General McAllister came up onto the hilltop. "What is it, Downey?" he asked.

"Possibly an explosion at Fort Guthrie, sir."

"You're sure!"

"Mark Lewis is sure it is."

The general reached for Holt's case and took out the glasses. He raised them and adjusted them. "Yes," he said quietly.

"Shall we go back, sir?"

"Impossible! We are encumbered by too many helpless people."

"Someone should go back, sir," said Holt. "They might need help."

McAllister bit his lower lip. "Send a few men back to see what has happened."

"I'd like to go myself, sir. It won't take long."

"I'll go too," said Mark Lewis.

The general was just about to scupper the idea when he saw the looks on the faces of the watching soldiers. They had messmates back there. It was their regiment. "All right, Downey," he said. "But mind you come back as soon as you have the information necessary for me to make a decision as to what to do."

"Yes, sir!"

The two of them walked down the hill and got their horses. Everyone in the camp was watching them. Some of the women and children had husbands and fathers back there. Nothing was said: there was nothing to say.

They spurred from the camp. Holt saw Kathy Nolan watching them. Just behind her was Annie Tulvis. Holt wondered if Annie was much concerned about her father.

———

MARK LEWIS SHIFTED A LITTLE. "Not a sign of life, Holt," he said at last.

The pall of smoke hung over the fort site, rifted now and then by the dry surging wind. The stench of burning horse and mule flesh mingled with the resinous odor of burning wood and the dry odor of scorched and baking brick and adobe.

They lay in the brush, with their horses concealed in a nearby hollow. Holt wet his dry lips. "It was the magazine," he said quietly. "We can't see the magazine site from here, but look how the colonel's quarters were smashed flat from the magazine side and how the east wall of the warehouse was driven in."

"Yes. You almost forecast that, didn't you?"

"I wish I hadn't."

The sun was warm on their backs. Beyond the area of

smoke-stained sky hung a lone ragged buzzard, held aloft by the wind, hovering a little, waiting, waiting... In a little while more of them would begin to gather, waiting for the fires to die down before they would glide in to clumsy landings on the parade ground for the feast they expected.

Mark Lewis stood up. "I'm going in," he said.

"You're loco!"

The scout waved a hand. "If the Apaches did it, they won't be around now. They don't like to stay near the dead. If they did the job they've been in and out of here long ago. They don't waste time in their killing. You know that."

Holt stood up and levered a round into the chamber of his Spencer repeating carbine. The two tall men walked softly across the dry ground with the stench getting thicker and more cloying in their nostrils, and brassier in their throats.

Then they saw the magazine, or the great bowl-shaped hole where the magazine had been. They saw the blast area. They saw the scattered bodies, and on some of them the curious lopsided looks from the smashed skulls they had suffered before or after the hard deaths they had earned by being frontier soldiers.

Mark Lewis stopped at the edge of the ravaged area and looked out on the parade ground. "Look," he said quietly. "They left one man alive."

Holt saw what they had left. A lean naked body which had been fastened to a cross formed of the flagpole and a splintered piece of timber for the cross arm. Even as they watched, the figure moved. He pulled himself up from a sagging position and then sank again.

Holt raced toward the suffering man. If there were Apaches watching him he didn't care. He had recognized Ben Loris on that crucifix, or what was left of him. Holt dropped his carbine and ripped free from its sheath the heavy knife he carried. He averted his face from Loris and cut through the lashings. He caught the bloody body as it fell.

"It's no use, Holt," said Mark Lewis quietly from behind Holt.

The adjutant had been so mutilated before being crucified that there was no chance of his surviving.

"They weren't satisfied with our Roman way of execution," said the scout. "He would have suffered far more agony if they had just left him to die on the cross."

"For Christ's sake, Mark!"

"Sorry, Holt."

The bloody lips moved. "El Carnicero," said Ben Loris, then he slumped in Holt's arms.

The well of hate for El Carnicero had always been deep and well filled within Holt Downey, but now the venom overflowed and kept on flowing. He stood up and looked down at his best friend, the man who had somehow been sent to replace Holt's brother Neville, who had also died horribly at the hands of the Butcher. The poor wreck at his feet moved a little.

Holt looked at the scout.

"I'll do it, Holt," said Mark Lewis.

Holt picked up his rifle and walked toward headquarters. He walked into the office and saw the body of Milas Fleming and the scattered sheets of manuscript. He had reached the back door when he heard the single sharp crack of the pistol. The hovering buzzards wheeled away as the echo slammed back and forth between the burning buildings.

The two tall men rode to the east and did not look back as the first buzzards coasted in on velvet wings and landed on the parade ground.

CHAPTER SIXTEEN

T he command moved out after dusk, traveling as quietly as possible through the thick hot darkness, led by silent Mark Lewis, who knew that country better than any other·man, with the possible exception of El Carnicero.

A pall of gloom hung over the column and seemed to travel with it. When Holt Downey had broken the news about the destruction of Fort Guthrie and its garrison he knew that lives had been ruined among those women whose husbands had been left behind to man the post. Some of them had begun to develop a strong hatred for General McAllister for taking them from their loved ones. They could at least have died beside them.

Holt Downey led the rear guard. It was the post of greatest danger, in his opinion. With the loss of Fort Guthrie there was nothing behind the column but country now controlled by the Apaches all the way to the distant Colorado. To the north was broken and impassable country. To the east were rugged mountains, waterless and not too well known. Due south was the Spanish Desert, which no man crossed in the summer months. There was one outlet toward safety: the way of maximum cover suggested by Mark Lewis. He had said it would be rough, and Mark Lewis usually understated things. This was surely one of those occasions.

By the time the moon came up two wagon axles had broken. One wagon was patched up, the other abandoned. An hour later another wagon smashed a wheel, blocking the way through a narrow defile in the hot windless hills.

Sweat dripped from the faces of the troopers as they tried to lever up the wagon without unloading it, but it was no use. General McAllister looked down at the wagon from the side of the defile, then looked ahead of the wagon. His dougherty led the lines of vehicles, and just behind it was a wagonload of baggage with a few infantrymen as guards. The remainder of the vehicles were lined up behind the damaged wagon.

Holt Downey crawled under the wagon and felt about with his hands. "It's no use, Lambert," he said at last. "The axle is cracked. Even if we got the wheel on, the axle wouldn't last more than another hour or two. Damn Lewis for leading us this way!"

Lambert spat. "In my opinion we'd have been better off out on the desert."

"Wid an Apache hiding behint ivry bush!" said Monahan.

"That's that damned Irish imagination of yours!"

"I don't need any imagination to know what will happen to us in here, Sergeant dear!"

The trumpeter's words seemed to ring and echo in the moonlit defile. The general shifted his feet and then wiped the sweat from his face. "Captain Downey," he said at last.

Holt crawled from beneath the wagon. "Yes, sir."

"Can't you get that wagon fixed, mister?"

Holt wiped his hands on his dirty trousers. "No, sir. We'll have to dismantle it to get the others through."

A trooper coughed. A mule snorted. Boots shifted on the harsh earth. Every man jack there wanted to pull leather fast and get the hell out of there the quickest way. If the Apaches caught them in there...

"How long will that take, Captain?"

"An hour. Maybe two. The wagon is wedged pretty tightly, sir."

Talbot McAllister looked to the head of the column. "I can't afford to waste that much time, mister."

The eyes swiveled toward the tall lean figure of the general. He rested his hand on the hilt of his sword. "I must get on to Fort Lowell. Captain Downey, I'll go on ahead with my dougherty and baggage wagon. I'll take two squads of troopers and a squad of infantrymen for the wagon."

No one said anything. Disgust was thick in the hot air.

"Mr. Sturgis will take command of my escort. Mr. Lewis will scout for us and lead the way." The general looked at Holt. "Miss Nolan and her *maid* will accompany us, of course."

"Of course," someone said *sotto voce* out of the shadows.

"Who was that?" snapped the general.

A warm breeze whispered up the defile. The general clambered down from his perch and strode toward the head of the column. Holt worked his way alongside the wrecked wagon. "Get started on it, Lambert," he called back.

Mark Lewis was standing at the head of the horses, with his reins looped over his arm and an unlighted cigar in his mouth. "Thought I had better brief you on the route, Holt."

"Thanks," said Holt dryly.

"The rat leaves the sinking ship, is that it?"

"We won't sink, Mark."

The scout smiled, showing even white teeth. "No, Holt. I don't think you'll ever sink." He squatted and traced lines in the moonlit dusk. "Follow this defile to a place where it widens out. Cone-shaped hill on the right. Turn sharp left from the road."

"Road?"

The scout grinned. "Well, track then... Aim for a notch due east. It will look like a solid wall of rock, but you'll see a dark sort of line running down the rock. That's the way into a winding canyon that trends southeast and brings you out near the head of Caballo Wash. You know the way from there."

"Yes. That sonofabitch! Leaving these women and children here in this damned trap!"

"Take it easy, Holt."

Holt stood up and looked up toward the dougherty. The wind was whipping the skirts of a woman who stood near the rear left wheel looking toward the two men. It was Kathy Nolan.

Lewis wiped the sweat from his face, took a fresh cigar from his case, and thrust it into his mouth. He chewed at it for a moment. "I'll get rid of McAllister and come back to give you a hand, Holt."

"Gracias, Mark. You're *muy hombre."*

Lewis laughed dryly. "I'm glad you think so."

"If it wasn't for you and those two women, *and* the good enlisted men you have riding with you, I'd like to see the Butcher catch up with Talbot McAllister."

"Take it easy, Holt! That's damned fool talk for a professional officer!"

Holt spat dryly. "If he's an example of a professional officer I'm not so sure I want to continue in the service."

The dark eyes studied Holt. "You will. There's a long road ahead of you in the service, Holt, if you live."

"The odds are piling up against that eventuality."

"Maybe so. With one or two exceptions, Holt, I think you are the man El Carnicero fears more than any other army officer in the Territory."

"How can you know that?"

The scout shrugged. "I've heard rumors."

Holt grinned quickly. "The Prophet been talking to you?"

Lewis took the reins from his arm and swung up on his horse. "No," he said quietly, "but if he had talked to me I would have listened."

"You still believe in this mysterious 'Prophet,' Mark?"

The dark eyes again studied Holt. "I do, Holt. And you had better believe in him too. He's as much of an enemy to you, and your kind, as El Carnicero is. Perhaps even more of an enemy, for El Carnicero may be killed in battle, while the Prophet will go on forever."

"The Invulnerable?"

Lewis nodded. "The Invulnerable. Adios, amigo!" And he kneed his horse away from Holt to join the rest of McAllister's party.

Holt watched them pull out. They could make good time now. Much of the baggage had been heaved out of the wagon to let infantrymen ride. If the wagon broke down the infantrymen could march at the pace of the horsemen and the dougherty, or be left behind, as Talbot McAllister left behind anything or anybody he had used to sufficiency and required no longer.

Then they were gone, and the defile was empty in the moonlight with a wraith of pale dust slowly settling on the rutted track. Holt put his hat on. Part of him had left the defile along with Kathy Nolan. He wondered if he would ever get it back, or even if he wanted it.

They pulled out as the moon went on the wane, leaving the pieces of the wagon scattered along the sides of the defile ahead of a litter of useless impedimenta and surplus baggage. Holt led the way at a steady pace, keeping his men close to him, with Corporal Donigan leading out as scout with two other troopers.

The wheels rumbled on the hard earth, mingled with the thudding of the hoofs. Dust rose steadily and hung in the windless air. There was a feeling of unholy haste in the command, but every one of them knew they could not afford to abandon a steady route march. The way was unknown, but the threat of the Apaches wasn't.

Hands grew greasy with cold sweat where they clutched carbine stocks. Heads swiveled from side to side, almost like automatons, as every gully, boulder, and bush silvered by moonwash was scanned for crouching warriors. It was getting cold, and the cold was aided and abetted by the icy fear of death which hovered over the slow-moving column.

———

It was dawn when they debouched from the track toward the notch on the horizon. Due east, Lewis had said. Holt was scouting ahead now, with Trumpeter Monahan riding just to his left and behind him.

The canyon widened out, and in the center of an oval area, ringed by boulders, there seemed to be some sort of dark growth covering the ground. An alien sort of vegetation in a country where only the hardy ocotillo and greasewood seemed to thrive.

"Holy Mother!" said Monahan suddenly.

Holt rode forward, keeping his eyes on the heights, until he was close enough to see for sure what was inside the rock oval, something he dreaded to see.

It was quiet in the shallow canyon, except for the faint rustling of the morning wind through the growths. It was quiet because the dead men in the rock oval could not greet the two men who sat their horses and looked down at them. Monahan's bay shied and snorted. "Quiet, Nelly!" he said.

The dead men looked peaceful enough. There had been no mutilation and their uniforms were untouched; but not a weapon showed about them, and only four dead mules lay up ahead with great gouges carved into their dusty flanks. Apaches are partial to sweet mule meat.

Monahan took off his battered campaign hat. "Looks loike they never knew what hit 'em, sorr."

Holt dismounted and took his carbine from its scabbard. The trumpeter took the reins of Holt's horse. Holt padded forward. There was no need to identify the bodies. One of the dead men was a big corporal, with a shock of flaming red hair and a swelling at his right biceps because of a bandage beneath his faded issue shirt. Corporal McCormick who had been with the general's escort.

Holt looked to the southwest. A skein of dust was rising far out there. He climbed up on a boulder and uncased his glasses. He had just time enough to focus them, and see the dougherty with its green Maltese cross vanish into a vast dip in the desert, but this time there were no campaign-hatted troopers riding escort. The escort wore headbands about their thick manes of hair.

Holt couldn't chase them. It was the border of the Spanish Desert. Their country. Beyond the desert was the mass of rocks and tangled growths that was known to be the hideout of El Carnicero. Holt looked down at the oval of rock. There were five bodies missing. General McAllister, Mr. Sturgis, Mark Lewis, Annie Tulvis, and *Kathy Nolan.*

CHAPTER SEVENTEEN

They came out of the desert, riding steadily, an officer, a trumpeter and a handful of troopers. They were all a neutral yellowish color, troopers and horses alike. Behind them was a small convoy of wagons, with dust dripping from their wheels like water.

Dragoon Station was a mote of civilization on the bitter edge of the Spanish Desert. The grotesque rock formation behind the low fieldstone buildings of the stagecoach home station held water in natural rock tanks. It was the only reason anyone would have picked such a place to make a stagecoach home station. From the largest of the buildings a thin thread of telegraph wire traced its way across the flats suspended from warped and splintered cottonwood poles.

Beyond the station, in the dubious shade of the rock tanks, was a little cluster of army Sibley tents. A tattered flag snapped in the hot dry wind. Horses were in a peeled-pole corral next to the rock-walled stagecoach station corral.

Trumpeter Monahan turned to Holt. "Troops there, sorr. A company from the looks av it."

"Damned small company," said Sergeant Lambert.

"Half a loaf is better than none at all, sargie."

"For Christ's sake, Monahan!"

"Shut up!" snapped Holt. He rode up beside the tents and swung down. A corporal saluted him. "Where's your commanding officer, Corporal?" snapped Holt.

"In the stage station, sir!" he said. "Lieutenant Owens, sir!"

Holt turned to Lambert. "Take over! I'll arrange for temporary quarters for the women and children!" He strode off.

Lambert swung down. "Jesus God," he said softly. "He's like a madman!"

Monahan nodded. He shifted his chew and spat. "Thayer is death in his eye. He has lost his brother and his fiancée and now his best friend and his new love to them red bastards. Nothing will stop him now. He will kill them or they will kill him."

———

HOLT OPENED THE THICK, iron-sheeted door of the station and walked in. An officer stood at the zinc-topped bar toying with a coffee cup. He turned to look at Holt.

"Mr. Owens!" rasped Holt.

The officer straightened up. "Yes, sir."

"Captain Holt Downey. B Company from Fort Guthrie. I have brought in women and children from that post. I am turning them over to you for safe conduct to Fort Lowell."

"But, sir, I'm here on guard duty. I can't very well—"

Holt cut him short with a brisk cut of his left hand. He could hear a telegraph key clicking in another room. "I want to send a message to Fort Lowell."

Owens nodded. He led the way to the telegraph room. Holt sat down and began to write the message while the telegraph operator and the officer eyed him. He was unshaven, gaunt and dusty, but his eyes seemed to strike like flaming blades. Holt shoved the message to the operator. "Jump to it!" he said.

Owens walked into the big common room with Holt. "Coffee? A drink, sir?" He shook his head. "You've had a rough time, what with the loss of Fort Guthrie and the capturing of General McAllister and his party by El Carnicero."

The eyes struck Owens. "How did you know all that?" Holt grated.

Owens stared at him. "Why, Mr. Sturgis and Mr. Lewis told me when they came in last night."

"What was that?"

"Mr. Sturgis and Mr. Lewis. They escaped when the Apaches attacked the general's party near the head of Caballo Wash. Didn't you know?"

"I did not." Holt gripped the edge of the bar. "Where are they?"

A door opened and Ronald Sturgis came in, fresh and clean-shaven. He stared at Holt, stepped back a little, and then wet his lips. "Hello, Captain," he said hesitantly. "I didn't expect to see you here. I thought you had headed for Fort Lowell."

In the moment's silence the ticking of a waggletail clock sounded like the beating of an Apache water-filled tom-tom. *"How did you and Mark Lewis get away when all the others died?"* asked Holt coldly.

"Mark was scouting up ahead. I was leading the escort. The Apaches came down on us from both sides and behind us. I was cut off. I galloped ahead to get Mark. I couldn't find him. By the time I started back, I could see it was no use trying to get through. It was all over. The Apaches took the dougherty, the general, and the two women. I—"

"You what?" interrupted Holt.

"I hid in the rocks. Later I escaped and ran into Mark Lewis. He guided me here."

"Where is he now?"

Sturgis looked at Owens.

"Well?"

Owens jerked a thumb toward a door at the end of the room.

Holt walked to the door and opened it. The stench of liquor struck him. The scout lay face downward on a sagging cot, with his left arm hanging over the side, the hand gripping an empty rye bottle which had poured out half of its contents on the sanded floor.

Sturgis spoke from the other room. "He had been drinking when I met him out on the desert. It's a wonder he found the way here."

Holt walked into the room. He kicked the bottle from the loose grip and then picked up a bucket of water. He soused the scout with it. Lewis stirred a little. "Mark!" said Holt. "Wake up, damn you!"

The man stirred and then sank down again. Holt gripped him by the hair and raised his head. "Damn you! Wake up, you filthy drunken bastard!"

"It's no use," said Owens. "He's been like that ever since he got here. Don't hit him, sir! He can't help himself."

Holt walked to the door. "Sober him up, you understand! One way or another, and you can half kill him if you like. But I want him sober enough to talk by the time I get my answer to that wire I sent!"

The two young officers listened to the grating of Holt's boots on the sanded floor. Owens smiled wryly. "Bit of a heller, isn't he?"

Sturgis flushed beneath his tan. Downey had a way of making him feel like an erring schoolboy. "I hate his guts. Everyone at Guthrie did. One of these days—"

"What, Sturgis?"

The shavetail drew himself up. "Nothing. We'd better sober Lewis up. If we don't, Downey will beat him to a pulp to get him to talk."

"Not while I'm here."

"Maybe not. But don't cross Mr. Downey, Owens. Not just yet. I've a score to settle with him."

The other officer shrugged. It was none of his business, and it wasn't his regiment. Regiments washed their own dirty linen in their own private way, and woe betide the outsider who interfered.

———

THE SUN WAS BEATING DOWN on the station like a molten blanket of metal. Not a breath of wind stirred. Holt Downey had washed and shaved. There was always plenty of water at Dragoon Station. The clicking of the key alerted him, and he walked to the little room. The operator finished with the message at last and handed it to Holt. He studied the burned hawk's face of the officer who was considered the best Apache fighter in the Territory. "Good news, sir?" he asked.

Holt folded the message paper and placed it in the pocket of his shirt. "Yes and no," he said. He took out a cigar case and opened it in front of the operator. The operator selected a long nine. "Thanks, sir."

They lighted up. Holt looked out of the window across the shimmering Spanish Desert. "I have permission to go out there," he said, almost to himself.

The operator blew out a cloud of smoke. "Out there? That must be the bad news."

"On the contrary. That's the *good* news. The bad news is that I can take only volunteers, and those must be men not necessary for escort duty to the women and children we brought from Fort Guthrie."

"Then you won't go, sir?"

Holt turned. He smiled, but there was no mirth in his agate eyes. "I *will* go." He walked from the room.

The operator shook his head, twirled a finger at his temple, then leaned back to enjoy his smoke.

Mark Lewis was sitting up on the cot when Holt

entered the room. He looked up at Holt, shook his head, then looked away again. "Get me a drink, Holt," he said.

"No, damn you!"

The scout waved a hand. "I thought we were in the clear. They came up out of nowhere. There was nothing I could do."

"Nothing but start belting a bottle."

"I'm sorry, Holt."

"You always are, Mark."

"What do you want me to do?"

Holt leaned against the side of the doorway. "I want you to guide me into the Lost River country."

Lewis laughed harshly. "Two men against El Carnicero and the Prophet? You're mad!"

"Maybe. Better two skilled men than a battalion of stumbling troopers."

Lewis felt for a cigar. Holt tossed him the silver case. The scout selected a cigar and placed it carefully in his mouth. He drew a block match across the plastered wall and lighted the short six. He eyed Holt through the wreathing smoke. "All right," he said quietly. "I've been living on borrowed time for the past five years. It was bound to come to something like this. You're absolutely sure you want to go?"

There was no need for Holt to answer. Lewis shrugged and walked out of the room with Holt. Owens and Sturgis stood there with a bottle of whisky before them. Holt took two more glasses and filled them. "Well, sir?" asked Owens.

Holt took out the message he had received. "I reported in by wire to Fort Lowell, and asked permission to pursue El Carnicero."

"The company is dead tired, sir," said Sturgis.

"I know. I can't take them in any case. Mr. Owens' company must stay here on duty. B Company must escort the women and children to Fort Lowell."

"That means you must go too, Captain," said Owens.

"No. Mr. Sturgis can take command."

Sturgis wiped the sweat from his face. He began to breathe a little easier.

"But he doesn't have to," said Holt. "Sergeant Lambert is perfectly capable of taking the escort to Fort Lowell."

Sturgis' face was getting white beneath his tan. He knew what would happen. He had been serving as aide to the general. He had pulled foot when the fighting was on, leaving the general and two helpless women in the hands of the Butcher. Then, too, he had run away from the Apache chieftain once before, at the Barrera Escarpment, and this slit-eyed bastard of a captain knew it well enough. Sure, Sturgis could ride into Fort Lowell, the safe and easy way, but his career would be blasted from then on. It was a small army out there, and a tough one, and a man had to measure up or leave.

Holt ignored the sweating second lieutenant. He placed the message in front of Owens and Lewis. They read it. Owens looked up at Holt. "According to this, the elimination of Fort Guthrie has left a big hole in the rings around El Carnicero's favorite raiding grounds. Headquarters was trying to round up enough troops for General McAllister to command. Seems as though the Old Man still has plenty of pull in Washington."

Lewis laughed shortly. "They'd probably like to see him out of the way—permanently."

Holt tapped the message. "The department hasn't enough troops right now to go in after McAllister, and by the time they did round them up it would hardly be worthwhile to send them in."

"You mean the Apaches would kill him?" asked Sturgis.

"No. Read the message. Headquarters received a message from an Apache *diyi,* or medicine man, who calls himself Dobe-gusndi-he."

"The Prophet," said Mark Lewis quietly.

Holt nodded. "He said he would keep General McAllister safe, but a prisoner in the stronghold of his people. In exchange for the general, he wanted repeating rifles, cartridges, pistols and other war munitions. He also wanted the release of all Apache prisoners."

It grew quiet in the room. Then Owens stared at Holt. "But that's impossible, sir! General McAllister was captured just yesterday! How could this Doby gusindi-hee, or whatever his outlandish monicker is, know that by the time he sent his message to Fort Lowell?"

A cold feeling ran down Holt's back. "How indeed?" he said quietly.

They all looked at each other. Sturgis refilled his glass.

Mark Lewis leaned on the bar. He seemed to have sobered up. "I warned you about him, Holt."

The room was sweltering, but a chill air seemed to have settled in it for a moment.

"Certainly the army won't meet his terms?" said Owens.

"It would be a helluva blow to them if they did," said Lewis.

Holt Downey raised his glass to his lips. He emptied it and wiped his mouth. He looked at each of them. "To hell with General McAllister," he said. "I'm thinking of those two women. I'm going out to round up some volunteers."

When he had gone the three men looked at each other. Sturgis smashed a hand down on the bar. "Damn him! I'll go with him!"

"Bravo," said Lewis dryly.

"That makes three of you," said Owens. "Three graves in the mountains—if they bother to bury you after they're through with you."

CHAPTER EIGHTEEN

It was the intense desert darkness before the rising of the moon that shrouded Dragoon Station. Four men were saddling their horses in front of the station. Holt Downey, Ronald Sturgis, Mark Lewis, and Trumpeter Monahan. It was quiet. Dim lights showed in a few of the Sibleys. Holt had ordered Sergeant Lambert to keep his men away from the station buildings, and the men of Owens' company were either on guard or patrolling the telegraph line.

Holt tightened the cinch and stood up. He had changed into a buckskin shirt and worn army trousers, and he wore a pair of Apache *n'deh b'keh,* the thigh-length, hard-soled, button-toed desert moccasins, the best footgear for the type of country they would enter. "All set?" he asked the three dim figures near him.

"Ready, sorr," said Monahan.

"Yes, sir," said Sturgis.

"Keno," said Mark Lewis.

Boots grated on the hard *caliche* earth, and a man appeared leading a saddled horse. "Captain Downey, sir?"

Holt stared at the man. "Yes, Caxton?"

"Asking the captain's permission to volunteer for this mission, sir."

"Almost too late, weren't you?"

Caxton shifted his feet. "I'm here now," he said flatly.

Holt nodded. "I don't know why you're going along. Are you sure you realize what may happen to us?"

"I've done a little Apache fighting before, sir."

Holt swung up onto his horse. "Then why?" he asked.

"Annie Tulvis, sir."

"Fair enough. Let's move out!"

The five horsemen trotted their mounts toward the southwest. They entered the edge of a vast depression of sand and thorny growths, laced with half-sunken rock ridges that stood up like dislocated bones from beneath the harsh skin of the ground. It was quiet and a hot, dry wind swept ceaselessly across the big land. The surrounding mountains were dimly seen, hunched and brooding, like sleeping monsters. It was the Spanish Desert.

———

THE PRE-DAWN LIGHT showed eerily over the eastern ranges, and a cold searching wind swept across the naked ridge. Two men lay side by side on the top of the ridge, concealed in a depression masked by greasewood that had somehow found root in the shallow earth.

Mark Lewis lowered his glasses and turned to look at Holt. "You see that notch on the second line of hills?"

"Yes."

"That's it."

Holt focused his glasses. The sharp notch swam into view in the cold gray light. It really didn't look like much from where they were, but close up it would be quite a gash in the tough skin of the rumpled hills. Beyond the hills were the mountains. The mountains marked "Unknown" on the maps. "What about water, Mark?" he asked at last.

"*Quién sabe?* There are *tinajas* in there, most of them

dry at this time of year. There is one place, Lost Tanks, which usually has water all year. I repeat—*usually*."

"We have extra canteens."

"Yes. Enough to get us in there. If there isn't any water in there, we'll never get back again."

The wind keened across the gray hills. Holt lowered his glasses. "El Carnicero is in there, isn't he? He has water."

"You have a curiously cold logic, *amigo*."

"Look, Mark! I'm going in there. I'm depending on you to guide us in there. I don't know of any other man so well fitted for the job, but if you want to pull out now, just go ahead."

The dark bloodshot eyes half closed. "I owe you plenty, Holt. I said I'd guide you in. I didn't say I thought we'd get away with it."

"You're an odd one, Mark."

"So they tell me. I was born with a caul."

"Can we get in any closer?"

The scout pursed his lips and studied the terrain to their right. "I think so. The way is covered. The ground is mostly bare rock, so we won't raise any dust. It will get as hot as the top of a stove in a few hours, but we can make good time at least until noon, and then hole up."

"Water?"

"Who knows? There are *tinajas* in there."

Holt wiped his lens and studied the land again. The last time he had seen it had been the day he had fought El Carnicero at the Barrera Escarpment, which was miles to the north. Now that he was at the very edge of the unknown he didn't like it. It was an ugly mass of varicolored rock, formed as though it had suddenly cooled while writhing and twisting in some vast sexual dance of nature in the days when the land had been shaped by the master builder. There was something obscene about it—a fitting lair for the Butcher.

They worked their way down the steep slope and led

the horses to the southwest. Mark Lewis was ahead, followed by Holt and Monahan, while behind them were Sturgis and Caxton, and when the last two weren't eying the stark terrain or the rough trail, they were watching the broad back of Holt Downey.

———

THE SUN WAS BEATING DOWN into the malpais country like an invisible outpouring of a great metal ladle. It reflected from the rocks and lanced up into the sweating faces of the five white men who were probing deep into the guts of a country practically unknown to white men. There wasn't any doubt in their minds that white men had been in there before their time, probably as early as the days of the Conquistadores, and there wasn't any doubt but that no white man had ever returned from that suburb of Hades.

Mark Lewis walked around a huge shoulder of naked rock that thrust itself out into *the* narrow twisted canyon the party was following. *"Bueno,"* he said shortly. He had stopped just in front of a slanting wall of rock which afforded hot shade. At the rear of the half-open area were some dark pools of water slowly filled from trickles running their course down the wall from some unknown source.

Holt eyed the water. It was greenish, and tiny pink and white bladders floated on the surface. "Well, it's not exactly Niagara Falls," he said dryly, "but it will do."

Lewis sat down on a rock and fanned himself with his hat. "We'd better hole up here. I'll scout ahead."

"I'll go with you."

"No. I've been in a little further than this and hope to work in beyond the last point I reached. I'd rather do it alone, Holt."

"Keno."

They watched the scout disappear around a turn in the canyon.

They watered the horses, then strained enough of the gamy stuff to quench their thirst. Monahan stood first guard, and the others tried to sleep in the natural oven in which they were held.

———

THERE WAS a faint suggestion of moonlight in the eastern sky, but the canyon was thick with darkness and heat. Mark Lewis looked at the others. "Rawhide horse-shoe covers will be a help," he said quietly, "but even so these devils have ears like animals. Walk like cats. They don't fight at night, as you well know, but they can track us through the darkness and hit us at dawn."

"How much farther do we go in?" asked Caxton.

"Not more than five miles."

"Then what?" asked Monahan.

They could see the white even teeth of the scout in the darkness. "It's in the laps of the gods," he said.

"Yeh, Apache gods," said Caxton harshly. "Yosen and Stenatliha."

The scout led the way through the dark trough of the canyon. It was uncanny how he could find his way through such a place, but there wasn't a better scout in the service than Mark Lewis, when he wasn't jousting with Johnny Barleycorn.

———

THE FOUR OF them squatted beside their horses, fingering their carbines. Lewis was probing the mysteries of the trail alone in the pre-moonlight darkness.

Holt looked up at the dark sky. He seemed to feel alien presences. Not humans, but alien gods, powerful here in their own country, for the area had been an Apache stronghold for centuries.

Joe Caxton shifted his chew. "Listen to the wind," he said.

The wind moaned softly through the canyon, but there seemed to be an underlying rhythm to it; a far-distant throbbing, more regular and insistent than the noise of the wind itself.

Holt stood up. He raised his head. *"Drums,"* he said.

The others stood up beside him, temporarily bonded to him by their fear. "We *that* close, sorr?" asked Monahan.

"Sound carries a long way in here."

"I wish it was a *helluva* long way, sorr."

Ronald Sturgis partially opened the breech of his Spencer to check it. "This is madness," he said.

"Go home then," said Holt.

"I'd never find my way out of here."

"None of us can now, sir," said Caxton. "If anything happens to Mark..."

They looked at each other. They had passed a lone skeleton a mile back; the white bones of the upper body rested inside antique Spanish half-armor, and a cabasset helmet was still on the bony skull. It was hard to get in there, but it would be harder still to get out.

In an hour the scout was back. "Come on," he said.

"We heard drums," said Sturgis.

"Why, so did I. Apache drums."

"You see anything?" asked Monahan.

Lewis shook his head. "I didn't have to. I heard them. Those aren't Thunder People playing those tom-toms, Monahan." He looked at Holt. "Well?"

"Move out," said Holt quietly.

The scout shrugged. "Leave the horses here. Don't picket them too tightly."

"Why?" asked Sturgis.

There was a moment's pause. "We may not get back

to free them. If they can pull loose, they may get back to water."

They moved out on foot, trailing their carbines. In half an hour Lewis stopped. "Look," he said simply.

They were close up under the great ugly excrescence that dominated the great masses of rock; a natural citadel, garrisoned by the fiercest guerrilla fighters in the world. The huge flank of the rock formation seemed to be writhing in lights and shadows. Holt was startled until he realized what caused the phenomena. "Fires?" he said.

Lewis nodded. "They don't care in here. Probably no white man has ever penetrated this far into their stronghold; if he has, he never lived to tell about it."

The scout looked at the four men in front of him. "If we go on, there isn't a chance in the world that we won't run into Apaches. You understand that, Holt?"

"You know why I'm here."

"Sturgis?"

"I understand."

"Caxton?"

The big soldier spat "I'm ready."

"Monahan?"

"Holy Mother! I'm scairt, but I'm Irish, superstitious and without a brain in me head for being here at all. Let's go."

Lewis turned without another word and led them steadily through a mass of shin tangle brush and up onto a transverse ledge which worked its way up a thick ridge, until they were almost at the great flank of the rock formation and the top of the ridge was just above them. "Drop," said Lewis casually. "Belly up to the top. Look down. Keep off the light line. You'll see why you came here."

They worked their way up to the top of the ridge. Holt's breath caught in his throat as he looked down. It was a vast natural bowl beneath them, stippled with small bosks of trees. A shallow and clear stream picked its way through masses of boulders. On a cleared space, just below the flank of the towering rock citadel, a huge fire leaped and flared. Beyond the fire area were many brush wickiups, covered with canvas or animal hides sewn together. But none of this held the attention as much as the figures which leaped and postured around the fire to the steady throbbing of water-filled tom-toms beaten with hooped sticks and the piercing note of eagle-bone whistles.

"Holy Mother," said Monahan. He swiftly crossed himself.

Caxton shifted his chew. "There's plenty for all of us," he said dryly.

Sturgis looked away, and his hands shook.

"Well, Holt?" asked Lewis quietly.

Holt looked to the right and then to the left. There was no way down to the left, or in front of them. But on the naked flank of the bulging rock formation was what appeared to be a thick, undulating pencil line. Beyond it, almost in the center line of the deep depression, was a place where the formation had been eroded. Talus slopes led up to it, and at the top of the talus slope yawned the mouth of a great, half-open cave. It was a natural place to sit and watch the dancing below. Holt stared. There were buildings there, built of the stone which lay so plentifully about. In front of the buildings was another fire, and a smaller group of people near it.

Holt steadied his glasses on the site.

"Well?" asked Lewis.

"Jesus God, Mark! There they are!"

"The general?" asked Sturgis nervously.

"Annie?" rapped out Caxton.

She was there with the others. The firelight danced on her lovely hair and skin. Kathy, Kathy, Kathy...

He shifted the glasses and his throat felt dry. He was there. El Carnicero—the Butcher—wearing his sacred deerskin shirt and his damnable horned helmet. Holt could have sworn the horns grew from the Apache's own skull.

Holt lowered the glasses and wet his lips. There was no use in going down into that depression. There must be at least seventy-five to a hundred warriors down there doing the victory dance. He eyed that intriguing pencil line above them and to their right. If that was a ledge, they could traverse it, and possibly reach the place where El Carnicero sat in primitive regal splendor with his captives and a handful of his chosen with him. Then it would be swift killing to free the captives. Possibly they could hold off a rush from below. They all had Spencer .56/50's, repeaters with seven rounds in the magazine, as well as issue Colts, six more rounds; sixty-five rounds to fire before any of them had to reload, and they were all good marksmen.

"Mark," said Holt.

"Yes."

Holt turned on his side and looked at his tiny command. Quickly he told them what he planned. Every eye was on that pencil line of ledge above them. Holt stopped talking and waited for their comments.

Caxton studied the ledge high above them. "Maybe," he said softly. "But if any of those bucks look up and see us flattened against that wall—they could pick us off like a Frenchman picks snails out of a shell with a pin."

"The beggars are too interested in their jigging," said Monahan. "They won't look up."

"If one of us knocked a stone or a rock over the edge..." said Sturgis.

"Ye might as well jump right down after it, sorr," said the trumpeter.

Lewis squatted down the slope and tossed a pebble up and down in his hand, then he looked at the eastern sky. "Moon will be up before long. We'd best get moving. Who'll lead the way?"

Holt slid down the ridge and picked up his Spencer.

He quickly formed a sling for it cut from a coil of light line he had brought with him. The others followed his example. Holt led the way along the ridge. Above them they could see moving shadows as the sweating dancers leaped and postured before the fire. The voices came to them now and then above the steady thudding of the drums.

"Like entering the suburbs av hell," said Monahan, "wid a welcomin' committee doin' the honors down below."

Holt felt the cold sweat running down his sides as he looked at that narrow trail which seemed to cling to the bulging rock wall. He did not look back at the others as he scrambled up the slope to reach the end of the ledge. It was a way of going for which there could hardly be a safe return.

CHAPTER NINETEEN

He was belly flat against the curve of the rock face, edging along, feeling each step carefully with his left foot before he went on, hoping to God that no stone would drop and that no yelling buck would look up from the victory dance and see five figures etched against the firelit wall high above the Apache camp.

Holt worked his way along the ledge. Stones dropped now and then. There was no way of helping that. But the hellish din below was getting louder and louder and the throbbing of the drums seemed to beat against the cliff side so that the clinging white men imagined the cliff itself was moving in time with the rhythm.

They would never get there. The thought was Holt Downey's. A moment later he saw that the ledge curved around a bulge, then dropped behind a knife-bladed ledge which gave hidden access to the area before the yawning cave mouth. Holt was just at the edge of the ledge when he looked down. The wild figures were still whirling and gyrating. Even as he looked a rifle cracked flatly, and he knew they had been seen.

Holt eased behind the ledge and pulled his Spencer from his back. They would die there. There was nothing else they could do. Caxton dropped beside him. He grinned. "One way or another. On the ledge or here. I had an idea we'd get it, sir."

Sturgis was next. "Oh God—oh God—" he mumbled. "We can't die like this!"

"You know of any other way right now—*sir?*" said Caxton sarcastically.

Monahan arrived. He wiped the sweat from his face just as another rifle flatted off. "Lousy shootin'," he said with a wide grin.

"Mark Lewis was last. He crouched beside Monahan with a dead cigar between his strong white teeth. "What the hell is this? A wake?"

"Ye heard the shootin'," said Monahan.

Lewis smiled. "Oh, that!"

"Yeah—*that,*" said Caxton dryly.

"They didn't see us. Some of the bucks are acting out their part in the recent fight. Shooting is part of the act."

Four sweating faces seemed to sag a little.

Holt looked along the ledge. Below and to their right was their goal. To their left was the broad slope that led down into the vast bowl where the main camp was situated. If they could surprise those near the cave entrance they *might* hold off the rest of them. But what would happen then?

"I wonder where that cave leads to," said Caxton as he checked his Colt.

"Hell," said Sturgis flatly.

"What now, sorr?" asked Monahan.

Holt raised his head. "There's no going back." He led the way on his hands and knees. When he reached the end of the ledge he was startled to see that the area in front of the low stone buildings was empty of people. For one horrible moment he thought they had gone down to the main camp.

"In the cave," said Lewis quietly.

Holt moved swiftly, darting across the open space to

jump behind the end building with ready Spencer. The others followed him.

"No one saw us," said Sturgis.

Holt glanced at him. The shavetail's handsome face was flushed, and his eyes were alight. *Might make a soldier out of him yet*, thought Holt.

Holt moved along behind the buildings until he saw the near edge of the cave. The fire crackled fifty feet to his left. There was no one in sight in the entrance of the cave. He looked back at the others. There was no need to say anything. They were as ready as they'd ever be.

Holt moved out, rounded into the entrance and raised his carbine. El Carnicero was lying at his ease on a big brass-bound bed, still wearing his damned horned helmet. A shambling Apache woman was holding a bowl of *tulapai* in her hands, waiting for him to take it. The general was sitting on a rock, with his hands lashed behind him, while Kathy Nolan and Annie Tulvis stood side by side against the eastern wall of the cave, looking at the horned beast who was eyeing them. Seven or eight warriors lounged or squatted at the rear of the cave. It was easy; *it was too damned easy!*

"Holy Mother," said Monahan softly. "Lookit the Butcher! Loike a bloody king he is, in his bloody palace!"

"Bloody is right," said Sturgis.

"Which one is the Prophet?" said Holt as he moved in.

Then the Butcher saw them. He sat bolt upright and started to claw for a weapon, then stopped and eyed the certain death moving in on him. He had guts, thought Holt as he swung his carbine to cover the chief.

"Holt!" cried Kathy.

"Quiet!" he snapped.

The other warriors slowly got to their feet to stare incredulously at the white men who stood there. It was impossible! No white men could get in there!

"We have 'em cold," said Caxton thinly. "What a bloodletting this is going to be!"

El Carnicero stood up and folded his arms. A small fire snapped and crackled not far from him, illuminating the set, lipless face of infinite cruelty.

Holt wet his lips. Surely they were going to fight! It was their way. They were hard to catch and would run from a fight if they had to, but if cornered they would fight like berserkers. It was the unwritten law.

Holt's finger tightened on the trigger. It was strange, the quiet way they stood there staring at the five white men, almost as though they had no fear of them.

"I don't loike the looks av this," said Monahan softly.

"Nor me," said Caxton.'

Sturgis glanced at Holt. "What's wrong, sir?"

Holt opened his mouth to call to Mark Lewis.

"Dobe-gusndi-he," said El Carnicero in a clear voice.

Then Holt turned slowly to look behind him, into the eyes of Mark Lewis, while the scout's Spencer muzzle moved in to rest against Holt's belly. The scout smiled thinly. "You have been wondering who the Prophet was, Captain Downey."

"You?"

Lewis nodded.

"I think I'm out of my mind," said Joe Caxton. He passed a hand across his eyes.

"Put down those carbines, gentlemen," said Lewis.

There seemed to be ice in Holt's veins. He could not move. It was unreal. It couldn't be. The hardships of the journey into El Carnicero's stronghold had unhinged them.

Sturgis dropped his Spencer, and it was picked up by one of the warriors. Monahan opened his mouth and then shut it, like a great gasping fish. "Holy Mother," he said as he dropped his Spencer. Caxton shrugged. He dropped his weapon. "I somehow knew this was a crazy business," he said.

One of the warriors silently walked up to the four prisoners and took Monahan's and Caxton's Spencers. He looked at Holt.

"Captain Downey, *if* you please, sir," said Lewis.

It was no use. He handed his carbine to the buck. Hands took the issue Colts from the holsters of the four men standing helplessly in front of the renegade who had led them in there.

The fire snapped and crackled. The Butcher smiled, or attempted what might pass for a smile. He spoke in slurring Apache to Lewis, and the scout answered in flawless Chiricahua.

"Listen to him," said Monahan.

Lewis studied Holt. "I couldn't resist my little joke," he said quietly.

"You double-dealing bastard!" Holt's big hands closed. "Now I'm beginning to understand. Who told DeWitt McAllister to patrol near the Barrera Escarpment against orders?"

"I did."

"Who planned the ambushes for Eaton and DeVoto? You?"

Lewis nodded. "I also killed that breed prisoner you planned to pump for information. I knew he'd talk."

"He planned the ambush that led to our capture," said General McAllister.

The dark eyes glanced at the general. "We needed bargaining material," he said.

Picture after vivid picture swept across the screen of Holt's mind. How Lewis always seemed to be on a drunken carouse when he was most needed. How El Carnicero seemed to know just where and when troops would strike, so that he shifted his attacks to unprotected areas. He looked at the impassive scout. "And the magazine?"

"It was easy, Captain. A long fuse. Long enough so that we were well away from Fort Guthrie when the blast came. El Carnicero was waiting for the blast. Neat, eh?"

"You filthy murdering swine," said Caxton. His big hands opened and closed.

"What happens now?" asked Holt.

Lewis leaned his carbine against the wall. He was safe enough. His red allies had their weapons covering the four white men. "I have no use for your three companions, Holt." He smiled. "Oh, they won't be tortured! They'll die quickly!"

"*Gracias,*" said Caxton dryly.

"And me?" asked Holt after a moment's pause.

The scout felt for a cigar and lighted it. "It's up to you. Throw in with me and you'll live like a king with the pick of the country. I can use a good war chief."

"Hear, hear," said Monahan.

"And the women?"

The dark eyes looked over the flare of the match. "Maybe you can remember an interesting conversation we held in the old powder magazine?"

It came back to Holt as quickly as the flash and explosion of the magazine had occurred, the conversation he had had with the scout. "*I've always had a theory about women. Nothing new really. It's older than recorded history. The ancients practiced polygamy and found it good. The Indians still do. Why couldn't a man like you, or me, for that matter, have several women?*" And a little later, concerning Kathy Nolan: "*She'd make the Number One wife. A strong, proud woman, who'd love you with everything she had.*"

"You're mad, Lewis," said Holt at last.

The dark eyes half closed. "Am I? I've shown these people how to win victories. They believe in me."

"Victories? They can't beat Regulars in a stand-up fight, and you know it!"

Lewis smiled. "Why fight that way? They've done pretty well so far haven't they? Look over there."

Holt turned. Crude racks held rows of repeating

rifles, Henrys, Winchesters, Spencers, and others. There were cases of ball ammunition piled behind the racks. Pistols were piled on a crude table. The firelight glinted on the brass barrel of a mountain howitzer.

Holt looked at the scout. "But they've lost their trump card, Lewis. The information you relayed to them on troops movements."

"How so?"

The cold question was enough for Holt. He knew now that none of the prisoners, with the exception of the general and the two young women, would live through that night. And the general would be used to gain more munitions, but he'd never live to see his freedom. Mark Lewis could go back as a civilian scout with no one the wiser. He was shrewd enough to get away with it.

"Move back," said Lewis.

"Here it comes, sir," said Caxton out of the side of his mouth.

El Carnicero looked like Satan himself as he stood there with his horned head and his shadow grotesque and dancing on the cave wall. He held a brass-bellied Colt in his right hand and a long-bladed knife in his left. He was ready to play.

The Apache squaw shambled to one side, and as she did so the firelight danced for a moment on her hair. Holt's blood went cold. The woman's hair was blonde. A dirty, matted blonde, but a true blonde. He stared at her. "Who is she, Lewis?" he asked.

"Move back!"

"Who is she, damn you!"

The woman looked up and her faded blue eyes seemed to light a little. "Holt!" she said in a cracked voice.

"Emily!"

El Carnicero raised knife and pistol, but the squaw threw herself against him, taking the knife thrust in her chest It was time enough for Holt to move. He kicked El

Carnicero in the groin. "Now or never, B Company!" he roared.

Caxton whirled and hit Lewis with his famed one-two, right fist in the gut, left up under the down-coming chin. The scout fell back against the wall like a rag doll. Caxton snatched the scout's carbine and turned. "Mona-han!" he yelled. He tossed the heavy weapon to the trumpeter.

Monahan grinned as he caught it He didn't bother to fire it. He gripped it by the barrel and waded into the yelling warriors like a farmer scything his hay.

Ronald Sturgis gripped a burning brand from the fire and brought it down hard on the skull of a buck. He darted across the cave, and just in time he smashed the brand across the face of a buck who was driving a knife down toward the pinioned general.

El Carnicero rolled over and raised his pistol. Holt kicked out at it, but it cracked just as it left the chief's hand. The discharge awoke thundering echoes which seemed to roll and gain momentum as they left the cave. The dance was ready, and the orchestra was tuning up. In minutes the swarm of dancers down in the main camp would be coming up the slope like army ants.

Holt gripped El Carnicero by the throat with a deep-throated grunt of satisfaction, tightening his hands, feeling the Apache's moccasined feet dance on the floor. But El Carnicero had a hideout knife, and he ripped it across Holt's left hip. The reaction caused Holt to hurl the chief to one side. The chief fell backward into the crackling fire and was silent for a few seconds, and then an animal scream broke from him. He rolled to his feet with fire smoldering on his deerskin kilt, battle shirt, and horned helmet of fur.

He slapped at it, but the flames began to lick faster. He screamed again and ran for the mouth of the cave. As he reached the outer area the wind whipped the flames into angry life.

Holt wiped the grease from his hands and snatched up a Spencer. He ran toward the chief, hardly conscious of the hand-to-hand fighting going on about him.

The warriors were running up the slope, staring at their famed chief as he leaped and slapped at the flames scorching his body. Holt raised the Spencer and fired at point-blank range. The heavy slug drove El Carnicero forward. He fell and rolled over and over with flames licking at him. His warriors leaped back. Before they knew what hit them Holt had emptied the six remaining rounds from the Spencer, drawing blood at every shot.

The Apaches broke for cover, but a knot of them charged from near the buildings. Holt reversed the Spencer to fight it out. A carbine rattled from just behind him and to one side. Then another joined in and the slugs broke up the charge, scattering the shrieking warriors like chaff until most of them were down and the others had fled down the hill.

Holt turned to see Kathy Nolan and Annie Tulvis standing there with smoking carbines in their hands. He grinned. "I could use you in B Company," he said. Then it was suddenly quiet in the cave, although the sound of yelling warriors and screaming squaws came up the slope from the main camp, Joe Caxton loaded the mountain howitzer and with the help of Mr. Sturgis and Trumpeter Monahan, trundled it to the mouth of the cave. He sighted it, inserted a friction tube, and attached a lanyard. He jerked the lanyard cleanly. The howitzer coughed, recoiled and sent out a puff of thick white smoke. The shell screamed like a banshee and burst just over the cleared area where the big fire blazed.

"Neatly done, Sergeant Caxton," said Holt.

"A pleasure, sir," said Caxton with a grin.

They watched the Apaches streaming across the great bowl toward the northern wall. "They won't be back," said Holt. He turned and walked quickly to Emily Locke.

Kathy was in front of the fallen woman. She looked up at Holt. "It's no use, Holt," she said quietly.

"Let me see her, at least."

"Not like this. Annie and I will take care of her. She can at least be buried like a white woman."

Holt wiped the sweat from his face. He walked to the general. Talbot McAllister was dabbling at a slice on his left forearm. He looked at Holt. "Fine work, Captain Downey," he said. "I can see now why they rate you as the best Apache fighter in the department."

"Luck, sir."

"It wasn't luck that got you here, sir! It was guts!"

"Let me help you with that arm, sir."

The general half closed his eyes. "I'll get that field command. I want you as my chief of staff, sir, and Mr. Sturgis as aide."

"If it is all the same to the general, sir," said Holt, "I'd rather go back to Fort Guthrie with B Company."

"There isn't any Fort Guthrie, and very little left of B Company, Captain."

Holt straightened up. "Someone has to rebuild Fort Guthrie, sir, and with what's left of the old B Company, we can sure as hell whip up another unit."

"The Battling Bastards of B, eh?"

"Yes, sir."

McAllister nodded. "I only wish I could do it with you."

"What about Lewis, sir?" asked Caxton.

"Aye, sorr," said Monahan.

Sturgis fingered a pistol and his eyes were like ice.

"Don't kill him," said Holt. He almost drove them back with the look in his eyes. "Smash up these weapons. Place the powder at the cave entrance and pile rocks over it. Run a long fuse back into the cave. We'll use one of *Mr.* Mark Lewis' tactics on his old allies."

"We can't touch it off in here," said Sturgis. "We'd be trapped."

Holt shook his head. "I think this cave opens into the channel of Lost River. Before we touch off that powder we'll make sure of it. Caxton, round up some horses. I don't think the Apaches will be back to bother you tonight."

Holt walked over to Mark Lewis. The scout opened his eyes and felt his left arm. "It's broken," he said thickly.

Holt spat to one side. "Get up," he said thinly. "Where does this cave lead to?"

"I don't know."

"*Get up,* Lewis."

The scout struggled to his feet, and the look in Holt's eyes blanched his face. "All right," he said. "But what happens to me?"

"You're alive, aren't you?"

"Yes, but for how long?"

"You'll see."

In two hours they were ready. They had buried Emily Locke, released at last from the hideous bondage she had been forced to endure for three long years. The ground was littered with smashed weapons and the sprawled bodies of the dead warriors. Holt tied the half-burned horned helmet and battle shirt of El Carnicero to his saddle.

They walked in single file with Mark Lewis leading the way with a flaring torch held in his one good hand. Caxton was at the rear. He dropped behind, and in a little while he hurried back to the column. "She's lit, sir. Are you sure that damned renegade won't trick us?"

"I'll get you out," said Lewis. His face was white and set under the light of the torch. He wanted to live too.

"You bet you will," said Holt.

He had not looked back. Emily Locke was gone now. The festering sore would heal. He glanced back into the great eyes of Kathy Nolan and knew she understood him.

CHAPTER TWENTY

The gray light of dawn shone over the eastern ranges. Behind the little party loomed the tangled masses of the place that had once been the lair of El Carnicero. Holt Downey dropped the reins of his horse and turned to look at Mark Lewis.

"Kill me," said the renegade. "Go on! I brought you out, but you owe me nothing!"

Holt looked down at the broken arm resting in its sling. He looked up at the drawn face of the scout. "No," he said quietly. "I won't kill you."

Lewis stared at him. "What kind of a game *is* this?"

"I'll give you a horse and water. You're free to go."

"I protest, Captain Downey!" snapped the general.

"Wait, sir."

Lewis looked from one to the other of the seven people watching him silently. "But why?" he asked quietly.

Holt raised an arm and pointed toward the stronghold. "You've lost any power you had with them. They'll torture you if they catch you."

Lewis swallowed and passed a hand across his sweat-dewed forehead.

"Wherever you go men will hunt you," said Holt

quietly. "Every white man in this country will turn you away or hunt you down. Too many civilians and soldiers have died because of you. DeWitt McAllister, George Eaton, Seb DeVoto, Milas Fleming, and many others. You're a pariah, Lewis. Go on! Get on your horse and ride. Ride anywhere. North, south, east, or west. It won't make any difference. They'll always find you out."

Lewis stepped backward and picked up the reins of a horse. His eyes looked like peepholes into Hell. Then without a word he turned and walked away toward the mouth of a canyon, still shrouded in shadows. They watched him until the stumbling figure vanished.

Holt turned. "Let's move out," he said.

He rode beside Kathy Nolan, and their hands were linked together. They had a job to do together. They were army. Man and woman, they were *both* army. There was still a lot of work to do in Arizona Territory. The bugles must still sound along the border. *The valiant bugles.*

TAKE A LOOK AT: THE COMPLETE DAVE HUNTER AND ASH MAWSON SERIES

Take a journey with Dave Hunter and Ash Mawson in this four-book western collection by Gordon D. Shirreffs. If the terrain doesn't kill them, the bullets certainly would...

In *Hell's Forty Acres*, Bounty Hunter Dave "Treasure" Hunter enters the Colorado River area searching for a lost silver mine, but finds a woman with a mysterious past, hostile Paiutes, and betrayal. It was rich with the promise of silver—and sudden death. In *Maximilian's Gold*, Hunter teams up with his buddy Ash Mawson to find the Mexican Emperor Maximilian's gold, stashed somewhere on the treacherous Chihuahua Trail. Gold can make a man as rich as a king. If it doesn't kill him first.

In *The Walking Sands*, South of the Arizona border is the Gran Desierto, a vast area of shifting sand hills. It is there that a church was buried beneath the sands, never to be found again. Hunter believes the Jesuits' treasure is there for the taking— but so do some other very dangerous people. And in *The Devil's Dance Floor*, Hunter returns, this time doing fancy footwork for a religious figurine. His search for the Virgin Mary figurine means crossing the Sonora Desert—the Devil's Dance.

The Complete Dave Hunter/Ash Mawson Series includes: *Hell's Forty Acres, Maximilian's Gold, The Walking Sands,* and *The Devil's Dance Floor*.

AVAILABLE NOW

ABOUT THE AUTHOR

Gordon D. Shirreffs published more than 80 western novels, 20 of them juvenile books, and John Wayne bought his book title, Rio Bravo, during the 1950s for a motion picture, which Shirreffs said constituted *"the most money I ever earned for two words."* Four of his novels were adapted to motion pictures, and he wrote a Playhouse 90 and the Boots and Saddles TV series pilot in 1957.

A former pulp magazine writer, he survived the transition to western novels without undue trauma, earning the admiration of his peers along the way. The novelist saw life a bit cynically from the edge of his funny bone and described himself as looking like a slightly parboiled owl. Despite his multifarious quips, he was dead serious about the writing profession.

Gordon D. Shirreffs was the 1995 recipient of the Owen Wister Award, given by the Western Writers of America for "a living individual who has made an outstanding contribution to the American West."

He passed in 1996.

CPSIA information can be obtained
at www.ICGtesting.com
Printed in the USA
LVHW092332240323
742479LV00004B/365